The Plagues of Pandora

(Matt Drake #9)

By

David Leadbeater

Thriller, adventure, action, mystery, suspense, archaeological,
military

Other Books by David Leadbeater:

The Matt Drake Series
The Bones of Odin (Matt Drake #1)
The Blood King Conspiracy (Matt Drake #2)
The Gates of hell (Matt Drake 3)
The Tomb of the Gods (Matt Drake #4)
Brothers in Arms (Matt Drake #5)
The Swords of Babylon (Matt Drake #6)
Blood Vengeance (Matt Drake #7)
Last Man Standing (Matt Drake #8)

The Alicia Myles Series
Aztec Gold (Alicia Myles #1)

The Disavowed Series:
The Razor's Edge (Disavowed #1)
In Harm's Way (Disavowed #2)
Threat Level: Red (Disavowed #3)

The Chosen Few Series
Chosen (The Chosen Trilogy #1)
Guardians *(The Chosen Trilogy #2)*

Short Stories
Walking with Ghosts (A short story)
A Whispering of Ghosts (A short story)

Connect with the author on Twitter: @dleadbeater2011
Visit the author's website: **www.davidleadbeater.com**
Follow the author's Blog
http://davidleadbeaternovels.blogspot.co.uk/

All helpful, genuine comments are welcome. I would love to hear from you.
davidleadbeater2011@hotmail.co.uk

This one is for the readers, for everyone who has ever enjoyed one of my books and for those who know every character within this one.

CAST LIST

THE SPEAR TEAM

Matt Drake, Torsten Dahl, Mai Kitano,
Hayden Jaye, Mano Kinimaka, Smyth,
Karin Blake, Komodo, Yorgi, Lauren.

ALICIA'S TEAM

Alicia Myles, Rob Russo,
Michael Crouch,
Zack Healey, Caitlyn Nash.

THE DISAVOWED

Aaron Trent, Adam Silk, Dan Radford
Claire Collins.

THE PYTHIANS

Tyler Webb — Leader and Founder
General Bill Stone — U.S. Army
Nicholas Bell — Owner of Sanstone Building and Builder.
Miranda Le Brun — Oil Heiress
Clifford Bay-Dale — Man of Privilege
Robert Norris — Principal SolDyn Board Member

David Leadbeater

PROLOGUE

Some said that age clung to the crumbling relic like a filthy, protective shroud. Others likened it more to a house of insanity, and that the shroud was protecting the villagers from the place itself rather than the other way around. Over the years it had represented many things to the maturing community; from the proverbial haunted house with its rambling, untended gardens to a symbol of their own steady decay to a representation of hate in harder times—the dying, blazing sun setting behind it, pouring its terrible fire through the jagged, cracked windows straight down into the center of town. The children harbored many a fear and undertook dares and monster-quests nearby, but they were fine and their parents were fine and the place eventually passed beyond their concerns, its illusory image overshadowed by responsibilities and life changes, television and wine. And of course most children are always fine . . . until maturity makes the dares and the challenges they set themselves take on a darker, more adult nature.

But when the sun started to go down, and the darkness sent its black fingers creeping like giant spiders across the land; when the devil's fire—as the elders called it—started to glimmer and glow through those knife-edged windows and ragged cracks, it was easy to remember why the place was shunned, why nobody ever bought it or chose to visit, and why every member of the population harbored the same uncanny thought deep, deep inside their hearts where most feared to go.

The house on the hill had always been there, and for one purpose only.

Its purpose was to kill.

The village was aghast when, in 2014, the house was purchased by an unknown buyer. A public meeting was held, its attendees so shocked they could barely offer speculation. Comment and gossip was rife throughout the community; the main consensus being that bulldozers would soon roll in and raze the eyesore to the ground. And one day heavy machinery did indeed roll in, on the back of huge Mack trucks, but not a wall or even a brick was disturbed.

What were *they* doing up there?

It was always *they*—the faceless, shadowy owner or organization behind any new project. And there was always a faceless, shadowy organization. The money men rarely kick-started anything without some kind of profitable agenda.

In early March 2014, the village was brought to its knees when each household received an invitation to attend a celebration up at the house—an opening ceremony of sorts where the new owner would meet and explain his plans for the prominent place.

It is widely believed that the phrase "curiosity killed the cat" didn't exist before the world's first woman, Pandora, was given a box and told, by the very real gods themselves, never to open it. Upon doing so she released all the sins of the world, including sickness, crime, vice, poverty and plague. Pandora's Box is an origin myth—an attempt to explain the beginning of something.

The villagers, although horrified, amazed and fretful,

were hugely curious. What could go wrong on a warm and sunny afternoon in America? What could happen when a man or woman was surrounded by hundreds of their peers, in the course of celebration?

The only odd thing about it all was that no children were specifically invited. The cards all read: *Anyone between the ages of 16 and 100.*

Odd, they speculated. Maybe the new owner was a touch eccentric, with a smattering of loon in his nature. A movie star perhaps or a writer. Nay, an ex-president. The speculation continued.

But curiosity compelled most of the township to accept the mysterious invite. Only the die-hard pessimists and worrywarts held out. And human nature obliged many of the attendees to believe the blanket invites had been misspelled—why shouldn't they take their children to what amounted to a Sunday afternoon barbecue?

The day arrived; the night before one of those blood-red sunsets that sent swords and lances of dripping red light stabbing and piercing toward the heart of the township, straight from the cracked and crazy visage of the house on the hill. The Sunday itself, though, was one of those days when even the brisk breeze warms your heart, the children's laughter is light, and the unexpected smile of a stranger can lift your spirits. Many were nervous and laid off the caffeine, perhaps wishing for something a little stronger. Kids of all ages caught the mood of their parents and became more somber as the time approached. Like a funeral procession the villagers began to march through their town, each person looking up at the ever-nearing fractured glass eyes that had watched over their town for at least fifty years.

In one form or another they had all visited the house before and although experiences differed between the timid and the daring, heads were filled with trepidation, expectation and most of all—curiosity.

And just like the world's very first woman, made of clay, on the command of the god Zeus, they would go forward and open the box.

Into the newly landscaped grounds they marched, amazed by the splendid remodeling, which served only to make the house's continuing ugly and threatening visage all the more hostile. Several turned away at that point, to the indecisive looks of their friends that stayed. More eccentricities followed, as a sumptuous banquet had been laid out, a rich and wealthy buffet, but no waiters to serve it.

And no host.

Only the townspeople and their fascination.

As the sun blazed down from on high, as the townsfolk ate and kept watch on that legendary house, as their children drifted inexorably toward the goblets of red wine and platters of assorted chocolates—their parents more concerned with keeping them away from the haunted bricks and mortar than the everyday alcohol and sugar—as conversation passed and frustration began to set in, a voice finally boomed out from within the house itself.

"I will be with you shortly," a voice that clearly belonged to a well-manicured, well-educated man spoke out. "But first, won't you join me in a toast to celebrate the passing of the old regime and the beginning of the new?"

The villagers thought they understood. A drink to represent the house's upcoming demolition. *What a good idea*, they thought. Many poured wine and champagne, fruit juice and glasses of water. They were about to meet their benefactor, a symbol of their future, a man that would now be inextricably entwined with the name and renown of the place where they were raised.

As one, persuaded by the promises of the unseen man, the attending township raised glasses to their lips and drank.

After a while only the cries of babies remained.

CHAPTER ONE

Tyler Webb, a weapons billionaire well on his way to establishing his own notorious, murderous and immensely powerful secret order, studied the faces of the men and women seated around him.

"We are the Pythians," he said. "What news today?"

Before anyone could speak he flicked a glance sideways, taking in the spectacular view offered through the trees by the eternal falls, never changing, all enduring. In a way, he hoped his new secret order might go the same way. Conversely, thinking of the time when he grew too old to manage and lead it forward anymore, he already felt a pang of jealousy toward the nameless figure that might.

General Bill Stone of the US Army spoke up. "The 'house on the hill' scenario has played out. We have announced our presence in the United States. We have announced our resolute intentions and the gravity of our actions. We have an army—recruited around the world and being deployed as we speak, and," he paused, "our first foray, the Pandora plague, is underway. We are starting to mobilize. Three sites have now been identified—London, Paris and Los Angeles—"

"Wait," Nicholas Bell, owner of one of the world's biggest construction companies, and least liked of the Pythians, interrupted the general. "I was the only one here that stood opposed to the 'house' operation. I'd like to know the true depths of what we wrought."

General Stone hesitated, clearly unwilling to articulate and unused to being disrupted mid-flow. Tyler Webb stepped in smoothly.

"My friend, my friend," he addressed Bell. "The Pythians do not discuss the trivialities of who lived and who died. Of *how many*. We set our path to ultimate power in motion and will not be deterred. The so-called innocents will die to facilitate our rise. That," he spread his hands magnanimously, "is how it should be."

Webb noticed that Bell looked a little sickened before he turned away, nodding amicably. His immediate thought was to bring the man closer, much closer. "Nicholas, why don't you move to DC for a time? Bill is the architect of both the 'house' and Pandora projects. If you were closer to him you might be better able to affect the plans."

His manipulation worked. Nicholas Bell, the rough multi-millionaire builder, nodded, seemingly appeased.

Immediately, one of his other minion-associates, Clifford Bay-Dale, the energy boss and the man nobody liked, raised his voice. "And my own project is next, I'm sure?"

Webb nodded slightly. "The lost kingdom sounds intriguing, my friend. We will table your presentation as soon as Pandora shows success."

"What about my galleons?" Miranda Le Brun asked, the jaded oil-heiress finally showing a spark of interest.

"In good time." Webb smiled. "Your enthusiasm for our battle suffuses me with delight. We will all have our day, to the cost of the poorer world, until the pinnacle of our desires can be found. It will all end, one day, with Le Comte de Saint Germain."

The interest he saw in the eyes of his collaborators gave

him a rush of almost sexual desire. They didn't know the full plan yet. Only he, the great Tyler Webb and nano-weapon expert, knew that.

General Stone, he noticed, didn't look at all pleased at the prospect of hosting the somewhat uncouth construction magnate in his home town. Not a single protest issued forth though, a testament to the general's iron discipline and willingness to bow to the man in charge.

"How goes it with the second- and third-degree members?" Webb asked.

"Kendra Nelson," Robert Norris, executive of SolDyn, said. "Is on board. A second-degree asset that, I have hopes, may be groomed one day to rise to first degree."

Webb frowned. "We will never have more than six first-degree members."

Norris also smiled. "I know."

Webb took his meaning and fought hard to keep his mouth from broadening into a grin. Plans were afoot, layer upon layer; the intrigue and insider play was good.

"Alex Berdal," Miranda said. "Third degree."

"Zoe Sheers," Bell added. "First degree."

Webb urged himself to triple check that last offering. He nodded and added one more name to the list. "Lucas Monroe," he said. "First degree. Primary."

They all stared at him, perhaps wondering why his nomination should be the primary, perhaps wishing they were his equal, but only Nicholas Bell spoke up in that crass way of his.

"What friggin' reason do you have to offer Monroe as a primary?"

Webb ignored the question so completely it surprised the

entire room. "On to our final item of business." He eyed the falls again, conjuring the image of a diverting evening planning some random unfortunate's demise over a bottle of expensive brandy, a Sony laptop, a bevy of criminals and a wealth of technology, whilst sitting before the great floor-length window in his bedroom with the spectacular real-life cascade as his hanging picture, his muse. His latest stalking victim was a blond couple from Missouri, innocent, fresh, just starting out in life. His pleasure would be to personally destroy them.

"How comes the factory?"

Again Bill Stone answered, this being his project. "Prepared but not yet operational. Some of the more . . . sensitive . . . items and staff are taking a little, um, procuring."

"By any means," Webb told him. "Make it happen."

"That is my maxim, sir. Our main obstacle is its obscure location. Greece isn't the easiest place in the world to recruit from, no matter the means you use."

"Understood. There is still time before we're able to advance with the plague pits. But use your time well, Bill, for once we hit the 'go' button—nothing on earth should be able to stop us."

"For now," Bay-Dale sniggered, his visage and conduct like that of a sneaking rat, a cowardly bully. "Let us revel in the outcome of the 'house' project and what fear it has wrought among our enemies, our subjects and even among our associates."

"The Pythians have arrived." Webb lifted a glass of red wine, fully aware of its symbolic representation to his associates in the matter of how the villagers had been poisoned. "A toast."

They drank.

They filed out.

"We will meet again very soon," Webb told them in parting. "For the official launch of our first real project. Before we own this world and all its sins, we will set it alight."

The converted nodded to him.

"A pyre for our pleasure."

"To raise a new empire," Stone said. "You must first burn the old one to the ground. History has taught us that."

Webb placed a hand on the general's solid shoulder. "The fires have already begun, my friend. And they are unstoppable."

CHAPTER TWO

Matt Drake leaned forward and reached out a hand, tentatively, questioningly, wondering if he were about to die.

Komodo handed the soft, dumpy object to him.

Drake sniffed at it carefully. Mai rolled her eyes. "What? Do you think it's about to explode?"

Drake looked non-committal. "Dunno, love. It's a bacon sandwich made by an ex-Delta soldier, an American, in Washington DC, *inside* the Pentagon. How can anything good come of that?"

"Yorkshire ain't the only place that makes a good sarnie," Karin spoke up in defense of her beau. "T-vor here can make 'em just as good. Go on. Try it."

Drake laid the bread on the table, beside the local steak sauce and a proper bottle of HP. "It just . . . doesn't feel right."

"For God's sake," Dahl exclaimed. "Eat it or I'll stuff the bloody thing down your throat."

Drake felt his lips turn sharply upward. It was good to get the entire team back together, especially since they weren't in any immediate danger or about to undertake a deadly operation. Lately, they had been hopping from one danger to the next. But now . . . two weeks had passed since the demise of his greatest nemesis. The gods had seen fit to reward their success with some much deserved downtime.

Still, shadows were never far from their hearts and

minds. Mai remained distant, focused on some past terrible deed and occupied full-time with Grace's welfare, as if she owed the young girl more than she could ever repay. Deep grieving mode returned to haunt them all at various parts of the day as they were reminded of loved ones they had recently lost. Indeed, Drake and everyone else experienced a form of guilt at *not* thinking of Ben Blake or Romero or Jonathon Gates in the passing of an entire afternoon. The life of a survivor was never an easy passage.

Drake bit into the sandwich, savoring the taste of the crispy bacon with its accompaniment of brown sauce. "Not bad," he murmured. "Not bad at all."

"Coming from a real Yorkshireman," Karin said, "that's high praise."

Komodo proceeded to hand out a tray of sandwiches and bottles of water, their first food inside their all-but-impregnable latest HQ. Provided by the new Secretary of Defense—Robert Price—the large, well-equipped office inside the Pentagon was just what they needed at this point. The SPEAR team had been bombed, assaulted, wounded and torn apart. Two weeks convalescing and quietly occupied with learning the ins and outs of a new routine was more than a soothing balm, it was a major part of the healing process.

Of course, the team wasn't complete. Not without Alicia Myles. Drake ranked her absence as dangerous to all mankind—not just because of the person she was but for the simple fact that she had never once slowed down, never mourned, never departed from the long, well-travelled road to allow time and losses and circumstance to catch up.

The time was coming when it would, and the outfall from

that particular nuclear explosion would taint them all.

Drake finished his sandwich and turned to Mai, attempting again to engage at least a part of her interest.

"Any news on Grace?"

"Nothing yet." The unknown seventeen-year-old that Mai had rescued from a terrible captivity had been called to a meeting with investigators today. Maybe they had unearthed something from her past. Drake hoped so. Mai had wanted to accompany Grace, but the child, independent, angry and guarded to the last, had insisted she go alone. This was part of her past and her future, part of growing up and moving on.

What else haunts you, Mai? he wanted to ask. All he knew was that Mai believed she had murdered a man that worked in part for the Triad, and that the memory was tearing her apart. In the words of those that often felt responsible for deeds beyond their control: *Blame all your life on me.*

With no more information coming and, judging by his girlfriend's face, no more about to be offered any time soon, Drake turned his mind to happier thoughts. Hayden Jaye, wounded in the final battle with the Blood King, had healed well and was now back up to full strength—if a little sore. One of the main reasons that she had recuperated so quickly sat beside her now—the Hawaiian mountain—Mano Kinimaka. With a sandwich in each hand and an eye to his colleagues, Kinimaka failed to notice the sauce slipping out from the bread. But Mano was used to accidents.

At the back of the large room, Smyth leaned against the wall, a cantankerous look stretched across his features. Drake knew the man well enough by now to know that didn't necessarily mean he was in a bad mood; it was a sign that all was well in the land of Smyth and could even mean he was daydreaming about the Easter Bunny.

Hayden, reinstated as leader of their elite group, called the meeting to order. "I hope you've all had a good rest because the devils of this world won't stay inert for long, and already we're seeing the beginnings of new troubles. Not with us today are Yorgi—the suits don't want to issue a Pentagon pass to an ex-Russian thief and jailbird—and Lauren, who has undertaken a mission for Mano, more of which I'll explain some other time."

"Why?" Smyth asked touchily. "Why not now?"

Hayden stared. "Because the nature of the job she performs for us is somewhat delicate, and if it doesn't pan out, then it will remain undisclosed."

Smyth snapped his mouth shut. Kinimaka cleared his throat. "You do well to keep quiet, Smyth. Even I don't know what she means."

Smyth looked unconvinced. Hayden continued, "With the final demise of Coyote we believe all remaining threats of the Blood King's vendetta against us and our families have passed. I guess you could call this a new era, even a new beginning. Now, before concentrating their efforts on Coyote, Drake and Mai travelled to Russia, chiefly to Zoya's abode."

"The crazy grandma," Kinimaka put in.

"The best footballer in Russia," Drake added.

Hayden took a breath. "Anyway, in addition to their findings relating to the Ninth Division and Coyote's identity, they instructed us to smuggle out as much of the woman's treasure pile as we were able. That included relics and artefacts which we haven't yet been able to identify, in addition to dossiers of information on a treasure trove hidden by crusaders, a lost kingdom, and this new group— the Pythians. Zoya appears to have collected a wealth of information and dirt on just about everything, and the worst of her labors will bear our team the best fruit for years to come."

"Do we have any credible threats?" Smyth asked, as if trying to make Hayden come to the point.

"They're all credible," Hayden answered. "We recovered enough information on the Thule Society to keep two analysts busy for a month. The problem comes in deciding which one needs our attention most."

"The Thule Society?" Kinimaka asked.

"A German occultist group and secret society within the Nazi party. Their ancient myth research arm, if you will. They were even named after a mythical country from Greek legend and spent millions of Reichsmarks and countless lives searching for places such as Atlantis, Mu, Hyperborea and other lost civilizations that they believed might hold the origins of the Aryan race. Members included people such as Rudolf Hess, Hans Frank, Goring, Himmler and, probably, Hitler."

The Hawaiian pinched the bridge of his nose. "I guess they were serious about their lost kingdoms."

"They were more serious about their Aryan origins. But are they the prime threat here today or tomorrow? I think not."

Dahl shifted in his seat. "I'm guessing you have more than just idle speculation on that front."

Drake held up a hand. "In the Queen's English he means 'which one?' "

Dahl furrowed his rows. "Since when did the Queen come from bloody Yorkshire?"

"Since your wife came to DC, started keeping you up all night, and turned you into a whipping boy."

Dahl rounded on Drake. "I don't see how that's any of your business!"

"You're not denying it then."

Dahl gritted his teeth. Hayden intervened. "In answer to both questions—yes. We're taking the Pythians most seriously. In fact, more seriously than any other threat in recent memory."

That made Drake do a double take. *"What? Why?"*

"We already know they're recruiting big. Trying to make a name for themselves. Not interested in staying secret. They're the new breed, the very real face of terror that no longer wants to hide behind a mask. But we don't believe they're terrorists as such, they're power-mongers, intent on pulling the strings that make the world turn. We gathered as much from Zoya's notes and the interrogations of mercenaries rejected or hired by their network. We know they have unlimited funds, government-level resources and leverage the like of which we've never seen, not even with Kovalenko. We know they're searching into the legend of Pandora, though in what way we can only guess. Maybe it all leads toward this 'greatest mystery of all time'."

"It doesn't necessarily make them more dangerous than the next bunch of crazies on our list," Mai said gently.

Hayden nodded. "Yesterday I would have said 'you're right'. But then . . . this." She hung her head and flicked a controller at the TV screen, saying no more.

Drake watched a news report from the Fox channel, the

coverage restricted to events that had transpired in a small, secluded town in mid-America. In one afternoon, 90 percent of the admittedly small population had been poisoned. Men, women, children. All attending some kind of celebration, all dead within minutes of ingesting a deadly liquid.

When it ended, Drake turned to Hayden. "It's horrifying, but I can't see how it relates to our secret organization trying to rule the world. Was one of the dead a Pythian? Did they find something in his house?"

Hayden shook her head. "No. The Pythians claimed responsibility for the killings."

Drake was speechless. One look around the room told him the rest of the team shared similar feelings of disbelief.

"To what end?" Dahl asked. "What could they possibly gain from such slaughter?"

"Notoriety," Hayden said quietly. "A deadly status. Their intentions and the depths they will sink to have been clearly defined. We don't know if they're home-grown or foreign but they're now on *everyone's* radar. Following this and threats in many countries, the Pythians have quickly become world enemy number one."

"And they already have an army," Drake recalled. "Christ, if this is their opening performance what's their first act gonna be like?"

Hayden nodded. "And, it bears the question, their *last?*"

"Women." Dahl stared at the TV screen. "Children. We will destroy them all for this. And anyone that has even a dirty fingernail in their organization."

Drake found his voice again. "We will."

Hayden turned the TV off and drank from a bottle of water. "The Pythians are a global threat," she said. "We just don't know their extent or true numbers. To that end, Drake, I'd like you to enlist Alicia and her new team in our efforts."

Drake felt a surge of pleasure, but didn't let it show. "Alicia and Crouch and their team just found a horde of Aztec Gold after destroying half of Vegas and Africa. I'm not sure they'll be ready for something like this."

"Something like this?" Hayden echoed. "Alicia is always ready for anything, and the sheer size of it means they *have* to be ready. Perhaps they won't be called upon, but contact Crouch, Drake. And Alicia. Put them on standby. It has to be said—they would want you to."

"Damn good point," Smyth rasped. "I sure wouldn't wanna get on Myles' bad side."

Drake and Mai shared a look. "It's a nasty place to be," he admitted and Mai grunted her affirmation. "I'll make the call."

"One more thing before we start," Hayden said, her blond locks bobbing vigorously as she felt a galvanizing sense of purpose swamp her system. "Not necessarily related but worth a recap. Whilst I've been convalescing and most everyone else was playing their little tournament with Coyote, something Jonathan said kept creeping back to me. Something I think may be important."

At the mention of the old Secretary of Defense—their murdered friend and benefactor's name, the team sobered, Drake in particular. It was hard enough to find a true friend in this world, let alone a trustworthy official, but Jonathan Gates had proved to be both. No doubt Jonathan had harbored his secret demons, but who didn't? The poor man's wife had been killed by the Blood King, early on in

Drake's SPEAR campaign, and then the man himself had been gunned down by Kovalenko's men as he started to accept somebody new. Some had even whispered about a possible presidential campaign.

"What was it?" Kinimaka broke Drake's reverie.

"Remember General Bill Stone? The man that stood against us during the whole tomb of the gods saga? He wanted the tombs for the US alone, or perhaps for himself, and actually won the support of the White House."

"I remember," Dahl said quietly.

"Well, luckily he didn't get to fulfil his plan, but something about him raised Jonathan's antennae. Jonathan said 'Bill Stone is into something, something deep'. An ulterior plan. He requested that Lauren Fox find out what it was, then changed his mind in the interests of . . . decency, I guess. Stone is the worst kind of leader." She shook her head. "One that believes people are his playthings and are beholden to him. The world is his gaming board."

"He's not the only one out there," Mai said.

"Agreed. But he's the only one on our radar, for now. There's one more thing. Jonathan told Lauren something in confidence, something she imparted to Mano only after Jonathan's death. He found out that the government actually said *no* to Stone's request."

Now even Smyth's face fell, the permanent frown replaced with shock. "But that means—"

"Yes. That Stone ignored the White House and went into those tombs without their knowledge. On his own, and with hired men. Why did he still want to go ahead at such huge risk?"

Kinimaka spoke up. "Whilst you guys were messing

about in the UK, Smyth and I undertook a mission of our own."

Drake gave the man a half smile. "Messing about in the UK?"

"Wandering the Dales. Visiting the funfair. Destroying hotels. Whatever. Our old HQ was raided by a team we believe worked for the Pythians. One of their men told us they wanted to grab everything on Jonathan's computer that related to General Stone. Everything."

Now Drake did a double take. "The Pythians? What could they possibly want with General Stone?"

"That's the question," Hayden said. "And one of the few leads we have on the group, despite Mano's heavy-handedness."

Kinimaka grunted, embarrassed. Even as an adult he retained the clumsiness of a three-year-old.

Smyth rose to his defense. "We did what we had to do. Under fire, we extracted information, what more do you want?"

"*More* information," Hayden said. "If you get the chance again I want these people brought in to be interrogated properly. This global threat could be the worse we have ever faced and we're humiliatingly short of information."

"To be fair," Drake added gently, "that's mainly because they haven't engaged in any kind of real action yet. We have nothing to follow."

Hayden opened her mouth to reply but the door to their office opened and Lauren Fox walked in. All eyes turned to her.

She gave them a smile that didn't touch her eyes. "For better or worse," she said, "we have a plan."

CHAPTER THREE

Lauren Fox stood before the SPEAR team, unwilling to call herself a fully fledged member and wondering just what the hell she was doing there. Before the man had attacked her in New York, before she became unintentionally linked to a North Korean terrorist plot, before she met Jonathan Gates, she had been a successful two-thousand-dollar-an-hour escort with no more hang-ups than your standard call girl. Back then she had lived next door to a retired hooker who took it upon herself to offer unending sage advice. She was sharp, streetwise, quick-witted and headstrong. She found it hard to apologize. Growing up in a string of grueling foster homes would do that to you.

What the hell am I doing here? she thought again.

But the answer had already passed through her thoughts.

Jonathan Gates, she thought. *I'm here for Jonathan.* The Secretary had shown her kindness when it might have harmed his standing; had helped her and counted on her when circumstances proved that he should not. He'd even offered her a way out—of sorts. Or at least a safer way.

Now she wasn't so sure.

Hayden was the first to approach her, hands held out as if sensing the self-doubt. "Drink? We have coffee."

"They have caffeine in all its sinful forms," Dahl said, holding up a bottle of water. "Here. Catch this."

Drake paused with an FBI emblazoned mug held to his lips. "Sinful?"

"Yeah." The Swede nodded. "Do they sell pure water as far north as Yorkshire yet?"

Drake grunted. "Sure, it's made it up to God's country. We still manage to get by with our mugs of instant coffee though."

Dahl shook his head. "Heathens."

Drake nodded. "And happy."

Lauren took a long swig from the water bottle, grateful for the refreshing taste. She sat at the head of the table, conscious of all eyes upon her—not in a nervous way but in the hope she could help fulfil Jonathan's last request of her.

"General Stone," she said. "I've seen the bastard twice now and do not believe he suspects me. But I'm always careful, confident, and professional. You may remember at one time we believed that Stone might be skeptical of me. But no. Our first meeting was tentative, cautious—" She thought back. Bill Stone had requested they meet in a room situated on the first floor of an expensive hotel, arriving alone and in an almost laughable disguise. At that moment she had known the general was oblivious of her true intentions. Quiet, courteous, almost shy, Stone had requested the Nightshade routine. She had treated him gently, carefully, and with infinite vigilance, scared for her life in the obscure room but determined to see it through.

For an old guy, Stone didn't look bad naked. Yes, the gut was a little saggy, the pecs undefined, yes he was one frightfully hairy specimen, but she had entertained much worse day after day in her line of work. And he didn't want her to touch him. Not with her hands in any case. First the whip and then the restraints. This was a man of the Army who wanted an opposite experience of everyday life, a role reversal. With pegs, cuffs and rope she treated him well, until he begged for release. Even then she refused, bringing out the vulgarity in him, the haughtiness. From the shy man to the arrogant boor in thirty minutes, and beyond. Stone loved it, in the end begging for more.

But no. Their first session was over. Inevitably, such treatment led to a request for a second. This time Stone was less cautious, meeting her in a hotel less than a block from his office, and actually taking calls as their session progressed. The arrogance of the man shone through, the sheer superiority and self-knowledge that he was a being at the top of the evolutionary pile—the stalking predator.

Lauren tied him hard, trying to make him hurt, but Stone only embraced the pain, grunting for more. Of course there was a limit as to how far she could go, and she didn't want to destroy the inroads she'd so carefully made, so the diamond-studded choker wasn't *too* tight, the Saran wrap full of tiny holes in the vicinity of his mouth, and the nut-crunchers set to 'medium'.

The second session ended with Stone taking his third call of the evening, worry suddenly mixing with the ecstasy on his face, and the first real development in her operation. In true egotist style he spoke whilst ignoring her presence.

Now, glossing over the details of the evening—which she knew by the look on Smyth's face was a major disappointment—she brought the group up to date on her discoveries.

"Last night he recommended me to his 'partner', a man called Nicholas Bell, I believe, since Gates referred to him by both names in separate conversations. Now, normally I would decline but because Stone referred to this man as his 'partner' on more than one occasion, I feel it might be beneficial to see the man."

"Partner could mean so many things," Hayden said. "Could you get the gist of his meaning?"

"Well, he's not bi-sexual and didn't sound over friendly. That leaves business associate, which works for us."

"When does this Bell want to see you?"

"Wednesday night."

"I hate to say it," Drake spoke up, "but this sounds awful dangerous, Lauren."

"I've entertained two men before."

There was a short lull to enable Smyth to reel his tongue back in and for Drake to wait for the inevitable Alicia comment before remembering she wasn't in the room. Funny how you didn't really miss someone and their habits until they were gone from your life.

He zoned back in. "Not what I meant, love. We're talking at least one, possibly two, corrupt men that might be targets of the Pythians. How dangerous can you take it?"

"I'm a born and bred New Yorker." Lauren shrugged. "I always take it to the limit."

"We could follow the two of you," Kinimaka suggested. "Stay close."

"It's hardly necessary." Lauren raised her hands. "I'm doing this as much for Jonathan as you guys. If Stone's dirty I'm going to out the bastard in public. For all his goddamn sins. And this Bell? Stone spoke to him three times just last night, *whilst* we were in full-on role-play. One time, I even had to hold the phone close to Stone's ear because the handcuffs were too tight."

Smyth's chin finally hit the floor. "Oh my God. Will you be my girlfriend?"

Drake grunted. "Please say yes. It'll distract him from *other* hobbies that involve blaming auto-correct."

"Despite it all," Lauren went on. "Stone still plays the army man with me. He has no shame. No scruples. If chance had taken him in a different direction a man like that could easily have become a psychopath. He has no conscience beyond that which he pretends to portray."

"All right." Hayden took in the team's reactions with a glance. "It seems Stone and Bell may have something to hide. I say we follow Lauren's lead and remain on alert. Allow her to do her job. We'd do the same for anyone else in this team."

Drake nodded quickly. Hayden had hit the proverbial nail right on the head—it didn't matter that Lauren came by her intel a little differently to the rest of them—Jonathan had made her a part of SPEAR for a reason and, so far, she was holding up her end.

As the affirmations rolled in, Kinimaka's phone rang. He took a quick look at the screen and frowned.

"Damn, it's Agent Collins from Los Angeles," he said aloud. Claire Collins was a first-rate FBI agent that had recently helped crack a worldwide terror plot involving the Serbian mafia as well as saving Kinimaka's sister from the hands of the Blood King's men. "What the hell could she want now?"

CHAPTER FOUR

Claire Collins spoke in a tough, no-nonsense manner, brooking no interruptions and no speculation. Kinimaka put her on speakerphone and let the room listen to what she had to say.

"Mano, first a heads-up. Your sister is on her way to DC, with a belly full of fire and brimstone. She no longer needs protective custody now you and your gang of lightweights finally took down Kovalenko. Best team in the world? Not in my book."

Hayden, their leader, took that one. "Not that we ever asked for the accolade, but do you know a better one?"

"My team just took down a Serb madman threatening half a dozen of the world's leading capitals with unending terrorism. In one day. The white-knuckle ride of a lifetime. Can you top that?"

"You're talking about the Disavowed." Kinimaka nodded. "I heard they were good."

"*We're* good." Collins corrected him. "And faced with Threat Level Red, we're tremendous."

"Are they there?" Kinimaka asked. "I wanted to thank them personally for saving Kono's life."

"One of them is," a deep voice spoke up. "Aaron Trent. And it's fine. Enjoyed the opportunity to rid the world of some trash."

Trent spoke in a clipped manner, serious and to the point, as if time was always precious. Drake had heard the story of how his team had been set up to be disavowed by the president, and of how they had lost friends, wives and fellow brothers in arms in their struggle to right such a great wrong, and of how they had prevailed. Still, he couldn't fully respect a man's abilities until he'd seen him in action.

"It seems there's a new threat," he said aloud. "You guys ever heard of the Pythians?"

"Newest set of evildoers by all accounts," Collins broke in quickly. "And who is that? Mano? Don't tell me I'm on friggin' speakerphone with your whole damn team."

"Don't worry," Dahl said. "Alicia Myles is missing."

"And this is Drake," the Yorkshireman spoke up. "Matt Drake."

Collins didn't miss a beat. "Okay then. Well, we're the FBI, Drake. We know all about the house on the hill killings. The global recruitment of mercenaries. The massive movements of funds. We're also privy to what the NSA are monitoring—that there has been a huge surge in the amount of mercenary and terrorist chatter in the past week over all known channels and others we aren't supposed to monitor. We know—"

"Something's about to happen," Hayden finished. "Yeah, the rumors are everywhere. Trouble is—we have nothing concrete."

"The chatter will narrow down. Localize. Then we'll know."

Kinimaka had been trying to process the imminent arrival of his sister, Kono, and what it might mean for his health. Never easy to get along with, his sister now blamed him for their mother's murder and her own new misfortunes. The fact that she left Hawaii years ago for the lure of a seedy world, and in doing so broke their mother's heart, didn't seem to matter anymore. Everything was now Mano's fault.

He snapped back to the present. Kono would have to wait. "Well, Trent, thanks again. And the same to Silk and Radford. I know what you guys lost to Blanka Davic. We've been chasing that bandit down for years."

Drake remembered taking Davic's father down during the quest for the bones of Odin. It struck him then how small the world and the circles that they all ran in actually were; either that or they had all been a part of somebody's master plan from the very beginning.

Come together at last.

"Trent, this is Drake. You probably know this bloody Pythian thing is escalating. Whatever you can learn, it would be appreciated."

"We're on it."

Collins ended the call by reminding Kinimaka of why she'd called. "Watch out for that one when she lands, my friend. I know she's your sister, but she's trouble."

Kinimaka nodded to himself. *Try telling me something I don't friggin' know.*

CHAPTER FIVE

Drake was with Mai when Grace returned from her time with the private investigator. By not saying anything the Japanese woman had requested his presence. For that alone he was grateful. For two weeks now this private investigator had been searching into Grace's past, trying to stitch together the tattered patchwork quilt that was her memory. *Two weeks. Surely he must have dug up something,* Drake thought. But seventeen years was an awfully long timespan to have to trawl through, and Grace herself said she could remember nothing beyond her time with the Tsugarai and her master, Gozu. Drake knew they were bad times. Best forgotten. Mai Kitano had saved Grace's life the moment she untangled those bonds, in more ways than one. Then Mai had made herself personally responsible for Grace's welfare and future, a development Grace seemed not entirely happy about. So when Hayden offered to help by introducing Grace to an off-the-books investigator, they had all leaped at the chance. Perhaps Grace could get some real closure; maybe she could start to live again. Even find her parents. A fresh start and all that. In particular, maybe he could do something the DC doctors couldn't—help find and revive her past memories. Grace needed to be made whole again.

In any case, he could search for her *physical* past.

Drake knew that Grace regretted her refusal of Mai's offer of companionship the moment he saw her. The normally upbeat outer veneer crumbled and a tear fell from the corner of her eye. Drake feared the worst.

Mai stepped forward, taking her in her arms.

"You are seventeen," she said. "You have been through hell. Standing up for yourself is one of the ways you will begin to step back into the real world."

Drake had met Aiden Hardy very briefly before they allowed Grace to visit alone. He remembered the man as in his early thirties, rugged, with a day's growth covering his big chin, and a smile that made his eyes twinkle, which was a quality someone like Grace would hopefully take to.

Grace pulled away from Mai, staring down at the floor and letting her words rush out in a flood. "He said that Hayden called him in to find answers. Nothing official, but something done quicker and dirtier than usual. That's kinda my specialty, he said." Grace sniffed. "He called me in because he found something."

Mai stroked her hair. Drake had never seen her so soft, so nervous. He knew that Mai was being bombarded mentally on two fronts—from feelings for Grace and the family of the man she had killed.

"Hardy stopped smiling after a minute," the young girl said, "and told me that I was probably a runaway." Tears caught in her throat. "I have no family history up to the age of twelve that he has yet found, which is probably when I ran away. But after that, there's more than enough. At twelve I was a streetwalker, bought and sold. These men, these animals that control the slave trade, they know what they're doing. They keep you pliable through a cocktail of alcohol and drugs, and probably brutality, that's what Hardy told me. I was one of the lost, ready to be used up and thrown away. I was failed, adrift. Treated as garbage. Of course, the dark streets of most major cities are awash with stories like mine. I was somebody's daughter, I guess, but that somebody is unknown."

Drake saw Grace's show of confidence slipping. "I don't even know if my mother loved me." She sniffed.

Drake swallowed hard. Mai held the girl in strong arms. "Your mother loved you," she said. "I know it."

Now Grace's voice grew harsher. "You haven't figured out the worst part have you?"

Drake frowned. "You might still be able to find them."

Grace wiped her eyes. "It's not that. Finding them is a dream that might save me, but *not knowing* what happened to me from age twelve until now is one thing. *Remembering* it is going to be . . ." She began to wail, burying her head.

Drake felt a slice of horror stab his heart. What could be worse that having horrific old memories return? The memories she had so long craved for would serve only to ruin her again.

Drake fought to speak. "As the memories return perhaps you can get counselling. Or—"

Grace shook. "All the memories that will return to me are . . . are . . . horrible ones. And there's nothing I can do to stop it. All I can do is . . . quit."

Mai spoke for the first time. "So I'm suggesting that you start living your life. Now. For the present and the future because the past *will* one day return and you will need great new memories to help combat those long regressed nightmares."

Grace shook her head slowly, clearly unable to believe her quandary.

I'm an empty shell," she said. "A blank sheet. Love is dead, long live vengeance. Where do I belong?"

Drake responded to the thin voice, the devastated tone. "To the here and now," he said. "Make yourself a life full of shiny new memories."

"Here? Now? At seventeen? But once I was a child! *I am somebody's daughter! I am. And my mother loved me!*"

Drake nodded. "So rise again. Find them. And be stronger than those chains protecting your heart and soul. Be a fighter. I mean, you're in the right company, love."

Mai met the girl's complex dilemma head on. "So here you are, at memory-age three weeks, and having to deal with a decision-making event that would faze most adults. The question is—would a person *want* to remember such horrifying events? If a man could forget what he had seen in war," she glanced up at Drake, "or if a woman could forget the night of her rape. If a police officer could forget just a few of the shocking and terrifying scenes they are forced to witness month by month, year by year, would they choose to do so?"

Grace stared in silence, maybe filing the question away for later consideration. The answer, Drake knew, was moot. Grace had no control over the resurrection of her memories. But she did have strength. And purpose.

She did have a future.

CHAPTER SIX

Lauren Fox started the most dangerous night of her life by choosing the right kind of high heels, ankle bracelet and stockings to wear. The length of her skirt, the color of her nails, the severity of her makeup. Nightshade could be created in minutes, but it took hours to form her masterpiece. Friends would not recognize her, let alone colleagues like Smyth and Hayden Jaye. By the time she was finished she felt a little sorry for the boys and men out walking and sitting with their girlfriends that Wednesday night.

They could not help but look.

Lauren grabbed her overlarge handbag, called a cab, and told it to take her to the Dupont Plaza Hotel via Constitution. She enjoyed the ride along the wide stately road, the poignant and evocative views helping her relax. Tonight the traffic was light, the areas around the monuments were almost empty and the sidewalks were barren. She directed the cab driver up 18th and across Connecticut, not because she thought he was new to the game but because she craved a little self-rule before entering a room where two powerful men awaited. Six months ago the scenario would not have bothered her. Now, knowing what she knew about Stone and Gates and the SPEAR team and what could be at stake, she already knew several shots of fortification would soon be required.

The cab dropped her outside the hotel. Lauren climbed

out, drawing the long heavy coat about her outlandishly clad body to avoid attracting prying eyes, a maneuver she was long familiar with. Even then, passers-by gave her more than a second glance, some of the creepier ones trying to make extended eye contact.

Lauren pushed through the front doors and headed purposefully for the elevators, ignoring the front desk. Within a few minutes she was heading up to the eleventh floor, ignoring the stares of the bellhop, unable to shake the feeling that everything was about to go wrong. Damn, she should be confident—this was her job, her only profession. The mechanics weren't exactly complicated. Both Stone and Bell would be putty in her hands. But for that to happen she had to feel more than confidence, she needed to exude it, discharge it like a weapon.

Usually, by now, Nightshade had taken over. Lauren found herself knocking on the general's door with doubt lingering at the forefront of her mind.

Quicker than she expected, it opened. Stone stood there, glaring, his eyes as hard and black as obsidian, evaluating everything.

"Well, well," he said. "Do we have a problem?"

Smyth exited the Pentagon soon after Lauren, stating to Hayden that he needed a few hours off. The team were in full information-gathering mode, not exactly Smyth's strong suit, and nobody thought it unusual when he left. Besides, the others needed the odd break from his relentless, steady irascible snappishness, they all told him that often enough.

Smyth took a car, a black nondescript Chevy, and tailed Lauren back to her place, then again in the cab. Traffic was mercifully light. All the while he was wondering just what the hell he was doing.

Lauren didn't need his help. She would beat him down—vocally at least—if she found out he was tailing her. The rest of the team hadn't raised any major concerns, although Smyth had noticed Drake's uncertainty. An unaccountable need to help reflected clearly in the Englishman's dark eyes. But he hadn't voiced anything: no promises, no requests. Clearly this team had evolved to the level where if you didn't ask for help you didn't get it.

Smyth didn't truly believe that. Real life always got in the way, and real life now involved trying to head off a major international crisis encompassing these Pythian assholes and something about Pandora. Quickly, he reined in his wrath, knowing it was unfounded.

Why then did he feel the need to follow Lauren?

Well, who wouldn't? was his immediate, flippant answer. But that wasn't it. Lauren was part of the team and the only one in danger tonight. Smyth just couldn't allow himself to let her take this on alone. After the loss of Romero . . .

Smyth gritted his teeth, fighting down an urge to strike the wheel. Quick to anger he was also quick to forgive, although kept that questionable value to himself. The image he portrayed was fine by him—it gave him solitude when he needed it and was always handy to end a tricky conversation. Conversely, it also allowed him to follow orders, which was Smyth's highest goal in life. He would make a show of disliking them but would always fall in line, because that's where he wanted to be—out of the limelight.

When Lauren's cab cleared the Dupont Circle and stopped outside the Plaza, Smyth allowed his Chevy to drift over to the opposite curb. Illegally parked and finding it hard to care he stalked across the road to her blind side. Concerned that he remain hidden from her sight, he needn't have bothered. Lauren's eyes were fixed firmly ahead, as much in an effort to avoid appraising glances as a way of getting her head in the game. Through the hotel doors they went, then Smyth saw his first major problem.

Elevators.

As Lauren headed across the large lobby, Smyth scoured the room for an ally. The first that caught his eye was a short bellhop, dressed in the hotel's smart livery. With a bound Smyth was at the guy's side.

"The woman heading toward the elevators." He didn't need to elaborate. Judging by the bellhop's eyes there *was* only one woman in the lobby at that moment. "I need to know the number of the room she goes into."

He flashed a twenty, then a second, secretly hoping the little ass would just get a move on.

"Hooker?" the bellhop asked. "Or cheating wife?"

Smyth wanted to slap him. "Both," he hissed. "Now, hurry. You'll be helping out a good man."

The bellhop, already sold, snatched the bills from Smyth's hand and surged forward, pushing a half-loaded suitcase trolley. Smyth nodded in appreciation.

The bellhop grinned. "Not my first rodeo."

Smyth didn't smile back. His lips stretched thin and his eyes clouded as he watched Lauren enter the elevator.

Something was going to ignite here, in this hotel, he was sure of it. Something big. Lauren was only fanning the flames, heading into the heart of the fire. For the first time that he could remember, he just hoped he would be proved wrong.

Lauren reacted fast. Luckily the bellhop was plodding by at that moment, pushing his half-loaded trolley. Her eyes flicked from Stone to the bellhop and she stayed silent.

Thank God for the bellhop.

The general winced a little, perhaps realizing he'd come close to being spotted, perhaps not caring one iota. In his game, at his level, any kind of publicity could be doctored, spun, and put to good use. He held the door open.

Lauren squeezed inside, distinctly conscious that Stone made no effort to move aside. When their bodies touched he grunted, licking his lips. These were the times when Lauren really had to rein in her true nature. The everyday New Yorker persona was confident, outspoken, streetwise and more than a little caustic. Her professional façade kept those qualities under wraps, preferring to express them in other ways once she got her most obnoxious subjects under lock and key.

Or Saran wrap, she speculated.

For now, Stone was the client. She jammed herself into the room, expecting and immediately seeing a lavish apartment. Would somebody like Stone charge this to the taxpayer?

She almost laughed aloud. Stupid question.

Fiddling with the buttons on her coat, Lauren drifted over to the ceiling-length windows, pretending to be entranced by the lights as she gathered her courage. Tonight, she was sure, she was working for the good guys against the enemy. And that simple adjustment to her standard Nightshade character made all the damn difference.

In less than a minute, Stone was behind her, hands by his

sides. "Before we get started," he said. "Maybe you should meet my associate, Mr. Bell."

Stone placed a hand on her shoulder, turning her around. Nicholas Bell stood to one side, grinning. Lauren's immediate thought was *Shit, have we got this all wrong?* Bell looked like a nice guy: great smile, hard body, laughing eyes. The complete opposite of Stone. Lauren was immediately drawn to the man, a rare event in her line of work. Was he really working with Stone? And what did the goddamn Pythians want with these two?

Bell stepped forward, right hand held out. "Nicholas Bell. Builder. Pleased to meet you."

Lauren smiled and shook. The only chink to this man's agreeable armor was that he had given her his real name and, possibly, occupation. *Builder?* Maybe not. Only those with ludicrous superiority complexes would give the game away at first contact.

She remained on guard. "Nightshade," she said with an arched smile.

"The bane of many a good man." Bell offered her a glass of champagne.

Lauren never drank in a strange apartment. She declined with a wave of her hand. "Shall we get started?"

Bell bowed. "I am yours to command."

Stone retired to the lounge, leaving them alone. Bell leaned in and whispered in a conspiratorial tone. "Thank God, I thought the old bastard was going to stick around and watch."

Lauren tried to hide the quick grin but failed. "Are you ready, Mr. Bell? Before we get started I always like to agree on a safe word. You know, if things get a little too . . .

challenging? Does *purple* work for you?"

Again the diverting smile. "Whatever you say."

Lauren hesitated. "Has Stone explained to you what I do?" Twice in the past she had visited clients that had been "set up" by their so-called friends, men that had run screaming when the nipple clamps came out.

Bell only nodded.

Lauren unbuttoned her coat, letting the material pool to the floor. Bell gasped appreciatively. Underneath she wore black stockings, a leather skirt that fell to mid-thigh, shiny boots that ended at the knee and a matching jacket with a shiny silver zip, undone to maximize her cleavage.

"Lady," Bell almost panted. "That's—"

Lauren cracked the whip. "Shut your mouth," she said. "And get down on your knees."

As she acted out her routine Lauren found her mind wandering. It wasn't worth speculating on why a man like Bell would pay for her attentions. Men were complex beasts, impossible to ever fully understand, brimming with all sorts of primeval needs. Men buried their secrets deep and that was why Lauren found it difficult, impossible even, to form any kind of relationship with one. Yes, she was jaded, cynical, but then she *had* seen the opposite sex in all its degradations.

Take Nicholas Bell as a prime example. Rich, powerful, very good looking. No doubt he drove an expensive car, prowled the streets through the day and hit the clubs and private receptions at night, leaving with a girl draped over each powerful shoulder. A playboy. A celebrity in his own small world.

Take away the wealthy trimmings and Lauren might have been attracted to him. Add the dash of darkness and every ounce of perception in her body screamed out in warning. The trouble was, where men were concerned they always did.

Canned laughter drifted through from the lounge, Stone watching some kind of regimented comedy. Lauren straddled Bell's back, scraping blood red fingernails down the length of his spine. The man shivered. Lauren swiveled and continued around the swell of his buttocks, the sensitive backs of his legs. With the tip of her whip she brushed the soles of his feet. Bell, confined, could only grunt and roll. Lauren climbed off and taught him the error of his ways.

Two hours passed. Lauren alternated between pleasure and pain, always leaving Bell guessing as to what was coming next—the gentle tickling touch of her long dark hair across his chest or the sharp sting of the whip; the bite of teeth, human or otherwise; the delectable tip of her tongue. A time came when Bell barely knew which century they were in and didn't care. The sounds of his elation finally drowned out the monotonous TV.

Later, they lay on the luxurious couch together, one of them sipping wine. Lauren found Bell, now wrapped in a thick white robe, laid back and relaxed, taking time to listen to her as well as address her comments. For those moments she felt like she was the only thing on his mind, but she couldn't help but know otherwise. The man was a consummate player, or an unwitting innocent. Lauren could only guess as to which. Again she was struck by how different he was to Stone—Bell lying around half-naked and growing gradually drunker whereas Stone was always reserved, inflexible, as taut as the suspension wires on the Brooklyn Bridge.

It was only when the general walked in that Lauren fully remembered her mission. Hours had passed and she was no closer to any kind of truth. On the plus side both men seemed to be at ease with her.

"In a moment," Stone said. "I shall take a turn but in the meantime I need to talk to Mr. Bell here. Privately."

"Wait right here." Bell patted her hip.

"Oh, I don't think she's going anywhere," Stone bellowed. "I think the girl enjoys our little trysts."

Lauren shrugged, pouring herself another glass of wine and stretching along the couch so that her long legs were revealed. The two men walked back into the lounge with lingering looks, mere clay dolls for her to manipulate. When they closed the door Lauren swallowed down her anxiety, tipped the wine into a nearby plant pot, and headed across the room.

The best part of her job as Nightshade, she reflected, was that she didn't actually have to lie with men like these. She was broad-minded to say the least, but some requests still shocked her and powerful characters like Stone and Bell acting out submissive role plays didn't sit right. Now she placed her ear carefully to the closed door and thought a silent *Yes!* when she heard Stone mute the TV.

"Enjoying my gift, Nicholas?" Stone's voice was faint, but Lauren could still hear the superior tones. She pressed herself closer to the door, angered by his superciliousness.

"Passes the dull hours of waiting," Bell answered without any emotion to his voice. "I'm still at a loss as to why Webb suggested I should come down here instead of returning home."

Lauren remembered the name. Stone's laugh was cold. "Perhaps it's to keep you safe."

Bell didn't have Stone's deep sense of sarcasm and condescension. "You think? I thought he might be trying to keep an eye on me."

Stone didn't respond. He went silent for a while, prompting Lauren's heart to miss a beat. Was he approaching the door? If she left it too late she wouldn't be able to make the couch in time . . .

Then he spoke again. "Whilst you were . . . occupied . . . I took a call from Mr. Webb. Things have moved along."

Lauren heard footsteps. With a trusted instinct born of years of vetting clients she bounded back toward the couch, draping herself at the last second. The lounge door opened and Stone stuck his head out.

"Have everything you need, dear? Don't you fall asleep on us, now."

Lauren made a practice swing with her whip. "Just keeping it warm."

Stone withdrew, closing the door once more. Lauren immediately took her life in her hands and sprang across the room, again placing her ear to the smooth surface.

"Can't be too careful," she heard Stone say. "Like I was saying—things have moved along." Lauren now heard an entirely uncharacteristic and frankly bizarre tone of excitement enter his voice. "The factory," he said. "It is *finished.*"

"Really?" Bell sounded shocked. "That was fast."

Stone's utter elation shone through in his raised voice. Lauren found the sound of it more than creepy.

"The factory is finished. Pandora can now be weaponized!"

"Shit." Bell's voice betrayed his fear.

"What? Does that scare you?"

"We don't even have Pandora yet. It's too early. There's so much to do."

"Keep your goddamn panties on, Bell. Unless that whore stuffed 'em where the sun don't shine. Huh? Huh?"

Lauren felt her hands clench into fists.

"No, Bill. I mean the factory is everything. The hub of our Pandora operation."

"*My* operation," Stone cut in.

"Yes, and the factory's on the other side of the world. Beyond our control. Is Webb sure they got it right? For an operation that started off so slow it sure is gaining ground at warp speed."

"If you were a military man you would know operations do that," Stone said. "Slow to start, then a magnificent rush and you're done. Every one fluid, ever-changing. You have to go with the flow, ride the treacherous waves. Christ, man, that's the fun part."

"If you think I see this particular operation as *fun* then you're vastly more screwy than I first believed."

"Well, Miranda's up soon. Imagine what wonders that perverted bitch can conjure up. Between you and me, I'm looking forward to her offering."

Again, Lauren stored the name away. Whatever these people were up to it clearly wasn't a shopping trip to Macy's and they appeared to have associates. Then she heard a comment that almost stopped her heart.

It was Stone's callous voice. "If the governments don't fall into line thousands will die. Hundreds of thousands. This Pandora plague . . . it will make us."

45

Lauren didn't hear what else was said for at least thirty seconds. That single word, despite its apparent absence in any standard worldwide form for centuries, still struck a hot white lance into most people's hearts.

Plague.

The word conjured rotting bodies in the streets, horrible, agonizing pustule-based death, no chance of immunity and that dreaded waiting . . . waiting to see if you or your loved ones contracted it.

Lauren pushed the terror aside, forcing herself to concentrate on what was being said inside the lounge. Now more than ever the information she gleaned tonight was imperative.

". . . time to find the three plague pits," Stone was saying. "If we fail there we fail with the entire operation."

Good to know, Lauren thought.

"And then Miranda?" Bell's voice shivered.

"Maybe. I heard Clifford's looking hard for this lost kingdom," Stone said, unreserved in his glee. "But first— it's my turn. The factory will start up in earnest as soon as we provide samples. So let's get to it. Our network of soldiers is immense, and each regiment, even each cell, believes it is working for somebody else, and that *that* person works for the Pythians. Ingenious, yes?"

Again Lauren missed Bell's response. Pythians? Was that why the secret group were interested in Stone and Bell? Because they were besmirching their notorious name?

Then Stone said, "Back to our pleasures."

And Bell answered. "I'll leave you to it. We are the Pythians."

Stone's answer was just as reverent. "We are the Pythians."

As footsteps came toward the door, Lauren's jaw hit the floor.

CHAPTER SEVEN

"Excuse me, my dear, but I think we can double your money." Stone exited the room whilst speaking, then locked eyes on to her position. "What are you doing?"

Lauren turned from the window, empty glass in hand. "Admiring the view, Mr. Stone. Would you like to do the same?"

She struck a pose with the lights of DC shining behind her, the handcuffs hanging from her belt and brushing her thigh, the jacket now fully unzipped.

Stone indicated the bag containing the tricks of her trade. "Want to do both of us at the same time? That's five grand for you."

It took all the years and every ounce of Lauren's experience to affect a lascivious smile. "Nightshade would be pleased with that."

Stone advanced, followed by Bell. Lauren noticed a wide smile replacing the sick look coating his face. "Round two?" he asked.

"The final round." Lauren couldn't help but return the smile.

Hours later, Lauren walked away as the two tired, sore men shrugged into luxurious dressing gowns. Seeing another opportunity she swigged from a champagne bottle, draining it dry so that they would think she'd consumed more than an entire bottle that night. The three sat and talked quietly, now breaking out the Bourbon, Stone with his typical conceited reserve, and Stone with his open charm. Lauren had to admit that together they made a very complex team. What did that mean for the rest of the Pythians?

Feigning exhaustion, she mentioned leaving and then sleep, taking a full double-shot of Bourbon and pretending to pass out right there on the couch. The ball was in their court. They would either make her comfortable, call her a cab, or take some kind of advantage. Lauren was covered in every way, she could always feign waking up. Not only that but she believed Bell would protect her honor.

A warning tone went off. *Are you mad?*

Probably. How else could I have survived this long?

In any case, the need for information now came before anything else, including her dignity and, above all, she abhorred the idea of ever seeing Stone again in private. Her debt to Jonathan was paid. The general was a monster, straight from his own mouth.

"The girl is passed-out drunk," Stone said matter-of-factly. "So I guess she doesn't get paid."

Bell grunted. "Don't be any more of an ass than you already are. A diversion like her for men like us? She's gold. You should encourage her, not drive her away."

"Perhaps. But in any case, we have a little more to discuss before retiring. Let her sleep it off awhile."

Lauren heard movement, felt a pat on the rump from Stone's heavy hand, and then footsteps crossed to the lounge. A door closed. Fear gripped Lauren's soul as she opened her eyes and rose. She was standing so close to the edge she felt herself teetering. If Stone found her this time she could very well be dropped off the outside balcony.

Lauren wavered. It was only when the snippets of information she'd already uncovered flooded back that she felt galvanized to move. *Pythians* . . . *factory* . . . *weaponized . . . plague!*

Damn, if only she had backup.

Placing her ear to the door, and ensuring her route back to the couch was free, she resumed her earlier role of . . . the thought crossed her mind that she'd played so many roles tonight there was a chance she'd forget her own identity. But then voices filled her head.

Stone was in full flow, ". . . London, Paris and Los Angeles remain our three areas of necessity . . . the freshest graves."

Lauren recalled from Kinimaka's briefing earlier that the SPEAR team already knew the Pythians were highly motivated by those three particular cities—something about mercenaries being recruited and offered ridiculous money to await instructions at the one of their choice. SPEAR had garnered the information from mercs that had later declined the Pythians' offer. Hearing Stone say it now only confirmed what they already knew.

Then Bell said, "As you know, General, I don't have to work. I'm available to oversee any of those cities, if required."

"I'm aware that you don't work, Bell. That fact is clear in your vitality alone."

"Is that a compliment?"

"Not at all."

"Ah. Silly me."

"Look, Bell. Why would you even want to oversee those operations? Do you forget that I organized them personally?"

"You mentioned a while ago that the three plague pits are the most important part of your operation. Doesn't it just make sense to have a leader oversee each one of them?"

Stone didn't respond for a while. Lauren imagined he was considering Bell's words. The information she had already collected was enough to get her killed. At least twice. As much as she wanted to stick around and learn more, Lauren began to wonder if she might have pushed her luck just about as far as it could go.

Nevertheless, her allegiance to SPEAR and Jonathan kept her ear glued to the door.

"My commanders in the field will do just fine," Stone eventually said. "They're all vetted and most importantly they're all ex-military Special Forces. I doubt that a newly rich builder could hold much of a candle to them."

"Self-made." Bell stood up to the general for the first time. "I earned every penny of it. Can you really say the same, Bill?"

"I'm not sure that I understand."

"I meant your authority. The power you wield. Earned it on the field did you? Or was it some kind of Harvard hand-me-down?"

Nothing was said for a moment and Lauren, concentrating hard, missed her cue. Of course she should have imagined the egotistical general storming out, all bluster and self-righteous anger. She might then not have lost everything in his murderous hands.

Stone pushed open the door so hard it struck Lauren and propelled her backwards into the room. At first the look on his face was a Polaroid moment, utter disbelief and shock, but then surprise turned to absolute rage.

"You bitch! You goddamn bitch. I knew you were too fucking good to be true!"

"I was just . . . I was just coming in to fetch you."

Stone swung at her, missing. Bell was at his heels. "Wait. Wait! She could be telling the truth."

Lauren backed away toward the door. Stone lunged and stuck her chest with an outstretched hand, knocking her off balance. As she fell he pulled out a walkie-talkie. "Get in here!" he screamed. "We have a big problem."

Lauren struck the wall, the impact smashing the breath from her body. She exhaled with a cry. Some kind of instinct kicked in. She remembered when the Koreans had sent a brainwashed soldier to silence her back in New York and how she had fought tooth and nail with that killer, eventually sending him over the balcony. That same fire, that same voice, rose within her now, ordering her to stand and fight, to make an account of herself. Quickly, she rolled and bounced to her feet.

Just as the hotel room door burst open.

Men rushed inside, weapons drawn but held down by their sides to escape corridor CCTV. Lauren saw the whisker of a chance and leaped forward immediately. Once that door was closed she was dead.

CHAPTER EIGHT

Her attackers wore suits and ties. Feeling a little ridiculous, the woman clad in leather and thigh boots struck out at them, first yanking a man by the knot of his tie so that he stumbled past her, then blasting another between the legs with an uninhibited kick. Her left hand grabbed for the door, flinging it wide, and her right jabbed clumsily at the nearest gun. Yes she had been trained, but only in a dojo where mistakes were never punished by death.

Not like this.

As she slipped toward the gap in the door, alongside the startled men, she felt an enormous impact in the center of her back. Somebody's boot. Stone's boot.

Unable to stop herself she flew forward, colliding headlong with the door jamb; the edge of the frame drawing blood from her forehead. A man clamped her neck before she fell completely out into the corridor, another hooked and dragged at her legs.

Still kicking, screaming, Lauren was pulled back into the hotel room. Sensing the end and more worried about imparting the information she had learned than her own welfare, she planted both feet and pushed back. The men around her staggered. Lauren wrenched free of their grip, tearing clothes and a lock of hair and ignoring the flare of pain. She was alone, she was SPEAR, she had been chosen for this.

With a kick she disarmed one man, drove an elbow into

another. When a third struck at her she caught his blows on her biceps, twisting into them and then unleashing a strike of her own. A space developed, a path to freedom. Lunging, she cleared three men, already feeling the fresh air of freedom as she skipped between their flailing legs, but others remained. They couldn't use their guns, not in this hotel, but they could use their bodies. Perhaps sensing her imminent escape and their own terrible reprimand they dived in front of her.

Unable to dodge out of the way Lauren went tumbling, entangled in a mass of arms and legs. As she lay panting, a fist drove into her ribs, another into the back of her neck. Stars exploded in front of her eyes. She slumped. Now, in front of her she could see Stone gloating, Bell appearing confused, and a man already heading purposefully toward the French windows.

"The balcony?" a voice said. "The way she's dressed it's almost expected."

"Sure. I don't care," Stone said dismissively. "But wipe her down first. All that leather and PVC might have retained our fingerprints."

Lauren struggled wildly, kicking shins, rolling away from uncertain grips. The men grappled with her. Bell voiced concern. Stone told him to get the hell over it, the bitch was taking a midnight dive.

Lauren swiveled once more, her face striking the room's carpet. As she landed, almost blinded with pain, she caught a last glimpse of the rapidly closing hotel room door.

Someone stood in the gap, someone she knew.

Was she hallucinating?

Smyth raced forward, one man against seven, but this

man was ex-Delta and a member of SPEAR. What men like Smyth could do was kill or incapacitate with a single strike, grab a weapon and squeeze off three kill shots out of three. He proceeded to do so now, but Stone was already radioing for backup. Smyth saw that these guards were better trained than the usual fodder, and he unleashed his anger, concentrating his attack on the men that held Lauren.

"Who's this?" Stone said stiffly. "Her pimp?"

Smyth broke the wrist of the man holding Lauren's waist, gliding in as she fell and taking her weight. As he moved he assaulted the rest. He could see their unease, their bewilderment. Who was this new attacker? Since he had fired first could they now return the favor?

Stone's orders were non-existent. Smyth broke a larynx and a nose, plucked up a gun and fired off an untargeted shot. As expected, Stone and his men reacted with fear, immediately guessing all and sundry would be calling the authorities. Smyth used the added confusion to nab Lauren and disarm two more of Stone's men.

He retained the gun, leveling it at Stone's face. "Don't move. Any of you."

"You'll regret this," Stone said. "Whoever you are. And Nightshade too. I did wonder about you from the very beginning."

Lauren fought to stand, but found her battered body couldn't quite manage it. Damn, she wanted to help her rescuer. Never had she felt so inadequate. Without warning two men broke from the group and ran at them. Smyth, still supporting her, shot one in the thigh whilst ensuring the last ran into an elbow.

Smyth back toward the door. "First one to stick his head

out gets it blown off." With that the short-tempered soldier pulled Lauren out into the corridor. "Sorry about the whip," he said. "Didn't have time to grab it."

"It . . . it's okay. I'll get another."

"Do you mind if I pick you up?" he asked with more courteousness than she could have believed possible. "Over my shoulder? We'll move faster." He threw a guarded look back toward the hotel room.

"Whatever you have to do, Smyth. Just get me out of here!"

"Yes, ma'am." Smyth bent at the waist, heaved Lauren over his shoulder, and sprinted forward. They raced down the hallway as one, stopping at the first bank of elevators.

"How the hell did you find me?"

"Followed you here. Used the bellhop to get Stone's room number. Sat on the comfy seats there—" he indicated a set of deep, leather couches positioned opposite the elevator doors. "Until I heard all the commotion. I always figured if Lauren Fox were in trouble she'd put up one hell of a fight."

Lauren let her head hang, trusting that Smyth would protect her. "Thank you," she said. "Thank you so much."

"Not needed." Smyth maneuvered them into the elevator. "You're a part of my team, Lauren. You're family."

"I am?" She caught a look at herself in the highly polished walls. "Christ, I look such a fright they could hire me out as a Halloween ghost."

Smyth, defying all that she knew about him, kept his eyes on the ground. "Maybe a kinky one."

Lauren slipped off his back and landed on her feet, groaning. "Thank you."

"Like I said. You're family."

CHAPTER NINE

Drake took the call in the dead of night, instantly awake. This early, Hayden's words were a little fuzzy but he got the gist.

"*Get down to the freakin' HQ! Now!*"

Mai was already awake, staring up at the high ceiling. "Time to go?"

Drake sat up in bed, rubbing his face. "Aye. Have you slept?"

"A little. I'm worried about Grace and . . . other things."

"I know. I thought, during the last few weeks, we might have broached that subject a little more."

Mai glanced at him. "A little more?"

"Well, just once would be fine."

"It's my mess, Matt, and if it comes back to bite me . . ."

"We'll deal with it together." Drake hugged her close. "I knew I should have gone to Tokyo with you."

Mai pulled away and rose, keeping her back to him as she dressed. "Really? And what would you have done so differently?"

Drake sighed, realizing he was on shaky ground. "I dunno, love. You haven't told me a bloody thing. Any road, if we're quick, we can cadge a lift off the Mad Swede."

Mai gave him a quick, long-suffering smile. "You talking gibberish again?"

"Oh, sorry. In the Queen's English—put a spurt on, my dear, and perhaps we can share Mr. Dahl's vehicle."

"That's better."

Together they rushed out of the room just in time to see Dahl, who rented the large apartment opposite their somewhat more conservative one with his freshly arrived family, struggling to extract himself from his wife's embrace.

"Need a hand, pal?" Drake asked drily.

Dahl managed to free one arm.

"We can wait two and a half minutes if you like."

Then Dahl was free, but Johanna snagged his hair at the last second.

"Seriously. We'll wait in the car."

The Swede caught them up a short while later, giving Drake a sideways glance as he fell in. "Not a bloody word."

"Me? As if . . ."

DC was quiet in the absolute dead of night; office buildings, museums and monuments still blazing to give it all the appearance of a functioning ghost town. Mai stared out the window as they made the short journey to the famous five-sided concrete structure, her mood also affecting the men. None of them knew why they'd been called in but, with the current unrest and hypothetical fallout from the Pythian threat, the prospects were bleak. Not knowing where in the world they would be by this time tomorrow, Drake made a point of addressing Dahl.

"Seriously though, mate, is Johanna enjoying DC?"

Dahl made a non-committal face. "It's like picking my way through a minefield with them. So far, they're treating it as a holiday. But when the novelty wears off, who knows, especially now since the Blood Vendetta has been lifted."

"You did the right thing." Drake said with eyes fixed

forward. "Bringing them here."

"Try telling them that," the Swede grumped.

"Doesn't matter, mate. Sometimes the best thing to do is the one that upsets someone the most and you can't explain why. They'll get over it."

Mai chose that moment to catch his attention. "Do you believe that?"

"Of course."

"Good." She turned away again.

Drake shared a couple of raised eyebrows with Dahl and fell silent. Soon, they were entering the Pentagon and making their way toward their new HQ. Drake was still getting used to the diverging hallways and highly polished floors, the black-suited and military-garbed men striding the halls, medals catching the light, the endless walls of security. At last they entered through an oak door.

The first thing Drake saw was a disheveled, bloody Lauren Fox. Then the peculiar sight of Smyth hovering protectively behind her, also looking battered.

Hayden walked to the center of the room. "Lauren's mission went a little . . . awry." She proceeded to give a potted account of the night's events, focusing mainly on the conversations Lauren had overheard. Drake was amazed by the scope of information, happy to see several scrappy clues fall into place.

"So London, Paris and LA are the locations of the three plague pits and they're going to attempt to weaponize whatever they find in there? Score one, two and three for Miss Fox."

He saw Smyth nod and put a hand on the woman's shoulder, then suddenly think better of it. "We should all have been there," Drake said softly.

Hayden held up both hands. "We'll save the blame for later," she said. "Right now, those cities are in grave danger. We must focus our efforts on them."

"What about this factory?" Dahl asked. "Take the factory out immediately—destroy the threat."

Lauren shot him an apologetic look. "Sorry, they didn't reveal its whereabouts."

"No need to apologize," Dahl said. "This is a great step forward. Jonathan never trusted the general and because you saw his opinion through to the end, you're allowing him to help us even now."

Lauren's face broke out into a smile.

"We have a lot of work to do," Kinimaka said from behind a wooden desk. "Nicholas Bell; this Webb guy and Miranda Le Brun—they need identifying."

"And the plague pits," Karin added. "Where exactly are they?"

"We have no clear-cut ideas," Hayden admitted. "But on the plus side, the Pythians won't know who Lauren and Smyth are or how they relate to SPEAR. If we're finally going to get a step ahead of our enemies, this is the time to do it."

"Can I ask—" Komodo spoke up from his position at the back of the room. "What exactly is a plague pit?"

Karin was beside him. "They relate back to bubonic plague and the Black Death," she said. "If you imagine two thirds of the population of Europe being wiped out you can see how hard it would have been to dispose of the bodies. Eventually the recognized patterns of burial collapsed, leaving us with plague pits during major outbreaks. During times like these graveyards quickly filled, with their graves used only by the wealthy."

"And these plague pits are still there?" Komodo asked in surprise. "Under the streets of London, Paris and Los Angeles?"

"Well, yes. There's one in Knightsbridge and another in Soho. Several around Paris and all the other major European cities. It's commonly accepted that plague-like organisms would not survive this long, but it was also believed that all those that died were infected only by the Black Death, until recently. Now they're speculating on other diseases too, including anthrax. What's in the plague pits could be a mixture of several deadly, ancient diseases."

"They intend to weaponize an ancient plague?" Mai suddenly declared as if waking up. "Are they mad?"

"If they are all like General Stone," Lauren put in, "they're off-their-head crazy, depraved sons-of bitches. No conscience."

Smyth patted her shoulder to help settle her nerves.

"But also immensely powerful," Hayden said. "Let's not forget that."

Hayden started as the landline rang. "I've already put in a call to Robert Price," she said for the latecomers' benefit, referring to the new Secretary of Defense. "I want authorization to move immediately on this, and to move big time."

Hayden spoke fast, bringing the Secretary up to speed. "Everything we have is essentially unverifiable, sir, but it's actually rock solid."

"You realize that's two total extremes don't you?" Price knew that she did and went on, "Anything further as to what happened in Drago?"

Drake knew he was referring to the "house on the hill" atrocity. The entire US was united in tracking down its perpetrators, from the highest level of government to the lowliest step above the worst of the social media trolls.

"No, sir."

"All right. Do we know where they'll hit first?"

Hayden coughed. "Excuse me, sir, but that's one of the reasons I called you so quickly. We believe they're going to hit *all three* at the same time."

Price was struck dumb for a moment, then: "The Pythians are hitting three major cities at once? Do they have that kind of manpower? That kind of organizational ability?"

"General Stone, despite his failings, is a first-class strategist. And who knows who else they have on their payroll?"

"Of course, of course. Jesus, this is going to get very big, very fast. I'm going to have to make some international calls, smooth out some rough ground. How are we for manpower? Homeland. The FBI. Do you need teams?"

"We believe we'll be okay for now, sir. We have people in mind, but a high alert in the targeted cities would be appreciated."

"After I convey this information the entire world will be on high alert."

"Right now, that's not a bad thing, sir."

Price's voice took on a tense strain. "I'm also assuming you want Stone left alone?"

"It's the best way. He's still our best way into their inner circle."

Drake tuned out as Mai drifted over. The Japanese

woman's eyes were downcast, her bearing lackluster. "What's the problem, love?"

"I can't get Grace out of my mind."

"Her past is not as rosy as she wanted but we can't change that. And we'll help her through it all. It's bloody bad timing too."

Mai stared. "What do you mean, bad timing?"

Drake didn't back down. He knew his words hadn't been spoken maliciously. "Haven't you been paying attention? Catastrophe is on the loose and heading to town with a mean motherfucking attitude, leaving nothing but destruction in its wake. We have to deal with that, Mai."

"We're always dealing with *that*, Matt. Don't you remember Babylon? Hawaii? My goddamn trip to Tokyo?"

Drake pulled her aside, feeling the others beginning to take an interest as Mai's voice rose. "You never did fully explain that trip. What happened?"

"I told you. Weren't you paying attention?"

"I don't believe you *murdered* a man, Mai. The term implies intent and desire to kill. He wasn't an innocent, by your own admission. Did you even have a choice?"

Mai glanced up at him from beneath her brows. "That's the problem, Matt. I did have a choice. I could have left Tokyo. I could have said no, abandoned the search for my parents."

"But he was your only way into the Tsugarai."

Mai nodded. "He was."

"And you rescued Grace, and others besides."

"And he also had a daughter. A son. A wife."

"He was playing with their lives the second he accepted blood and drug money from bad people."

"Some people have no choice."

Drake fell silent, realizing Mai was referencing her own parents and how they had initially sold *her* to survive life with their first-born daughter, Chika. He was arguing a losing battle. No way could he win this.

All of a sudden he realized Hayden was talking to him. ". . . as soon as you can."

He blinked rapidly. "What?"

Dahl shook his head. "Ask him again. Takes a bit of processing for a Northerner."

Drake didn't even register the insult as Hayden again asked him to make the call to Crouch and Alicia. "We need them now," she said. "If they're not in place soon they may be too late."

Drake nodded, taking out his phone. Enough impossible questions, theories and bad tidings were amassing to give him a headache. Crouch was essentially working for himself these days and wouldn't jump in to help unless he believed things were deadly serious. Maybe what he really needed was a chat with Alicia. That might help release the tension a little.

But he didn't feel comfortable enough to cross blades with the feisty heroine right now.

A man's voice answered his call. He spoke in highly stressed tones. "Are you free? Are you finished?"

Crouch paused a second, then said: "We are."

"Then we need you. I mean, all of you, and more. This Pandora thing's gone intercontinental; we're fighting a war in four countries now."

"*What?*"

"Drake?" Alicia's tones floated over the connection.

"You're not making any sense."

Drake gripped the bridge of his nose. "It's the end of the world, Alicia. The plagues of Pandora. The Pythians are everywhere. We're losing. This is going to take every single resource, every ounce of brainpower, every grain of courage. We're all going to get bloody or dead on this one, Alicia."

"We've faced Armageddon before, and recently. More than once."

"Not like this." Drake felt as troubled as he'd ever been in his life. "Something this big comes along just once in a lifetime. Survival isn't even on the bloody menu. Saving our society, that's all that matters."

Alicia went quiet, seemingly lost for words. Drake then heard her say: "We have to help them."

Crouch spoke again, his voice as resolute as iron and stone. "My team is all yours, Matt. What do you need?"

Drake thought about what Hayden, Price and Lauren had already brought to the table. "First of all head to Europe. You'll be our response team there. We're in the process of appointing others."

"Europe's a big place, mate," some smartass put in. Drake didn't recognize the voice.

"I realize that. We don't have the right intel yet, it's a fluid operation. Start with Rome. I want you on the mainland."

Hayden stared at him. "Why Rome?"

He cupped the mouthpiece. "Pretty central. Who knows, the Pythians could even now be leading us up the garden path. If it turns out to be Paris, Crouch can make the hour-long trip on SPEAR's coin."

"Done," Crouch said. "I'll be in touch when we've landed."

"Thank you. Oh, and guys?"

"Yes?"

"If you have loved ones and relatives, I'd call them before you land."

Drake ended the call, meeting the eyes of everyone in the room. "What?" he said. "Don't you feel it too? This is pure fight or die. We've been here before, more than once, and I remember every ounce of pain and anxiety and emotion. Every time-sensitive heartbeat."

The way they all nodded, as solemn as men facing a firing squad, showed him that they felt the same way.

CHAPTER TEN

Hours later, and the SPEAR team was again in touch with Crouch.

Hayden had waited until the ex-Ninth-Division man's team were cocooned inside a fast jet with full audio and undivided attention before relating all the details. The SPEAR team were working hard inside their HQ, gathering all and any information on everything that might relate to the mission.

"We're heading to London shortly," she said. "But despite what we know, we're still working almost blind. London is a city built on bones; there are dozens of plague pits. Why do the Pythians keep referring to a *Pandora* plague? How does it all fit? There are clues here, we just have to solve them."

"Can I just clarify . . ." a young woman's voice spoke over the connection. "And sorry, this is Caitlyn Nash. When you say plague pits you're talking *bubonic* plague, yes? Like from the Black Death and half the world's population wiped out?"

"The very same, Miss Nash," Dahl said. "And may I say, very nice to meet you."

Drake snorted. "Get out of her pants, Dahl. You've enough on your plate satisfying one female."

"I meant nothing . . . I'm happily—"

Drake shook his head. "God, you're such an easy target."

Alicia broke into their banter with typical aplomb. "Cut it

out, you two. Never bloody changes does it? Besides, I get first crack at Miss Nash."

"Jesus." Smyth looked like his legs were about to collapse beneath him. Lauren turned to stare. "You carry me out of a battle zone . . . on your back . . . and *that* makes you weak? *Men!*"

Smyth turned bright red. "I . . . I . . . damn."

Caitlyn's voice drew them back to harsh reality. "And what exactly do we know about the Pandora myth? Mostly it's related to the box, which was a lethal gift of the gods to mankind. They say Pandora was the first woman, a punishment from Zeus in retaliation for Prometheus stealing fire from the gods and giving it to men. Pandora was fashioned from clay, a beautiful goddess, then each god gave her a virtue—grace, boldness, persuasion, curiosity, and more."

Hayden stopped her. "Why do we need to know all this?" Karin, the SPEAR team's own resident genius, nodded in agreement even though she had probably been about to launch into a similar monologue.

"Because it leads us into how all the sins of the world were loosed and how they might relate to what we're up against."

Hayden pursed her lips in surprise. "Okay."

"Using the name Pandora could be anything from the Pythians employing a simple code word to them using the entire myth as clues to something . . ."

"Really?" This time Crouch interrupted, sounding interested.

"Of course. Megalomaniacs love revealing their intentions, even if it's in the form of a riddle. Anyway, once formed the gods gave Pandora a box and told her not to open it."

Drake made a face. Smyth laughed. Even Dahl grimaced. "Not the best plan."

"No. And Pandora was tempted, just like Eve with the apple. Do you see now? Pandora *is* an origin myth. Just like Adam and Eve."

"An origin myth that's also an apocalypse myth?" Karin wondered.

"Now you're with me. Anyway, they say Pandora pretty much invented the phrase 'curiosity killed the cat'. She opened the box and let loose evil and plague upon the world. Crime. Poverty. Pain. Hunger. Sickness. Vice."

"I understand." Karin said. "You're saying the code word Pandora relates to one of these vices, particularly sickness I would think, and that her story may provide more clues."

"Exactly. Everything from an origin or apocalypse myth to reasons and locations."

"We'll start with the plague pits," Crouch asserted. "I think somebody should also start investigating how someone might be able to weaponize ancient bubonic plague."

Karin patted Komodo's arm. "We can do that. And we already have all agencies tracking down the other Pythians that were named."

Hayden signed off with a muted goodbye. She turned to address the room. "The pure, uncaring evil of this staggers me. Even today, when we know what goes on in many parts of the world. Even now, I am stunned that wealthy, learned people, no doubt many with families of their own, can do this."

"A boy born into power, wealth and privilege does not necessarily find it easy to accept," Dahl said quietly. "He's born into a predetermined world with predetermined values. He has no freedom, no boyhood or youth. He's expected to follow a requisite path, laid down by his father and their forefathers. One day . . . he may rebel."

Drake blinked at the Swede's words. "That sounds like it came from the heart, mate."

"I was privileged," Dahl said. "And I rebelled. How else do you think I came to be here?"

Drake shrugged softly. "Always wondered why that fancy accent didn't come with an officer's placement."

"Because I became my own man. And went my own way."

Hayden stared at Dahl. "That doesn't give anyone the right to commit genocide."

Dahl glared right back. "Don't you think I know that? I'm right here beside you, fighting the same fight, remember?"

Kinimaka came forward and put a massive arm around their boss's shoulders. "Everything all right, Hay?"

Hayden sighed. "I think I need more painkillers."

Drake stared around the room. "I think the feeling's pretty universal."

CHAPTER ELEVEN

Tyler Webb straightened his laptop, taking care to precisely align each side so it was perpendicular to the edges of his dark oak table, before clicking a button and settling back into his sumptuous seat.

"We are the Pythians," he said. "What news have you?"

Five mini-screens sat before his eyes, each one filled with the face of a fellow conspirator. This was the first time they had tried video-link, but summoning every member in person whenever they needed a meeting was fast becoming problematic, not to mention annoying.

"Threat level has risen in the three plague cities," General Stone reported. "No credible reason as to why."

Webb detected an underlying tone but let it go. Perhaps the general was pushed for time or, more likely, irritated at being turned into Nicholas Bell's nursemaid. "Don't they have ways of monitoring chatter?" Webb said off-handedly with a tired gesture. "The threat level goes up and down all the time as a response. I shouldn't need to tell you that, Stone."

"Sure."

"And that's by no means a bad thing," Miranda Le Brun said smoothly. "Makes the game all the more interesting."

"Since the factory is now up and running," Webb continued. "I think it important that one or two of us oversee the operation. Yes, yes, I know it's a long flight over there but the task will help stop boredom setting in.

With that in mind I was thinking—Miranda and Nicholas? What do you think?"

Bell was quick to jump in. "I'm happy to do that!"

Webb concealed a smile. Perhaps the builder was as exasperated with Stone as the general clearly was with him.

Le Brun smoothed her hair. "I suppose so," she said with an air of tedium. "Anything to help the cause."

Webb could have happily throttled her, but calmed his anger. The Pythians were working surprisingly well together, and Le Brun herself was up soon with her own little project. If she didn't prove herself then perhaps his most recent fantasy could become a blissful reality. *Of course,* he thought. *You don't simply throttle someone, even Le Brun. You have to tenderize them first. Make them afraid. Derail their life.*

Stalk them.

"Once the factory is productive," he went on quickly. "We will need another meeting by the . . . falls. In the tower." Despite the highest security allowing real name references and the net of secrecy cast over their campaigns, Webb still remained cagey about referencing his exact location over the wires.

Stone was talking off-screen, most likely to Bell, and turned back. "Sorry, it's not like Bell and Le Brun have jobs is it? Maybe they should both stop trying to pretend they're doing us a huge favor by . . . flying over there."

Webb sighed. "All right. Are we really bickering now? General—you are a public figure. Until you're compromised—which we all hope is many years from now—you should remain in that position. I don't have to remind you how helpful it's already been to our cause."

"Yes, sure. I'm good."

"In the end," Webb made sure he kept the floor, "thousands or even hundreds of thousands may die to further our cause. But for now, let's look at our upcoming projects." His observations were mere gusts of air, of no real consistence and without conscience, meaningless figures to the ears that listened. "So sayeth the king of maniacs," he then added with a harsh laugh. "Glossing over the facts, making light of the crushed bodies we will trample beneath our feet, ignoring their pain and suffering. But hasn't it always been that way?"

"Amen," Le Brun said heartily.

"The weak will be crushed beneath our boots like dying leaves," Stone said, a little too flamboyantly for Webb's taste.

"You mentioned our upcoming projects?" Robert Norris, the SolDyn exec, checked his watch. "I have a meeting I just can't get out of in fifteen."

A little deflated, Webb understood the exec's dilemma. "It's fine. We'll talk in more depth later. Just to say that Clifford's 'lost kingdom' theory is already bearing fruit and Miranda's 'galleons' concept, if it proves to be true, sounds utterly intriguing—"

"I've always been fascinated by them," Le Brun put in.

"Galleons?" Stone asked with an arched smile.

"These *particular* galleons," Le Brun said. "You'll see."

"And over all," Webb said grandly, "Saint Germain. The Wonderman. The occultist. The Prince of Transylvania. The philosopher—"

"Can we get on?" Norris asked.

Webb fought down an even stronger urge to throttle

someone. ". . . and the greatest adventurer with more treasures, relics and artefacts than any man, any museum, has ever known," he finished as if he'd been meaning to conclude that way. "Which have never . . . ever . . . been found."

"Fantastic," Stone said drily. "The sooner we can get three or four of these undertakings going at once the happier I will be about the final scheme."

"The other reason I called this video conference," Webb continued emotionlessly. "Is to officially announce that we're ready to push the button on the Pandora project. I thought you all might want to be present the moment we start rolling on the three plague pits. This is a magnificent moment for the Pythians." Webb swelled out his chest and gave the magnanimous wide smile. "All assets are in place. The factory is ready. The backup facility is prepared—" he glanced around. That last statement was a little premature, but hopeful. "Are we ready?"

Excited nods and statements of approval told him he had chosen well.

"Then let's begin."

CHAPTER TWELVE

Alicia Myles felt the oddest moment of uncertainty when Crouch cut their connection with the SPEAR team. More than longing, she felt *certain* that she should be with those guys, a part of the team that had essentially saved her, changed her outlook on life. It was okay running headlong down an ever-winding road, but what if the people you left behind were the people you were meant to be with?

She studied the faces around the jet's enclosed cabin. Their boss, Michael Crouch, sat in deep thought, head in his hands as he studied a small laptop before him. The soldiers, Zack Healey and Rob Russo, sat behind Crouch, looking distinctly uncomfortable. Healey still looked fresh-faced and innocent—an appearance that invited many harsh ribbings—whereas Russo's outer shell was as hard as a mountain and twice as craggy.

Nevertheless the two were good friends, a comradeship born in warfare, liberation and adversity. Healey had recently been rescued by Russo and Alicia from the hands of a barmy African crime lord after helping locate the long-lost golden treasure trove of the ancient Aztecs, a mission that had brought action and mayhem to Mexico, Las Vegas and Arizona. Alicia had bonded very well with the two soldiers, already sure they would guard her back in any future situation.

There should have been two more people aboard the plane. One was missing, an odd addition by any terms, Laid

Back Lex, the misfit that had been a part of Alicia's old biker gang and one of its only survivors, had been left out of this dangerous mission. With so much at stake, Lex's inability to conform, and the lure of the motorcycling Nirvana around Vegas, Alicia had persuaded him to sit this one out.

The last was a young girl, Caitlyn Nash. Though sporting a colorful, dubious history—she had already burned out once whilst working for MI6 at the tender age of twenty one—Caitlyn had proved herself during the Aztec Gold mission under intense torture and by helping solve the clues along the way. It was she that had coined the phrase The Gold Team for the group. Alicia felt a little protective of the girl, but couldn't help but tease both her and Healey when the two showed signs of a budding relationship.

And to Caitlyn's credit, especially in Alicia's book, she had started showing signs that she could not only take a good ribbing, but give it back too.

Alicia sat back and listened to the discussions. The first decision had been made a few minutes ago; that they would divert from their planned Rome heading and set a new course for Paris. Caitlyn and Crouch were discussing plague pits and how many there might be scattered around Paris.

"Several sites have been identified," Caitlyn said, already tapping into surveillance feeds and analyzing the data—her prime function over at MI6. "Too many. And if we wait for the Pythians to strike, we'll be too late to stop them. In addition to that, there may be other less famous sites. To pick up from where we were earlier, it is now widely believed by experts that not all the pits are full of the victims of the Black Death, *Yersinia pestis,* but that they also contain other diseases such as anthrax, leprosy, and something else that is particularly frightening—signs of extremely lethal and highly contagious viruses similar to the *filoviruses* that cause hemorrhagic fevers."

Crouch turned a horrified gaze upon her. "Are you saying . . . ?"

"Yes," Caitlyn nodded, "Ebola."

"These experts are saying Ebola could have been behind the Black Death epidemic?" Alicia asked with some skepticism.

"It has been suggested at levels higher than this."

"We hear an awful lot about this Black Death," Russo grunted. "The plague. But isn't it just a disease that our ancestors didn't have the technology to stamp out? Would it really be so damaging today?"

"Hard to say," Caitlyn said. "Depends on the strain, the virulence, and if it's weaponized or not. The Black Death itself killed the majority of the population and rushed across the continent. Yes, they may not have had any prior exposure to this strain of the disease which inevitably makes the infection worse. But the first ever recorded outbreak of bubonic plague was in AD 541-542, later called the Justinian Plague and known as the greatest pandemic in history. There was a third pandemic that began in China around 1855, killed over twelve million in that region alone, and was still considered active until 1959."

Alicia let out a long breath. "Jesus."

"Absolutely. But again, this only helps dispute the belief that the Black Death was caused by rats. A plague outbreak is always preceded by the presence of a great many dead rats, since they are also susceptible to the disease. Now, unlike in Asia, in Europe there are no plague-resistant rodents that could act as a breeding ground for the disease and a distinct lack of accounts mentioning dead rats in any medieval literature. Also, despite two outbreaks of plague in Iceland in the fifteenth century rats did not settle on the island until much later."

"So if not rats . . ." Alicia said. "Humans?"

"And we're back to Ebola," Caitlyn said.

"What about all this talk of weaponization?" Healey interjected. "Is it even possible to weaponize an ancient disease?"

"We were just coming to that," a familiar voice interrupted, causing Alicia's heart to race.

"Jesus!" the Englishwoman said. "Have you been listening all along?"

"Of course," Karin said. "Why, were you missing us?"

Alicia snorted. "Oh yeah, like I'd miss an ugly wart on my face. And speaking of that, how's the Sprite?"

"Ummm . . . very quiet. But you're on speakerphone now, guys, so let's move on. Obviously a million different theories exist as to the weaponization of most diseases so let's start at the top. In the case of any bioterrorist event involving plague, the healthcare system of a region will be easily overwhelmed. Yes, I said *will*. Especially if strict isolation is implemented indiscriminately for most patients. The *Yersinia pestis* virus can be destroyed with drying, heat and ultraviolet light, making weaponization a very tricky process. Would you believe that in World War II the Japanese bred infected fleas by the billions and released them over northern Chinese cities, initiating unspeakable epidemics? Plague has been prevalent in those areas ever since."

Healey let out a long breath, fresh face screwed up. "*How* do these people get away with it?"

Crouch stared over at his young protégé. "Don't ask stupid questions, Zack. You may not have been around the block as many times as, say Alicia, but you know how governments work."

Alicia blinked in surprise. "Hey . . ."

But Karin was already continuing. "Initially the United States dismissed plague as a bioweapon threat, because the disease endures in the area, and would cause deaths on all sides long after the primary attack. But . . ." she paused.

Russo leaned over toward Alicia. "You gotta admit, you *have* been around a bit."

"Just makes me more experienced."

"Yeah, well, so long as that experience doesn't come near me we'll keep getting along just fine."

"Oh, Rock-Face, are you sure? Just imagine all that sweet *rock* music we could make."

Russo turned away, almost squirming. Alicia loved to embarrass the stand-offish, and—truth be told—rather prudish soldier, but then the same could be said of Healey for entirely different reasons. The younger man had fully intended to ask Caitlyn out on a date, meaning to woo her in the "proper and correct" manner before shagging her brains out, as Alicia had put it. Healey had mentioned the fact as Russo and she rescued him from a hell pit in Africa. But then Drake had called and the Pythians had struck, upsetting everyone's plans.

Fucking megalomaniacs, she thought.

She now leaned over to whisper in Healey's ear. "Do you think she looks hot, tapping away on that computer? I know I do."

Healey squirmed away. That was two out of two. Alicia sat back, relaxing. Job done.

Karin's dialogue went on unbroken, ". . . reports that the Soviets developed a dry, antibiotic-resistant, environmentally stable variety of the plague organism. This brings us up to date and to the American CDC, who have now categorized weaponized plague as a Category A agent."

"Fucking boffins hiding away in their windowless labs and the soulless men that control them," she heard Dahl say. "Wish I could get my hands on a couple of them."

"Maybe we will," Drake answered, sounding equally disgusted.

"Okay, well, according to this colonel the nastiest form of weaponized pneumonic plague was developed in Russia, employing canisters that released it in a powdered form from cruise missiles. Hard to detect." Karin's voice faltered as she spoke. "It's . . . horrendous what the human race can concoct. In aerosol form pneumonic plague reaches its zenith, the most terrible, easy-to-deploy world killer out there, all down to the contagiousness of the disease, its resistance to dozens of antibiotics and, at least up to early 2000, no vaccine was available to combat the aerosolized form."

"So now they're creating diseases without a vaccine?" Crouch shook his head.

"Well, according to the CDC, plague has been used as a weapon since the Tartars catapulted infected corpses into the city of Kaffa in an effort to spread the disease. It is said . . ." Karin again wavered, "that the Soviets have fifteen hundred metric tons of the stuff."

"And what's the casualty rate?" Hayden asked.

Karin could be heard tapping away. "If fifty kilograms were released over a well-populated city in aerosol form, pneumonic plague would occur in roughly two hundred thousand people. And, Jesus, a footnote right here . . . no early warning system is in place."

Crouch chose that moment to stand. "Well, we're a good few hours out from Paris yet. I suggest we use these hours to get some rest."

Alicia saw an opportunity for jest, but the last glut of information weighed heavy on her and she waived the pleasure. She met her boss's eyes and nodded.

"We're gonna need it," she said.

CHAPTER THIRTEEN

The moment Drake was in the air he knew the days of peace and quiet were long gone.

The plane was abuzz, Karin and Komodo in full research mode, Hayden liaising with the UK authorities via Robert Price, Kinimaka realizing in that lovably clumsy way of his that he'd left DC about three minutes after his sister, Kono, touched down on her way to see him. Dahl hovered over everyone, taking stock and offering happily accepted advice, Smyth made eyes at Mai and Lauren, but in a rascally way. Only Mai stayed apart, quiet at the back of the fast jet.

Drake was glad to see the team back in action.

There were three more people aboard. Lauren, Yorgi and Grace. The team had decided they might need Yorgi's services and Lauren's memories. Grace was there on Mai's insistence. The Japanese woman just couldn't leave her new charge on her own—especially in light of yesterday's new information.

Drake focused on the flight and the flood of facts and figures. Preparation was an imperative. They would land and then hit London's streets running, no holding back.

Karin was at the forefront of the information charge, naturally comprehending what type of intelligence they would need and in which order.

"Plague pits of London," she said. "There are many, leading some to name it the city of bones. From one end to the other you need only dig a few yards beneath the surface to discover its many hidden secrets—tens of thousands of bodies are buried beneath the sprawling capital, a land of skeletons. In addition to the Knightsbridge pit I mentioned earlier we have another at the center of Soho—Golden Square. Now a charming little area, it has a secret history as a plague pit. In 1685 Lord Macauley described it as 'a field not to be passed by without a shudder by any Londoner of that age'. Here, as the great plague raged, nightly cartloads of corpses were dropped and buried. It was believed that the earth was deeply infected and could never again be interred without the risk of infection."

"But all that has been proven wrong," Smyth said. "Right?"

Karin shrugged. "We thought so. The bacteria should have perished within weeks. But, as I mentioned, scientists have now noted the presence of other diseases too. Diseases that may not die."

Drake made a waving motion. "Any more pits?"

"Plenty. An interesting one lies on the Bakerloo line. At the south end of the London depot there's a junction. One line leads to Elephant and Castle, the other to a dead end and a runaway line for trains unable to stop. Behind the walls of this tunnel lies a plague pit."

Drake suppressed a shudder. "Think about *that* the next time you're on the tube."

"Another exists at Green Park, discovered when they were building the Victoria Line. And more . . . so many more. Hayden, Drake, we can't possibly cover every single one. Not by ourselves."

Hayden nodded. "Maybe the British police could help."

Drake held up a warning hand. "Be careful how you word it. London's on a high alert. If we send squad cars screaming to every location we're gonna cause mayhem, which will hamper our own search."

Hayden stared. "I'm FBI, Matt. I know how to be diplomatic."

Drake grimaced but said nothing. Dahl caught his eye with a similar frown. Hayden noticed the exchange and laughed. "Look at you two goddamn comedians. Do you have a better plan?"

Dahl nodded slowly. "As a matter of fact, I do."

Kinimaka sat down next to Hayden, protective as ever. "Please share."

"We monitor the chatter," he said. "And I don't mean how the cops do it. I mean how Interpol and the NSA do it. We know the channels they use, the methods they employ. Code words. More importantly, we know the identities of *dozens* of mercenaries allied to the Pythians, though not their whereabouts since they dropped off the grid. If we can establish any kind of close proximity for them—" Dahl clicked his fingers. "Game on."

Drake thought about it. "Jesus Christ, Dahl, that's not bad."

Dahl nodded toward Hayden. "Make the call. Let's go get these bastards."

Drake let out a long sigh. "I just hope London's ready for this."

"Not to mention Paris and Los Angeles," Hayden muttered.

CHAPTER FOURTEEN

As they came in to land, Hayden called the team they had chosen to assist in Los Angeles. Recommended by Michael Crouch and Armand Argento of Interpol, and the team that had saved Kono Kinimaka's life more than once, the so-called Disavowed were ex-CIA and an unlikely but competent bunch.

Hayden spoke to their self-appointed but now universally accepted leader, Claire Collins. "Hi, again. If you're up for some off-the-book, rollercoaster action where you'll quite possibly get yourself killed at least twice then you're one of the gang."

"We're up for anything and everything." Collins said. "At least twice. So tell us what you need in LA."

"Well, obviously you won't be the only ones out there. But we need you guys to play to your strengths. The Disavowed team were the best in the business at what they do, and could still be. We need them on the ground, working this thing from the streets."

"We'll get to it."

Hayden proceeded to impart all the information they had gathered, bringing Collins up to speed as her colleagues listened. When she was done their West Coast team sounded ready for action.

Hayden spent a few more minutes briefing them and then signed off. "We're counting on you guys. Don't let the Pythians or their agents out of that plague pit alive."

"We're right on it," Collins said. "If there's one thing we're good at . . ."

". . . it's kicking terrorist ass." Claire Collins ended the call and sat back in her seat, searching the eyes of everyone else gathered in the room, evaluating.

"So . . . what do you guys think?"

Aaron Trent perched on the edge of his chair. Trent was tall and dark-haired, spoke in a clipped manner, was slow to smile but always good-hearted. He had recently been fully reunited with his son after his ex-wife died at the hands of a Serbian whack-job called Blanka Davic. The readjustment, not to mention the grieving, was taking its toll.

"Search and destroy. But I can't leave LA for more than a day. Mikey's just too fragile to be without a dad right now."

Adam Silk, an ex-child thief recruited into the CIA, a whip-like man able to finesse his way into almost anything, looked concerned. "Maybe you should sit this one out, Aaron. Take some time."

"If it were less of a threat, I'd say yes. But not after what I'm hearing."

Dan Radford, the playboy and techie of the group who had recently come to realize he was head over heels in love with the wife he'd once happily approved of having an open relationship with, poured himself a coffee. "We need a list of plague pits in LA. We need equipment setting up or access to an existing room where we can monitor the airwaves. We need an open line to the authorities and promises of response if we shout. Not only that, but somebody should be setting up a think tank to find these

Pythians and their factory. We have their names, right? How hard can it be?"

"Has there ever been a case of the Black Death in the States?" Silk wondered. "I've never heard of one."

Collins looked blank. "I guess we'll find out. The Bureau's already on high alert, concerned over the significant increase in terrorist chatter these last few weeks. Nobody's sure what to make of the Pythians—a new group appearing out of nowhere and making such gigantic waves is unprecedented."

Trent was staring into space. "I know one thing about the bubonic plague," he said. "It's supposedly where the rhyme 'ring-a-ring-of-roses' has its darker roots. The children's nursery rhyme?" He intoned, "Ring-a-ring o' roses, a pocket full of posies, atishoo, atishoo, we all fall down'. Associated with the plague and Black Death, though I do believe true folklorists disagree. But, come on. Sneezing and falling down? A rosy rash was said to be a symptom of plague. And posies of herbs were often carried as protection to ward off the stench of the disease. And they still sing it to this day."

"Shit." Silk looked wide eyed. "Ain't you a ray of sunshine? How do you know all this?"

"I went to school. Didn't you?"

"Actually, no. Not really."

"Oh, yeah, sorry. Child thief and all that. Well, I also know that the line 'atishoo, atishoo' was in fact originally 'ashes, ashes'. A reference to plague-ridden corpses being burned. Then again," he smiled grimly, "it might just be a happy singing game."

"Okay, so maybe I could draft Susie in to help?" Susie

Brewster was Silk's new cop girlfriend.

"Oh yeah, the more I see of Susie the better my day becomes." Radford said, then realized his gigolo days were over and blushed. " 'Cause she's a good cop," he added lamely.

"Maybe your wife could help too," Silk hit back. "Since she's slept with the majority of LA's elite."

"Hey, that was mostly movie and music stars," Radford protested.

"So that's acceptable now?" Collins wondered. "I realize some couples have a laminated card with 'approved' celebs on it but Amanda's would have to be the size of a billboard."

The room fell into laughter, Radford taking the ribbing good-naturedly because he knew his own slept-with list was just as long, but then Trent rose to his feet, no hint of a smile on his lips.

"Whilst we talk, our enemies grow stronger," he said. "Let's get to it."

Collins saw her phone light up and clicked the 'accept' button. "Yeah?"

"Are you ready for this?" a voice asked. It was Armand Argento, their Italian Interpol contact.

"Ready for what?"

Collins saw every eye swivel toward her, sensing trouble.

"You should sit down. It is not good. Oh, no it is not so good."

"Armand! Just spit it out!"

"Am I on speakerphone? I don't want to have to say this twice, *amico mio.*"

Collins pressed the button. "Shoot."

"Word has just come in of a terrible development that concerns you." Argento said. "Oh, I am sorry. So sorry. The word is—that the Moose is working for the Pythians."

Not a breath was taken, not a hair stirred.

At last, Trent spoke. "Are you sure, Armand?"

"As sure as an Italian man can be. No we are not without our failings but we do find it hard to recall them."

"The *Moose?*" Radford recalled every moment of horror from their recent contact with one of the world's greatest contract killers. "Then this is personal."

Trent's face was like carved granite. "It'll never be more so."

The Moose had recently kidnapped Trent's young son, aided in the murder of his wife and tried to blow up Radford and Amanda. The killer had been contracted to Blanka Davic for a ridiculous sum of money, and had sent Trent on a terrifying chase across Los Angeles. After Davic fell, the Moose disappeared. Most had thought to retire—never to be heard from again.

Collins thanked Argento and then got to work. Her first call was to Hayden. "How close are you to London?"

The CIA agent's voice was tense. "Just coming in to land. London's sitting on a knife-edge now. We'll be . . ."

". . . in touch soon." Hayden stared out the window as she spoke, admiring the city's shimmering lights. All seemed calm down there, made more so by the manifestation of a faint early morning mist, but she knew it was anything but.

Cops and secret agents, terrorists and mercenaries roamed the streets. The public had no idea of the secret war about to erupt all around them.

Airplane tires squealed against tarmac.

"Here we go."

CHAPTER FIFTEEN

Armed with crucial new information the SPEAR team hit the quiet streets of London. A pair of extra-large taxis whisked them from Heathrow toward the city center at 3:30 a.m., finally stopping behind a tactical mobile HQ. The team's chief combatants were outfitted with weaponry, to the surprise of most of the assembled Brits, many not knowing of the deal agreed between the British Prime Minister—James Ronson—and the American Secretary of Defense. In these beleaguered times no sane country would decline an offer of such vital, multitalented help as the SPEAR team could provide. Not only that, their members consisted of ex-SAS and Swedish Special Forces, and Michael Crouch, their other benefactor, possessed influential contacts within the British government on a par with the country's leader.

Kitted out, wired up, they made their way over to Marble Arch, eleven stalwarts stalking what was left of the night. The first they saw of Marble Arch was the large green sign pointing their way ahead to the ring road, A4 and A3 and with Notting Hill Gate to the right. Beyond that they saw the Odeon cinema and then yellow and green trees emerged from the slowly dissipating mists. Drake caught just a glimpse of the famous white pillars and the great arch itself before Dahl turned their seven-seat Ford S-MAX off the four-lane road onto a relatively narrow side street.

"Eyes peeled," Dahl said.

"For what?" Drake joked. "Men wearing Pythian-monikered bomber jackets?"

"A few hours ago the exchanges between mercs known to be working for our new worst public enemy rose by 800 percent. Here," he waved his arms, "in hotels situated around Marble Arch."

"I know that. I also know they pinned it down to an area consisting of fourteen hotels."

Hayden tapped the comms unit attached to her right ear. "Latest is they've narrowed it down to two," she said. "Take a right up ahead."

Drake felt a surge of enthusiasm. "Two? Now that's more bloody well like it."

Dahl slowed as he turned the wheel. Cars were parked on both sides of the street, the entrances to hotels set back from the road. Underground car parks could be accessed down steep slopes, but most were gated off for the night. Small bakeries and eateries stood around, lights out in all but the hardiest.

"Now there's something you don't see every day," Kinimaka said, rubbing at his window. "A closed Starbucks."

Dahl idled along the ill-lit street, taking his time as their second vehicle closed up to the rear. Smyth was driving, his grumpy face hanging over the wheel and scrunched as if with road rage, no doubt being ignored by his vehicle's passengers—Karin, Komodo and Lauren. Drake adjusted the body armor he wore and glanced into the back seat.

"All ready?"

Affirmations came back, all except Mai. Drake suddenly longed for Alicia's return—at least the feisty warrioress could get something out of Mai, even if it was only uncontrolled anger.

"I think we should stop," Dahl said. "And scout out these hotels on foot. Get the lay of the land."

Within minutes the group were treading the quiet, gloomy streets after pulling voluminous black single-layer jackets over their combat gear. The first hotel was an upmarket, classy affair, made all the more apparent by having a Ferrari and an Aston Martin parked outside. Drake could also make out the front end of an orange Lamborghini through the lower car park bars.

"Just be a minute, guys."

Dahl clucked at him. "Leave it alone. They're just cars."

"Oh good God, you sound like Alicia. And they're not *just* cars. They're exquisitely designed masterworks of engineering."

"Can we focus?" Hayden drawled. "For just a second?"

The hotel reared up by the side of the road, a sweeping double-door entrance the only obvious way in. A service road ran down the left-hand side. As they watched, a car park attendant came to the open lower entrance as if in query. Drake waved him away. The hotel, though clearly staffed and operating through the night, was calm.

"I feel a little conspicuous," Kinimaka said.

Hayden gave him a knowing grin. "So what's new? But in all seriousness, I'm happy to be spotted out here. It'll spook the bastards into action."

They drifted along toward the next hotel. This one appeared even more opulent, with an entrance designed much like the Marble Arch and gold filigrees around the lower windows and entrance doors. A doorman with a top hat stood in the shadows, head down, checking his cellphone. The wide, sinuous parking approach held two more supercars that grabbed Drake's attention—a new Jaguar F-type Coupe and a Mercedes SLS AMG.

Drake stopped again, tongue practically hanging out.

Dahl stared along with him. "Must admit I do like the Jag."

"What is this?" Hayden asked. "Motor Show week?"

"No," Drake answered. "But it is London in the spring and summer. Foreign rich kids and mega-wealthy playboys, ambassador's sons, Saudi dignitaries and the like, all tend to migrate here for several months, bringing their specially prepared, one-off vehicles with them. It's becoming a kind of annual event."

Hayden was eyeing up both hotels. "Time is ultimately against us. What do you say we split up and check both at the same time? Mercs like these, they *have* to have some kind of security protocol in place, unless they're completely incompetent. A double breach should shake something loose."

Dahl nodded. "Sounds good to me."

Drake stood with Dahl, Mai and Smyth whilst the others retraced their steps. As one the SPEAR team pushed through both hotels' doors, ready for anything. Drake assessed the lobby with its gleaming floors and white walls, its marble-topped desk behind which a pretty receptionist sat smiling, the empty area of plush seating and the entrance to the bar. Nothing appeared to be out of place.

Still evaluating, he crossed the open space, sensing his companions at his back. If the receptionist noticed their sense of anticipation she gave no sign. Drake stopped before her, smiling.

"Callan Dudley." The name of a particularly skilled and vicious mercenary they knew had made several recent calls from this area. "Or Charlie Egan."

His voice was loud, carrying beyond the lobby. For a moment the receptionist looked blank, then asked if they were meeting someone.

Drake nodded, keeping his voice at a steady boom. "Callan Dudley."

Dahl leaned into his shoulder, whispering, "I've seen better acting at a school play."

Drake managed to swallow his retort, squeezing his lips together.

"I can't confirm the name of anyone staying here." The receptionist smiled. "But you could check the bar to see if your friend is there." She lowered her voice. "Been quite a few asking for Mr. Dudley tonight."

Drake saw how it must look. The receptionist had already fielded the same question a dozen times judging by how many phone calls Dudley had made. He turned toward Dahl and then saw a figure standing in the doorway that led to the bar.

"Yer lookin' for me?" Dudley's accent was pure, broad Irish. First impressions were daunting. Though whippet thin and tall, Dudley's bare arms were thick with corded muscles and covered in tattoos. The man's reputation was much worse. More than a shoot-first-ask-later kind of merc he was a trouble-causer, a hell-raiser, and nowhere more so than in his home country with his older brother and five other gang members, none of whom were even in the UK.

Dahl started to close the gap. "Are you Dudley?"

"So what if I are?" Drake struggled to understand the

brogue. Jesus, now he knew how Dahl felt.

Smyth backed the Swede up with Mai drifting around the side. Their approach was too ordered, too aggressive. Dudley saw through it in seconds. His eyes darkened and he shot back into the bar. Drake and his three teammates converged on the opening as Dudley and his men surged through.

"Have 'em!" Dudley sneered.

A fracas broke out, a pure brawl. Instantly on top of each other, mercs and soldiers piled in. Drake ducked a haymaker and felt knuckles crash into the top of his head. Although seeing stars straight away he ignored the lightheaded sensation and tackled his opponent around the waist. The two fell to the ground in a powerful tangle.

Dahl shoulder-barged his first merc back the way he had come, the man seemingly shot out of a rubber band and crashing into the door frame, cracking it from side to side.

Dahl shrugged. "Don't make 'em like they used to."

Mai skipped between her adversaries, dealing blows where she could but maintaining a small gap. Her strikes were debilitating, sending mercs to their knees or making them clutch at tender areas only then to be hit by a whirlwind called Smyth. Growling, he proved he could brawl with the best of them, taking the punches and returning them with more than an equal measure.

Drake rolled clear, using a side wall to pivot and jump to his feet. Another man came straight at him. Drake employed the Dahl technique, dropping his shoulder and striking at the throat. The man crumpled. Drake leaped off his falling back, using it as a platform to attack the next.

Dudley reared up before him. "Gonna tear yer feckin' arms off, mate."

Drake knew of this man, knew the reputation. On any given day he'd happily take his time teaching the maniac the error of his ways but not now. Not today. Too much was at stake. The man beyond Dudley was pulling out a gun. Drake smashed Dudley aside and reached for the weapon.

A shot went off. The receptionist, reaching for a phone, screamed and scrambled away. The bullet passed through the marble-topped counter before shattering a PC screen, sending computer fragments everywhere. Drake slammed down on the man's gun arm, releasing the weapon, then elbowed him in the face. Mai jabbed at his neck from behind, sending him to the floor faster than a sack of rocks.

Drake looked around. Dahl, predictably, had picked his opponent up and was holding him by the scruff of his neck. The man's legs were kicking ineffectively. Drake shook his head as Dahl launched the man against a wall.

"Show off."

The mercs were beyond the SPEAR team now, closer to the door of the hotel. Mai advanced, picking her way through the mayhem of groaning bodies and flexing legs.

"What a mess."

Drake shrugged. "Not too bad, love. I've seen worse Black Friday events at Tesco."

Smyth struggled in a far corner. With a snarl he hefted his opponent over a shoulder and hurled him among his teammates. Luckily for the man he landed well and rolled to his feet, none the worse for wear.

Smyth glared.

Dudley and most of his crew reached for weapons.

Drake sprang at them. More blows were exchanged. The mercs crashed into the hotel's front doors, nowhere to go.

Even immersed in the intense concentration of battle Drake felt a momentary rush of elation.

A good win. They would be able to . . .

Sudden gunfire shattered his senses. The glass doors of the hotel and the windows above blew in, shards dropping and exploding across the lobby. The mercs yelled and dropped as Drake and his colleagues did the same. Sharp fragments showered among them. Harsh yells blasted in from outside.

"Get the fuck out, Dudley! Fuckin' Five-O's here!"

Drake heard the sound of approaching sirens. As he looked up the mercs were backing out of the destroyed front entrance toward their comrades outside. Drake's immediate fear was for Hayden and the others who'd accompanied her into the adjacent hotel. Rolling to the right he tried to see beyond the running men.

"C'mon!" Dahl was first up to join the chase, feet crunching across the glass. Drake rose in his wake, wincing as a bullet whizzed within a whisker of the Mad Swede. The mercs pounded down the hotel steps and out into the road, most glancing left and right with frustrated eyes. But Dudley was not finished yet.

"The feckin' plan still stands!" he yelled. "Just earlier. Move it!"

Instantly the men, reined in and motivated by their leader, poured toward the slope that led to the joint underground car park. Drake was momentarily distracted as Hayden ran up.

"You all okay?"

"We're good. Assholes were packing enough firepower to assault Fort Knox. Took us by surprise."

Drake cast his eyes over the group. "Yeah, I'm thinking some of us should stay behind. Safe at the hotel."

Dahl was chomping at the bit. "Stay here if you like, ya damn Yorkshire sissy. I'm going!"

Drake bit back a tawdry reply. Instead he nodded toward Hayden. "Just you and Mano come with us. These bastards don't care about collateral damage."

Hayden nodded quickly. "Komodo, look after them."

The big soldier acquiesced with a grunt, clearly wanting to join the action but accepting his responsibilities. He ushered Karin, Lauren, Yorgi and Grace back toward the lights of the hotels.

Drake heard the roar of a powerful engine starting up, and then almost instantly, two more.

"Shit. That can't be good."

A swift assessment of their situation followed. Drake found his eyes continually drawn toward the vehicles parked outside the hotel. "We can do this," he murmured, then: "This way!"

He took off at speed, down the slope toward the roar of the approaching engines. Even Dahl shouted that he was crazy, but not one of his teammates hesitated for a second. They had his back. Drake powered down the sharp incline, skidding to a halt at the entrance to the car park and spying the attendant down on his knees, bleeding from the temple.

"Hey, mate. You okay?"

The attendant scrambled away. Drake was at his side in less than a second. "We're the good guys," he said. "Look. Just look. Help us. Those bastards are terrorists, and they're taking guns onto the streets of London. Look!" Drake brandished his SPEAR identification.

Mai was down on her knees at his side. "Please." She took the attendant's head in her hands and locked eyes. "Help us."

The attendant nodded, blood flying from his wound. Smyth cheered. "Good ole Maggie."

Drake made a disgruntled noise. "Is there anything you *can't* make men do?"

Mai smiled sweetly. "Not that I've found so far."

"Drake!" Dahl cried out. "What the hell do you want him to do?"

The roar of engines was very loud now, and Drake could see two black boxy shapes and a bright orange wedge coming toward them through his peripheral vision.

"Keys," he almost begged the attendant. "To the cars outside the hotel. We need them now or we're gonna lose these guys."

The attendant blanched. "I can't. We should wait for the police."

"The police aren't equipped for war in the streets," Drake yelled. "Not at this moment, anyway. We are."

"I . . . I'm sorry. I can't. It's more than my job's worth."

The first black shape, a Range Rover equipped with smoked glass, roared up. A gun poked through a partially open rear window. The first shot passed by with a whine, the second kicked up shards where Smyth had been standing a moment before. Drake grabbed the attendant and rolled behind the nearest car, Mai at his side.

"Keys," he said softly as more shots rang out and engines roared.

The attendant pointed quickly at a metal box attached to the nearby wall. "Tagged seven and twelve. Seven's the Jag. I couldn't stop you."

Drake jumped to his feet. Dahl stared down at the parking assistant, clearly worried. "Don't worry, the blood and bruises should help you explain how all these cars got stolen at once."

Smyth hesitated as they started to run. "You think it would help if we hit the guy again?"

"No!"

Outside, Drake rolled fast as a second Range Rover shot past him. Mai and the others were trapped on the other side but quickly scooted across as it bounced up the slope. Drake stopped rolling, hit a curb with a grunt and climbed to his feet. A third vehicle, this one accompanied by a roar louder than Satan's own personal steam vent, raced toward the exit. Drake sprinted up a patch of grass, keys in hand.

"Dahl," he shouted, flinging a set of keys. "The Mercedes is yours. Try to keep up."

The Swede grumbled, "I'd prefer the Jag."

"Are you kidding?" Drake shouted back at full sprint. "We're chasing a group of fully armed killers through London with God knows how many lives at stake and you're complaining about the car you get to drive?"

"The Jag's . . . better."

"I know." Drake grinned. "That's why I'm driving it."

They broke for the cars, Drake and Mai climbing into the white F-type as Dahl and Smyth reached the garishly yellow SLS. Drake clamped his foot down on the brake and pressed the Jaguar's start button, listening as the potent engine screamed to life.

"Wow," he said a little dreamily. "That's a helluva V8."

"Just drive!" Mai cried. "There's no time!"

Drake jammed the accelerator to the floor and squealed

into the road. Up ahead he could still see their quarry, still hear the echo and rumble of their mighty engines.

"Race is on now," he said as Dahl's Mercedes fishtailed into the road behind him.

The streets echoed with thunder and gunfire.

CHAPTER SIXTEEN

Drake powered the Jaguar up the narrow street, using the bronze paddles located behind the steering wheel rather than the automatic gearbox. When driving this fast he liked to at least feel he was in control. Parked cars flew by to either side, so close he clipped a side mirror.

"Matt," Mai warned.

"The guy was parked at a bloody silly angle!"

Dahl roared up behind him, almost a challenge. Drake flicked the minus sign on his paddle, shifting down; then streaked away, taking the revs to the red line before flicking up to third. He swung the F-type around a corner as the tailpipe popped and crackled. Dahl was already closing. Ahead, the orange blur came into focus as it was held up by the two bulky Range Rovers.

"What the hell is that thing?" Mai squinted.

"Aventador," Drake said. "By Lamborghini."

Mai held on as Drake drifted the F-type around the sharp corner that brought them onto the multi-laned road at Marble Arch. "Is it faster than ours?"

Drake coughed. "Like you wouldn't believe."

"How on earth can these mercs afford such expensive cars?"

Drake thought about it. "Maybe on the Pythians' dime? Maybe they just stole 'em. And you can rent a supercar for about a grand a day."

"Oh, is that all?"

Drake propelled the car around Marble Arch, the back-end fishtailing happily as it gripped tarmac just at the top end of Oxford Street and surged toward Park Lane. Dahl came alongside in the SLS Mercedes, its engine louder than anything Drake could have imagined. And now behind the Swede he spotted Hayden and Kinimaka behind the wheel of a cobalt blue Aston Martin DB9.

"Bond's back," Drake said with a smile. "And about bloody time."

Ahead, due to the lack of traffic so early in London, their enemies pushed on. Drake imagined they would certainly try to lose them, and since the SPEAR team had no clue as to the whereabouts of the plague pit they were heading for, this, their only lead, had to pay off at all costs.

The cars flashed toward Park Lane. A pedestrian, out on this cold morning, whipped his head around, mouth open in amazement. The bleach white Marriott Hotel zoomed past, and another building covered in scaffolding and protective wrap. Drake raced up to the back of the Aventador, pulling out into the next lane. The Lamborghini swerved to cut him off and an arm thrust out of its passenger window.

"Gun!" Mai shouted.

Drake hauled on the brakes. Dahl's yellow Mercedes shot by, tires squealing as he swerved out of the path of the bullet. White smoke plumed into the air. The SLS went broadside for a second but then Dahl managed to wrestle it back into shape. A bullet smashed into its lower bodywork. Hayden's Aston kept its distance.

The Lamborghini again squealed away, smoke emitting from under its tires, drifting up toward the lines of overhanging trees. Park Lane switched from three lanes to four. Drake pulled the shift-paddles once more, quickly revving and switching the Jag through two howling gear changes, reaching fourth in just a few seconds. Even the Lamborghini wasn't getting away, and the Range Rovers were somewhat slower. The vehicle's speed and instant response was violent, pinning Drake and Mai back into their seats.

Down Park Lane they raced, the famous Forstner car showroom zipping by. Without warning the three mercenary vehicles swung sharp left. Drake reacted instantly but still only just managed to make the turn, burning rubber.

Mai lost her grip on the leather covered door handle, the seat belt just stopping her from ending up in his lap.

Drake spotted the big red 'C' painted on the road. "Bloody hell! We're heading into a congestion charge area."

"You're worried about *that*? Really?"

"I'm a taxpayer. Of course the congestion charge worries me."

Drake threaded the needle between a parked lorry with orange lights across the top of its cab and an overloaded skip with a plastic-wrapped pallet sitting next to it. Plaster puffed in his wake, making it harder for Dahl to see. More buildings obscured by scaffolding stuck out like eyesores to either side.

"Guess the recession's well and truly over." Drake hadn't yet seen a city street where some kind of work wasn't being carried out.

"Just concentrate." Mai was focused ahead. "Drive."

The Lamborghini veered right, a harsh maneuver that made its back end drift. Drake stamped on the brakes in anticipation. As he did so the driver of the orange supercar aimed a gun out of his own window.

"Oh, bollocks!"

The merc only managed one shot due to speed and velocity but that shot was stupidly accurate. It smashed into Drake's side mirror, breaking it and sending it through his side window. Grimly, he hung on, covered in glass and plastic, hair whipped by the sudden gust of wind.

"Unholster your gun," he said. "But don't fire unless you're doubly sure nobody's around."

"At 4:30 a.m.?" Mai took her weapon out. "Even the Tower's ghosts will be asleep."

Drake flicked the F-type to the right again, heading back toward Park Lane by the side of the Aston Martin showroom. At the top end a line of trees marked the road. Two Range Rovers and four supercars roared past the corner, wheels scrabbling for purchase, engines roaring like angry monsters, smoke streaming and trailing around them in swirling plumes. The Grosvenor was next, its black painted sign flashing past, its doorman staring after them and shaking his head.

"Seen it all," Mai commented.

Drake nodded. "Park Lane ain't no stranger to the supercar prowl or odd race," he said. "Try walking down here at the weekend."

Flags flashed by, fluttering, clinging to the sides of the hotel. The Dorchester with its wide curved frontage came next just before a set of lights turned to red. The mercs completely ignored the signal, ploughing through. Drake saw a black taxi ambling up toward the crossroads and floored it.

"Damned if we're gonna lose these freaks!"

The cab came to a sudden halt, horn blaring. Drake, Dahl and Hayden shot through as the sounds of sirens at last began to split the night behind them. Ahead, the road and path widened as Park Lane met Hyde Park Corner. Ordinarily these roads were clogged with red buses, black cabs and tourists, but tonight they were mercifully clear. Drake saw the elephant at Achilles Way, perfectly balanced on the end of its trunk; a square green signpost that mentioned Knightsbridge flashed by too fast; and then the magnificent Wellington Arch—a sculpture showing the angel of peace descending onto the chariot of war—reared up ahead like an ancient vision.

Drake flung the F-type around Hyde Park Corner, hitting the apex and letting the back end glide the whole way around the enormous roundabout, straightening the front end as he almost brushed the Aventador's rear and the main arch itself flashed by. The SLS was right behind him, the Aston Martin almost touching the Mercedes' flank as they all passed two inches in front of a bus stop that read Hyde Park Corner. Drake flicked the Jag to the left, down the long straight of Grosvenor Terrace, trying to intimidate the Lamborghini into making a mistake.

Drake's phone rang. Mai jabbed at the speakerphone. "What?"

"Let me past!" Dahl's voice boomed. "I'm the better driver."

"You mean you'll take more chances," Drake hit back.

"We can't risk losing them," Hayden chimed in, joining the link.

Drake stamped on the brake as the outlandish Aventador swung into a side road, piercing the district of Belgravia like a vivid blade. Dahl shot past, missing the maneuver and then Hayden was suddenly on Drake's tail.

"Dickhead," Drake muttered.

Dahl swore loudly.

Drake pursued the mercs once more, passing dozens of buildings that all looked the same—white stone lower floors and drab brown uppers. Drake thought it might be the dreariest street in the capitol until he spun around another corner and crossed an intersection. Flagpoles jutted out from the sides of several buildings, each one a different color.

"Upper Belgravia." Drake said. "We're in embassy territory."

Around the wide, tree-lined square they shrieked, the Aventador shooting in front of the Range Rovers. Drake felt a quick rush of concern as the back window flipped open and the rear tailgate banged down.

Two men lay in the back of the vehicle, rifles nestled along their shoulders.

"Evade!" Drake screamed, knowing the phone channel was still open. He swerved left, accelerating rapidly to help narrow down the angle. Dahl trod on the brakes, front end dipping. Hayden swung her Aston Martin among several parked cars and vans, narrowly missing a collision. Bullets clanked off their bodywork and struck railings and lampposts, a parking meter and a pair of Renault Twingos. Belgrave Square echoed to the sound of double volleys, its prosperous peace shattered for the night.

Drake nursed the F-type back into position, wary now of the Range Rover but still able to keep it in his sights. The procession cut down West Halkin Street, the first Range Rover taking out one of the inverted-arrow keep-left signs, Dahl destroying the other.

Up Lowndes Street and Hayden was suddenly on the phone. "I know where they're going. Knightsbridge Green. It's the only known plague pit around here."

"Can we get there before them?" Dahl asked.

"Can we risk you guessing wrong?" Drake worried.

Hayden stayed firm. "We may not beat them, but we can take a better route," she said. "Follow us and get ready to fight. Things are about to get rough."

Drake snorted "*About to?*"

Dahl sniffed. "Stop crying and get out of my bloody way."

Drake nodded at Mai. "Whatever weapons we have, get them ready."

CHAPTER SEVENTEEN

Drake slowed as Hayden slammed on the brakes.

"Knightsbridge is a built up area," he said through the speakerphone. "Maybe one of these bloody hotels was built on top of the pit. Or Harrods."

"It wasn't."

"How can you be so sure?"

"Because it's the one they're heading for! Think about it, London's practically a charnel city, built on centuries-old bodies. If they're heading for this one it must be accessible, otherwise why not choose another? It also has to be *viable*, for whatever reason. The Pythians wouldn't have pushed the 'go' button without being sure."

It made sense. Drake stopped the F-type behind the Aston and waited for Mai to hand him his loaded weapons. Dahl roared up alongside, almost too close to get the door open. The Swede and Smyth jumped out first, grinning as they sauntered up to Hayden. Drake shook his head. "Kids."

Mai was already out. Drake squeezed through the tiny gap and made his way to the front of the Aston. Kinimaka was groaning and squeezing out the kinks in his outsized body. Hayden checked her satnav.

"A recent *Daily Telegraph* article puts the plague pit about four hundred meters in that direction." She pointed toward a dark corner, indistinct beneath the soft light of the street lamps. "Let's move."

With no sign of the mercs' vehicles, the SPEAR team set

out at high-speed, keeping close to the high railings and stone walls that bordered the surrounding buildings. Now, darkness was their ally. From far away the sound of sirens shrieked at the mist-shrouded night. Though time was not on their side the team hunkered down at the first corner.

Hayden peered around. "All right. I can see several vehicles parked at the roadside, nothing unusual there, but they're adjacent to a high wall where floodlights have been erected. It appears to be a builder's site—a great way to hide what you're really looking for. No activity though."

"Is it in the right place?" Drake wondered. "Last thing we wanna do is take down a bunch of men working overtime and swilling builder's tea."

"Gimme a minute."

Hayden checked her satnav again, marking the exact location from the *Daily Telegraph's* map and linking it to her digital map. She nodded. "That's it, I think."

Dahl sighed.

"Well, dammit, the coordinates are vague. The map is vague. What the hell can I do?"

"So we wait?" Drake said, rubbing his eyes. "Let's start a recce of the area."

Hayden was still checking her information. "Wow, remember what they said about the bacteria in plague pits vanishing almost immediately? Well, they published a list naming every disease where, if once-contaminated human remains are dug up, they might put people at risk of exposure to pathogenic microorganisms still carried by the cadaver. Plague is among them, as well as anthrax, smallpox, viral hemorrhagic fever and yellow fever. Even today," she put a finger in the air to make her point, "it is said that all planning applications for new-build properties on Shepherds Bush Common are continually rejected for fear of tampering with the plague pit that lies beneath."

Drake felt an involuntary shudder. "Jesus."

"Even the office blocks at Houndsditch don't occupy full plots due to the amount of plague pits in the area."

Hayden looked up. "The right hand says it's all good, the left remains wary. I'll stick with the left."

Drake cast his gaze up the street. Despite the intensity of the glare that escaped over the top of the wall, its beams speckled by the ground glass somebody had glued to the top, he could hear nothing.

Dahl glanced over at him. "You stuck to the spot or are you going to start that recce?"

"Shut yer gob," Drake answered with true Yorkshire aplomb. "I'm not waiting to cadge a bloody lift here."

At that moment all decisions were taken out of their hands as three cars approached the scene, at least one of their engines pre-announcing their arrival. The Range Rovers slewed across the road with tailgates still open, occupants pouring out. The Lamborghini powered its way to the front of the pack and tried to drive up the curb. The squeal of grinding alloy wheels grating across concrete made Drake cringe.

"If only for that they need their asses kicking."

Dudley was driving. As the Irishman slithered out, almost rolling onto the road, Drake and the team broke cover. Running, staying low, they closed the gap between themselves and their assailants with silent deliberation. Dudley and his men stopped outside a wide, arched wooden gate as one of them knocked. Dudley's voice could be heard with that now familiar twang.

"Get yer feckin' arses out 'ere!"

Drake slowed as the big double gate was suddenly flung open, unsure of what to expect. Through the great opening the mercs rushed and now Drake could see beyond them, into the floodlit area, to where they were working.

A hollowed out crater sat within the small, fenced off square, directly between a hotel and a row of offices. It wouldn't have surprised Drake if past hotel occupants hadn't stared out of their small windows, down at this segregated strip of land, wondering just why it was sealed off. Maybe they fancied it was a private garden, an underground junction box, a forgotten patch of greenery.

Never knowing . . .

The sides of the plague pit were jagged and vertical, uneven where men had jabbed shovels and scraped at the dirt. Those men were now arrayed around the rim, staring down. As Drake watched, more men toiled up a sharp slope, each one carrying a small white container that looked like an organ transplant box. Five men came up in all, depositing their boxes carefully into a larger one. Dudley strode over and clicked it shut.

"Grab it. Quick nigh!"

"Man, what an accent," Smyth complained.

"I think I like it," Mai said.

"Well at least he talks," Drake said huffily. "Rather than *texts.*"

Hayden motioned for silence. "One thing. Don't let those samples get away."

Dudley urged his men on. "Cops are comin'. Move it."

Drake exploded into action. Pistol raised, he ran forward shouting a warning. Predictably the mercs either turned to fire or ran in the opposite direction. Those that raised their weapons hit the concrete bleeding; those that ran were hunted.

Dahl and Smyth ranged around the parked vehicles, coming in from the far side. Hayden and Kinimaka fanned out to Drake's left. Dudley screamed an insult or two, now hefting the large box over one shoulder. "Move out," he said. "Give de feckers no quarter."

Drake skipped behind the house wall as the mercs opened fire. Fragments of brick blasted past his nose, speckling the Range Rovers. As he raised his gun a mass of men surged through the gate, barging each other and running as if they'd seen a plague-infested ghost. A shoulder smashed him across the face. Hayden shouted. Dahl, in typical form, rushed the entire group from the right. Mai was in their midst, bending and breaking.

Drake tripped and pushed men so that they tangled with others. Dahl smashed his way among them, a literal bowling ball, bashing the smaller pins to left and right. Some careened into the brick wall, howling; others fell against the cars and the spaces in between, faring no better.

Dudley slipped past the big Swede, as slippery and predictable as an injured tentacle, and rolled across the Aventador's low hood still clutching the box. Men scuttled after him, shielding his escape. Drake took two down with precise shots, then joined the chase. Dahl was hot on his heels.

Hayden's voice came through their comms system. "We're staying here to make sure it's not a decoy."

A man whirled in front of Drake, whipping a pistol around. Drake paused for one heartbeat, let the weapon swing by, and then slammed the off-balance man in the chest. Dahl overtook him, catching the next and lifting him by the back of his jacket, sending him sprawling face first into the street. Dudley turned around once more.

"Only pain 'ere, boys. Soldier boys never learn."

Dudley *threw* the big box high into the air, turned on the spot, and faced Dahl. The big Swede, clearly surprised by the unmistakable confrontation, slowed a little. Drake couldn't help but watch the box somersault through mid-air. Distracted, he folded when a merc tackled him around the waist, staggering backward but staying on his feet with Mai at his side.

Dudley came at Dahl, snarling. The box landed hard beside them, thudding into the street but resilient enough to endure without a scratch. Dudley punched hard and true, a boxer through and through. Blows to Dahl's ribs and arms made the Swede only flinch, rather than let his guard down. Dudley kept coming, snorting and puffing, drawling it up a storm.

Drake hefted his attacker by the shoulders and slammed him sideways into the wall. Still holding his pistol he used it to shoot another man about to take a potshot. Four were left around him; they grabbed the box and made a break for it. Drake watched them sprint up the road in the direction of the many shops and plush apartments that fronted Knightsbridge.

A nasty thought occurred to him. These guys didn't even need to escape the area. If the Pythians owned a piece of property around here—anything from a One Hyde Park hundred-million-pound apartment to a basement beneath the local Nero's—then the authorities were never going to find it.

Even a vehicle in a parking garage . . .

The more he thought about it the more realistic the idea sounded.

He clicked the comms. "Follow the guys with the box. Now!"

Hayden's voice came back instantly, crackling. "We're pinned down."

Drake glanced over as he ran with Mai, seeing the ex-FBI agents taking cover behind a Range Rover as assailants fired on them. The good news was that the wail of sirens was coming inexorably closer, now almost on top of the street battle.

The bad news: He was almost a man alone, chasing down the current most precious prize on the planet.

From behind he heard Dahl grunt and then Dudley cry out. But still the Irishman raged. Drake leaped aside as one of the men he was chasing peeled off and turned around, on one knee, gun drawn.

Drake dived as the weapon fired, hearing the shot but not seeing even a flash as the bullet fizzed past. Rolling, he came up feet first and planted them in the shooter's chest, breaking ribs and taking him out of the fight. Up and running he was even further behind now as another man broke away from the pack.

Another shot.

Drake dived behind a van, heard the bullet ricochet away, popped his head out and came close to getting it blown off by a second shot. The van's front headlight disappeared in a plastic blizzard. Flashing blue lights painted the surrounding walls. Drake sneaked a peek through the van's rear window, saw the remaining two men escaping with the box. It was critical, deadly serious if they escaped, but what could he do?

Getting his head shot to pieces was not the answer.

In that instant, for reasons he could not begin to fathom, Mai stepped out into the open. The gunman's aim swiveled toward her. Mai didn't move; just stood there as a distraction waiting for the bullet that may or may not end her life. Drake yelled at the top of his lungs and rose too, shooting through his entire clip. In that moment Mai breathed again.

"Damn."

Drake knew not what the curse meant, nor whether it was for a good or bad outcome, but he finished the shooter off and didn't hang around to ask. Head down, sprinting at top speed, he reached the dark corner ahead and slipped around it as carefully as possible.

Empty. The road was empty.

The men were gone. The box was gone. The plague had escaped.

Drake shouted with frustration.

In the aftermath, as Hayden fought to establish the team's credentials with an overenthusiastic inspector, Drake sought Torsten Dahl. The Swede was sitting with his back to a low wall, staring up at the skies. Drake threw himself down alongside him.

"How ya doin', mate?"

"Could be better." Dahl winced a little as he moved. "Little fucker packs a punch."

"He get away?"

"Yeah." Dahl sounded as gloomy as a man who'd

married for money only to find out his wife's real name was Colin. "Took off across the gardens like a stabbed rat."

"Is that supposed to be topically funny?"

"Not especially."

"Did he at least come out worse?"

Dahl gave him a stare. "Don't be a dick. What do you think?"

Drake grinned. At that moment Mai came up to them, standing next to Drake's outstretched legs. Her cell was ringing. "It's Dai Hibiki," she said. "Maybe he's learned something more about Grace or her parents."

As she spoke, Drake studied her with hooded eyes. Hooded because they were anxious. Hooded because they were terrified.

What the hell was going on with Mai Kitano?

CHAPTER EIGHTEEN

Los Angeles simmered at 8 p.m., basking in the heat amassed from another glorious day. Beaches and parks still echoed to the sounds of the spirited and the sprightly, all the more lonely now for losing the greatest gifts humanity could bestow—life, liveliness, energy. And innocence. Innocence existed here only in the young. Parents struggled to keep the real world from their children beyond the very last moment—and to help do that they took them to the beach. The park.

Let them run in the sun, luxuriate in the warmth, play to their hearts' content, live out their very real dreams before life intervened.

Los Angeles, the city of angels, savored the night. The Santa Anas gusted through the mountains, but at least the forest fires weren't burning tonight. More than two million people were living their lives in the great basin, day to day, night to night, meal to meal, TV show to TV show.

Aaron Trent was known by his friends and colleagues as the "serious" one. He was the leader, the one with the weight of the world on his shoulders. Every decision, every op and its outcome, was down to him. For many years the gods had seen fit to reward him, earning his three-man team a reputation as the best in the business. The Razor's Edge, they had been called, and every agency in the world sought their input. Their skills were legendary.

And then one night it had all shattered to dust. By then

his marriage was over, his boy—Mikey—living with his mother and her new boyfriend minutes from Rodeo. Trent and his team had become known as the Disavowed—three agents who took the fall for a country's failings. Later, they discovered the real truth—that they had been used, framed by a Serbian madman who found aid in one of the world's largest corporations. By then it was too late. The Disavowed had found a new purpose—helping those who could not help themselves, working for the weak who struggled to fight against the powerful.

Now, as the omniscient stars glittered knowingly and the warm air absolved the sins of yet another day in paradise, Trent knew there was something else in his life that had well and truly begun to matter. Her name was Claire Collins, and she was the Disavowed's FBI liaison, helping them work off the books now that their old friend, Doug the Trout, was dead. Collins was the new light in his life, the ballbuster with a soft edge, the midnight dancer with a fragile heart; she had all the complexities of a motherboard, all the sharpness of a samurai sword, and all the energy and sparkle of a six-year-old.

She sat to his right, enjoying the barbecue his colleague, Dan Radford, dished out.

Thoughts of Doug the Trout only sent his mind back toward Mikey. Doug had saved the boy's life very recently, dying in the process, taking the brunt of the explosion that was meant for Mikey. The perpetrator of that act, a terrible contract killer known as the Moose, had supposedly escaped into retirement and obscurity. Now, Trent suddenly felt the need to hold both his son and his girlfriend; he slipped an arm around their waists.

Mikey, eight going on eighteen, squirmed in protest but didn't pull away. This barbecue was a major step forward for the young boy—his mother had been kidnapped and murdered during the recent terrorist attack on LA, when everything had gone Threat Level Red; this was the first time Mikey had seen his dad with another woman.

Collins raised a glass. "Here's to us."

Trent reached for his juice and handed Mikey a glass. Radford and his wife, Amanda, both held bottles. Adam Silk and his new partner, Susie Brewster, were partaking of the red wine.

"Still standing," Silk said with a boyish smile.

"Still raising hell," Radford added and gripped his wife tighter.

"And ignoring the complaints," Trent said a little sternly.

"Just tell 'em to go fuck themselves," Collins finished the new mini-ritual off with a cough over the curse word and drank deeply. Trent watched her. Collins was more than a woman, she was a core of complexity—hard-ass, no-nonsense by day, party-goer and deviant by night. A dual identity. *No,* he thought. *A jewel identity.*

The warm winds drifted through and the hot food was devoured in earnest, the noise and laughter becoming louder as the night wore on. Time stopped on a night like this; problems were put aside as the magic of company mixed with the magic of Southern California, creating one blissful, eternal moment.

All too short.

Collins put a hand in the air as her cell rang out. "Have to take this," she hiccupped, trying to stop dancing at the same time. "No rest, wicked, and all that."

Trent glanced at his watch. "And past your bedtime, bud. We should be heading home."

Mikey pouted. "It *is* a school night."

"Oh, man. I'm the worst father in the world."

A strained note entered Collins' voice as she conversed over the phone, a note that piqued Trent's attention.

"Tell me what happened!"

Trent caught Silk's eye and rose. Radford joined them. Without being asked they all zoned in on Collins' exchange.

"And they lost the sample? All right. Where do we currently stand with LA and Paris?"

Trent saw Radford signal to his wife who moved toward Mikey. The whole team were aware of the global situation right now and had promised to help in any way they could. Skilful and capable response teams were their best chance of defeating this latest threat and Trent believed there were none better than his own.

"Now?" Collins burst out. "Shit, man. You sure pick your time. Sure, sure. We're on our way. Get me the location of that graveyard."

She ended the call, taking a moment before meeting the eyes of the Disavowed.

"Go grab your guns, boys," she said. "We need to take apart a few more terrorists. Right now."

Trent listened as Collins briefed them on the situation. Radford fired up the car and Mikey smiled a weak goodbye, tearing at Trent's heartstrings. This just couldn't go on. Eight was an impressionable age—what happened now would live in his son's memories forever. A solution had to be reached.

Immediately after they helped save LA.

Collins spoke from the back seat. "The Pythians just struck London. The SPEAR team lost the first sample."

"Dammit," Silk exploded.

Trent felt the hard veneer of battle fall across his face. "We're all up against it. Don't judge. The Pythians are on our pitch now and we have to step up to the plate. Take the bastards down."

"To break it down as simply as possible," Collins said with an impish glance toward Silk. "So we can *all* understand—a well-equipped, well-funded team of mercenaries are seeking to rob the graves of the long dead. Apparently it took a while to pin down but now they have a location and they're going for it big time, balls out. We have to stop them."

"And the rest of the security forces?" Radford asked.

"They'll help too."

"Who do we have on tech?" The technological side of every operation was Dan Radford's domain.

"There's no tech involved here, Dan. It's pure urban warfare."

Trent inhaled quickly. "Well, at least the recent ops prepared us for that."

"Tell us about these samples," Silk said from the front passenger seat as Radford hurled them onto the freeway. "What are the mercenaries looking for?"

"Old plague bacteria," Collins explained. "I don't know the details so don't ask. The relevant point here is that most of the leading governments of the world know of this threat and have agreed that nothing should be held back in trying to neutralize it. Nothing."

"Dance off?" Radford pressed. "That's your thing."

"I'm up for that."

"Continue," Trent urged.

The car barreled through the night, slipping through red stop lights as they switched from lane to lane, splitting the red flashing snake that ran from Hollywood to downtown. Collins tied her hair back with practiced ease. Radford eased the vehicle around 4x4s, sedans and a row of dumper trucks.

"Old bacteria may still be viable in plague pits," she said. "Or they have found some way of extracting what they need. These people are planning to weaponize the plague, a terrible encore to their 'house on the hill' demonstration."

"Wasn't the plague a Europe thing?" Silk asked, frowning. "Did we even encounter it over here?"

"The only known occurrences of human-to-human transference were in 1919 and 1924-25, way after the Black Death and other infamous outbreaks. An outbreak in Oakland first and then later in Los Angeles. At least thirty cases of bubonic plague, most of the victims were buried right in the cemetery we're heading for right now. Long Beach Municipal."

"Surely other pits would have been easier to attempt?"

"Why?" Collins swayed in rhythm to the car's motion. "It's away from the big city. Quiet. No security. And on US soil. Half these friggin' Pythians are American, for God's sake."

Radford pulled up, not too close. "We're here."

Most of the cemetery was built on a gradual slope, gray and black headstones running down to the roadside. Gray mausoleums stood around like lost souls, the great, outstretched limbs of untended trees pointing to things invisible and unnamable.

The team climbed out, noting the presence of SWAT vans, cop cars and other specialists already lined up. Collins groaned. "We're not in charge here. This is gonna be one messed up operation."

The team exited the car, trying to stay inconspicuous. The cemetery itself sprawled to their left, exposed, no fence or gate enclosing its expanse. A brown sign boasting a painted palm tree announced: *Municipal Cemetery, City of Long Beach*; an oil pump worked continually alongside as if trying to wake the dead.

Trent paused in the shadows. "Something's not right," he said, and turned around as if sniffing the air.

"It sure is friggin' quiet in there," Radford said with a fake shiver.

"No, not that. If I'm right—" he nudged Collins. "Patrol cars spotted two men believed to be working with the Pythians right here. Cell chatter is high for this area. But—"

"A pit takes time to dig, right? And they have to do it carefully."

"But we're in a cemetery," Radford pointed out unnecessarily, stressing the last word. "No one's gonna be bothered if they see anyone digging. That could even be why they chose this place."

"Sure," Trent said, still favoring the shadows beneath a sprawling tree and watching the bustle of activity near the road. "But we learned the Pythians were pursuing this Pandora thing only a day or so ago. The guys in London acted fast enough to *almost* thwart their plan. I'm guessing we're in the same ballpark. The problem is—*they know it too.*"

Silk stared across the pools of shadow and silvery light that hunched and merged between gravestones, trees and mausoleums. "If they have a backup plan," he said, "knowing the Pythians as we do, it ain't gonna be dancing in the moonlight."

Collins turned a wistful eye on him. "If only."

Trent frowned at the ground. "Later, maybe. What the hell are we missing?"

Although ex-CIA and FBI, although trained to be observant and notice the things everyday civilians didn't; although crammed with many years' experience, it still took the team several minutes to pick through their memories and find an answer.

Collins got there first. Maybe it was the sudden roar, the growling clank of heavy metal, but the bulb going off in her brain lit her eyes. "Damn! The dumper trucks!"

Trent spun. Like angry, newly resurrected monsters, four brightly lit trucks roared down the wide road that fronted the cemetery. End to end, engines screaming; Trent was put in mind of the four horsemen of the apocalypse come to devour the living.

"We passed them on the freeway," Collins said. "And if they're here now it can only be for one thing."

"Diversion." Trent ran back toward the road as if he was trying to cut the trucks off. To the left, some of the security forces had finally taken notice and were starting to shout. Trent cried out, sensing Silk, Radford and Collins at his back, trying to attract all the attention. Guns materialized through the trucks' open windows.

Trent dived and rolled, reaching for a weapon. Bullets crisscrossed the air above his head. Coming up on one knee he opened fire.

"Just another friggin' day with the Disavowed," Collins said in his left ear, already pulling her trigger.

"We sure aren't a hop-on, hop-off kinda ride," Silk said. "We're more of a twenty-four-hour endurance race."

"With a twist," Radford added.

"I think you mean twist*ed*," Collins said with a devilish grin.

The dumper trucks barreled past, breaking formation as they approached the SWAT vans and cop cars. Trent found himself left in their wake. His sober, analytical mind saw exactly where this was going.

"God help them."

One truck veered off the road, smashed up across the curb and over the sidewalk, entering the cemetery. Roaring, it proceeded to bounce and crash its way through gravestones, shattering each one to pieces as it climbed the slope. The remaining three trucks charged on, at last taking fire, but way too close to their target to make a difference.

Three hundred tons travelling at forty miles an hour is more than a daunting sight—especially when it's bearing down on you. Cops and flak-jacketed special units broke before the onslaught like waves before an enormous prow. The first truck rammed a cop car, destroying the front end and sending it spinning into the next. The truck then collided with the side of a SWAT van, lifting it off the ground with an almighty crunch and tipping it over to the side. Behind it the remaining two dump trucks smashed more cars and vans, and aimed deliberately for the running men.

"It's a fucking war zone." Trent watched the first truck as it crashed through the cemetery. "Come on!"

The four of them dashed from tree to tree, headstone to headstone, sprinting up the slope in pursuit of the speeding truck. It wasn't hard to follow. The sheer size and noise, the damage it left in its wake, the concentrated purpose of its route, left them in no doubt as to its destination.

Over the crest of the hill they ran. The truck was already hurtling down, gaining speed and jouncing from bump to bump so harshly Trent wondered if its occupants might end up with broken spines. One look behind told him they had no backup; the authorities had their hands full with their own pitched battle. He charged down the hill and saw their destination before they were halfway there.

An open pit by a fallen grave marker; the dark shapes of men standing around the rim.

"Waiting," he said. "They're just waiting for the truck. We have to hurry."

At that moment there was a fiery flash from the gravesite. Trent recognized the sign immediately but Collins spoke faster.

"RPG!"

CHAPTER NINETEEN

The team threw themselves left and right. The rocket scorched the air as it passed through, exploding against a nearby tree. Trent turned his face away from the sudden heat. A creak and a rustling of branches signaled the next threat—the falling tree itself. Radford squealed and Collins cried a warning as they both scrambled away. Trent half rose and crabbed his way clear, whipped by branches and twigs as the tree's extremities still beat down on him. Silk didn't manage to escape the felling, ending up prone beneath a rough layer of tree limbs. Trent and the others struggled over to help.

"Go," Silk said as he pushed his way clear. "Just go."

Trent broke into the open. Ahead, the truck had stopped and men were swarming around it. Trent knew that this cemetery opened out north and south onto other roads, no doubt a fact the mercenaries were counting on. Already exposed, he wasted no time in firing off shots, hoping to slow the mercs down. Men dropped to their knees and fired back, bullets whizzing far and wide through the darkness.

And then another dreadful noise. The howling approach of one of the other three trucks, storming through the graveyard behind them. Headlights chopped at the night behind him like demonic light-sabers, and then the truck was bearing down. Again Trent found himself rolling to the side, coming up hard against a grave with Collins rolling across his feet.

"Christ," she swore. "Found myself on my bloody back more times in the last fifteen minutes than in the past week." She grinned up at him. "And that's saying something."

Trent stayed attentive, ignoring her. Collins had always been about the job when she was working, saving the play for later. Since they'd got together though, her outlook had started to change.

Silk and Radford joined them. The second truck swerved in to join the first, carving great furrows through the grass. Trent could already see flashing lights approaching the scene, but with such an extensive, unfenced cemetery to cover they might as well try to stem the Pacific tide.

Forward again, the team ate up the ground between themselves and their enemies.

Trent was able to use the huge trucks' blind sides as extra cover, bringing him right into the enemy camp. Trained to kill by the CIA, he was not a man prone to leaving anything but bodies behind before the Razor's Edge were disavowed, but this scenario suited him just fine. Mercs rose and fell before him. He ducked behind an outsize tire as gunfire erupted. Silk took the man out. Radford, always the team member most likely to break something in combat, ran for the first truck with Collins at his side.

Trent saw logic in that. The samples these mercenaries had collected would surely already have been loaded by now.

He took off in pursuit, climbing onto the side of the truck by way of the wheels. As his fingers found their grip the truck started to move. Silk, alongside him, emitted a knowing grunt.

"Shit, this is gonna be bad."

The truck roared. Trent clung on as best he could. Most of the mercenaries were on the other side, largely unaware of their presence. Any passenger with more than half a brain would see them immediately, but they still had a chance.

Trent climbed, finding hand and footholds protruding from the vehicle's uneven bodywork. Within a minute he slipped over the top, staying low. Bullets strafed the truck's side, aimed at Silk, but the wiry man made it just in time. Collins, still below, took out the shooter with a single shot.

Trent shuffled forward as the vehicle gained speed. Only now did an unhappy memory return of its frantic, destructive journey through the first part of the graveyard. He swiveled to left and right, searching for a place to hold on to, then felt his body sliding backwards as the behemoth picked up speed.

"The good news is that the samples have to be on board," Silk called over from his precarious position near the edge. "Bad news? We forgot our metallic grappling hooks."

Something about what Silk said sent a prickle of unease the length of Trent's spine. *On board?*

"Shit!" *Of course they don't have to be on board, dammit! What would the cops chase—the three-hundred-ton, weapon-stacked ogre or the single backpack-toting individual?*

Trent rested his gun on the roof, gripped what he could of an exterior ridge, and scrabbled into his pocket for his cellphone. In predictable style he came up with chewing gum, his wallet and a set of keys before grabbing the plastic casing and wrenching it free. By now the truck was motoring and a steady breeze was getting acquainted with his face. One sharp dip and his body lifted clear of the roof, jouncing down again with a bang and a crunch of compacted flesh and bones.

Silk groaned. "This was a bad idea, man. A bad idea."

Trent fiddled with his cell. One handed, and being older than fifteen, the process of making a call was tricky. Mikey could probably have handled it in seconds. The vehicle's front end smashed through several gravestones, the concrete markers barely registering, but the ground was patchy and undulating. As Trent struggled he noticed Silk giving somebody a wave.

What the . . . ?

"Collins." Silk noticed his frown. "She started it."

Trent instinctively ducked as more bullets struck the truck, then hung on as it swerved to the right. He watched his gun slide toward the edge then stop. Finally, he managed to jab the dial button.

Another tremendous jolt and the phone was sailing away over the side leaving Trent squeezing his eyes closed in frustration.

When he opened them a pair of eyes was staring back at him. It took him a moment to realize men had started to climb the sides of the truck even as it swerved and careened through the graveyard, and by then the rest of the man was sliding onto the roof. Trent shot forward, head down, then launched himself feet first. Sliding across the roof his feet struck the merc dead in the chest. A wild scream followed him to the ground.

"To your right!" Silk cried, struggling with his own man.

Trent whirled. These guys were three bullets short of a full mag. But then they were also trying to escape and would do whatever was necessary. And all the time the man with the backpack and Collins and Radford were getting further away.

Trent smashed his man full in the nose, seeing it break. The man windmilled a little, but was otherwise unfazed, still coming forward. Another man raised his head above the side. Trent was close enough to kick him full in the face and over the edge. He grabbed hold of his current assailant by the neck and used a violent spin to hurl him into full flight.

He turned again. Silk had just defeated his own opponent, leaving him prone on the roof, and looked unwilling to kick him into space. Trent understood his restraint. They may be paid mercenaries, but the Disavowed were not thugs. If you didn't have to . . .

"Your cell," Trent panted, trying to survey every angle at the same time. "Get Collins on the line."

Silk dialed. It took a moment to connect but then the agent's fruity tones bombarded them.

"What are you doing? Get the fuck down from there!"

Silk shrugged. "Believe me, I wish I could."

Trent urged him on with a stern gesture.

"Oh and yeah, we figure that whilst everyone chases the big, noisy trucks the samples are getting away on foot. Probably with one or two men. It makes sense."

Collins didn't hesitate. "We're sticking with you," she said. "We'll call that in but we're with you all the way."

Trent sent another man pinwheeling off the truck. By now the second metal mammoth had maneuvered its way alongside. Cop cars weaved through the graveyard in hot pursuit. With the sprawled men and the damage caused by the trucks and the cars, the place looked like a war zone.

Silk stared back at the vehicles. "Wonder if Susie's out there?" His new girlfriend, the woman he had left his wife for, was a Los Angeles cop. The two were barely separable these days. Susie had helped him through the recent heavy trauma of revisiting his days as a child thief and recalling the people he had befriended and helped only to see them brutalized, loved and then lost. His greatest love had been murdered; his greatest mentor vanished without a trace. But they had caught the serial killer that haunted his past and although the ordeal had wrecked his marriage it had also given him a new lease on life.

"If not yet," Trent said, "then soon. She knows where you'll be."

Silk barely kept his balance as the truck cleared a hillock. "Yeah, smack bang in the middle of the chase."

Trent almost smiled. "Amen."

Ahead, the cemetery was finally thinning out. Trent saw the wide concrete strip of road and knew immediately what was about to happen.

"Hang on!"

The dumper truck cleared the cemetery, shot across the sidewalk and swung out into the road. Whoever was driving was good, because the back wheels slid all the way, a hundred-degree drift, but he held it with composure and even poise. Trent and Silk clung onto whatever they could, the edge of the roof, the aerial mast, the rear machinery. Bodies flung from side to side, they kept their heads down until the vehicle righted itself, hearing shouts as climbing mercs were thrown off by their own driver.

"How many of them *are* there?" Silk shouted.

"Enough," Trent said. "The Pythians don't appear to underestimate."

The dumper truck powered along the road now, its fellow tucking in behind. A swarm of power-sliding cop cars screamed in pursuit, lights flashing, sirens blaring. Trent looked back as their ride became easier.

"Ah, shit."

Men had climbed the sides of the truck that followed them and were now drawing weapons and taking a bead on the Disavowed.

"We're sitting ducks up here!"

The mercs opened fire.

CHAPTER TWENTY

Trent threw himself across the roof, Silk following. Bullets hit the high back with a metallic clang; others flew through the air with a supersonic whistle. Trent wrestled his own gun free, firing back just to give the mercs something to think about. Their own truck was hustling at high speed now, rushing by the odd civilian vehicle out in Long Beach at this late hour, jumping red lights and panicking pedestrians. Trent rolled again as another metallic flurry perforated the air, completely unsighted, and felt a rush of relief to find he wasn't dead.

Silk fired off a few shots. "Not my idea of a thrilling Thursday night."

Trent looked at him deadpan. "Oh, I dunno. Beats a CSI rerun."

Silk's cell rang. Rolling his eyes and putting down his gun for a moment he answered it. "Yeah?"

"Me!" Collins' high-pitched voice startled even Trent. "Bad news, boys. You won't believe this but the fucking Moose is out here tonight. He's back!"

Trent felt a ring of steel encircle his heart and fought hard to keep down a sudden rush of pure hatred. Along with Beauregard Alain he was either called the world's greatest or worst contract killer, depending on your viewpoint. The man who almost killed Mikey, the man who helped murder his ex-wife, the man who was willing and tried to blow up Radford in a diner full of innocents, the very man who helped orchestrate a terrorist attack on LA and got away with it. The Moose.

"I didn't believe it. How can he be so stupid? I thought he retired to a vineyard or something?"

"He did. I guess the Pythians have very deep pockets. Of all the cities to bring the Moose back to—LA? It's not only crazy, it's callous and outrageous."

"Seems they want everyone involved. Do you have a bead on the bastard?"

"No. That's just intel. But you can bet your balls he's here tonight."

This time, Trent felt a gust of disquiet travel through him, something that made all the hairs on his arms and the nape of his neck rise. "Jesus."

Silk squeezed off another shot, still holding the phone. "Anything else?"

"Yeah," Collins shouted. "We'll be with you in just a moment!"

Silk winced and held the receiver away from his ear. "What does she mean? And why the hell is she shouting?"

Trent shrugged, but then the reason became clear as a loud roar accompanied the sight of two big bikes powering up alongside the second truck below. Collins was visible astride the first, Radford the second. Collins held a gun at arm's length.

The truck swerved toward her. Collins flicked the bike away, maintaining distance. Radford hauled on the brakes, creating tire smoke. In another second he was shooting around the truck's other side. At the same time both he and Collins opened fire.

Trent held on as their own truck slid around another

corner. Frantically he stared around, recognizing the ocean, now running alongside, the beach and a row of houses. "East Ocean Drive," he said. "Man, any closer to the ocean and we'd be swimming in it."

Looking back he blinked hard as every other pursuing vehicle made the same turn—the second truck, the fast bikes, the stream of cop cars, and a black SWAT van. Pedestrians stared from the sidewalk and the golden ribbon that was the beach. Even the surfers were sitting on their boards, grabbing an eyeful.

Trent heard gunshots echo into the night and smash through Silk's phone connection as Collins again opened fire. The second truck suddenly swerved and a splash of red struck the windscreen on the passenger side. Silk managed to hit a merc on its roof, sending the man sprawling and then slithering over the side. His body bounced in Collins' wake, but only just.

"This is all well and good," Trent muttered. "But my heart tells me the samples are a long way from here, either carried by or protected by the Moose."

"Collins called it in," Silk cried. "Let's just stay alive."

Charging down East Ocean, the staggering convoy ate up mile after mile. The cop cars moved closer, but were now attracting fire from the mercs atop the second truck. Trent and Silk saw some breathing space and were about to rise when a new monster entered the battle. A police chopper, rotors thundering, swung into sight and headed, nose down, for the men on the second truck. Quickly, it gained on them, flying above the raging torrent of cop cars and both motorbikes. Guns bristled from its open doors.

Trent and Silk hit the deck near the back edge, watching.

Rapid gunfire slammed into the truck's roof, shredding men and piercing the metal, passing down into those below. Instantly the truck bucked, swinging sharply as its driver died. Collins and Radford made evasive maneuvers, Collins shooting to her right, up over the sidewalk and a little way down to the beach, Radford bouncing across somebody's front garden and then laying the front end down to avoid a parked car, whipping it back up in time to lay on the power and shoot back into the race.

Trent turned to Silk. "Guess who's gonna be perforated next?"

Silk nodded. "I'm already there."

As the second truck slowed and smashed up onto the sidewalk with mercs falling from its sides and leaping from its doors, Trent and Silk rose and ran to the front end. Once there, they paused, looking down. Trent caught a silver flash in the corner of his eye and looked right, saw Collins keeping pace with them, hair flying, and beyond her now a police speedboat, slicing through the ocean, matching their speed.

The rotors of the chopper grew louder.

Trent could see only one way out. Sirens and rotor blades slashed the air apart behind him. The truck's terrible roar battered his ears. Collins' powerful bike spurted ahead with a powerful roar. The speedboat bellowed.

A cocoon of peace enveloped him. "Just do it."

He leaped down onto the truck's cab and leveled his weapon, but it was already too late. The chopper thumped overhead, bullets spraying from its sides. Many found their way diagonally through the truck and into the cab; allowing the bird to pull up and away before the deadly stream caught up to Trent and Silk.

They were warned! he thought. *They knew we were here. Thank God.*

But that still left them in a world of difficulty. The driver, now dead, was no longer in control of the wheel. The behemoth slowed but it also slewed to the side. Cop cars shot past the right-hand side, careful to keep a wide gap between themselves and the runaway. Collins and Radford surged ahead. Trent hung on as the truck slid to the right, causing confusion among the cops. Several cars collided before a space opened up and the truck jolted through, striking the sidewalk and then shuddering onto the beach. It hit hard, its left-side wheels sinking, its right still spinning, and immediately tipped. Trent and Silk, clinging to the bulkhead with white knuckles, felt the heavy vehicle lift onto two wheels. Both let out involuntary cries. The whole world tipped.

A life flashed before Trent's eyes—the new life he wanted for his son and himself. This wasn't the way to do it. This was going to get him and his friends well and truly killed.

The truck lifted and lifted, Silk at the bottom and moments from death; Trent at the top and feeling his legs starting to float—and then the three-hundred-ton monster stopped tilting, its weight the final factor, and slowly slammed its chassis back down onto all tires.

Silk fell to his knees, the sudden loss of momentum as jarring as the horror he had just lived through. Trent clung to the bulkhead. For a moment they were both quiet, thankful, drawing breath.

The sound of sirens and the roaring of engines destroyed their fugue. Collins, minus her bike, ran up alongside.

"What the hell are you guys still doing up there? Get down here now!"

Trent sent a quick glance toward Silk. "We'd better do as she says. Nobody wants to survive a ride like that and then face Collins in ballbuster mode."

Silk nodded. "I don't know which is worse."

Trent steeled his resolve and wiped the blood from his face, then nodded down at Claire Collins.

"Coming, dear."

CHAPTER TWENTY ONE

Tyler Webb slammed the table in excitement, his exuberance getting the better of him. Alone in the office, but still faced by five live TV screens he struggled to keep from dancing around.

"We have two of them!" he cried. "What a start to the game, my friends. What a start."

Five confused faces stared back at him. Of course they were waiting for the customary greeting. Of course they knew less than he about proceedings in the three target cities. Of course, this was as it should be.

"We are the Pythians," he intoned.

"We are the Pythians."

"So, straight to business. Team London lost most of its men but still smuggled out the sample. Team Angeles, when warned of the oncoming raid, reacted superbly and threw attention away from the Moose as he liberated our sample. Team Paris is about to strike. I love the fluidity of all this, gents and ladies. Makes me feel very much alive."

"Los Angeles was touch and go," General Stone affirmed. "To say the least."

"That's what I mean!" Webb practically cackled. "We spent two days finding the right place, two days excavating and then outmatched the best of the US in a last minute escape. You couldn't write that stuff!"

Stone looked a little relieved. Webb wondered why for a moment and then remembered the thorn in their rosy situation. "This team in London," he said, "that almost beat us. They're called SPEAR, I believe."

Stone winced but covered it with a nod. "Yes, sir. I believe we first heard of them through Dmitry Kovalenko. It was they that thwarted the Blood King in his efforts to use the nano-vest on the president underneath Washington DC. Indeed, it was they that took him down. They also stopped Coyote," he smiled, "but failed to stop *her* using the nano-vest."

Webb pursed his lips. "I recall they also stopped several other attempts to test the vests."

"Sure." Stone shrugged. "I guess they're what you might call—our arch enemies."

"And the team in LA?"

"We're investigating. I believe the Moose, when he's safe, might be able to shed some light onto that question."

"Do they have anyone in Paris?" Nicholas Bell asked.

Stone raised both brows. "I can't imagine there will be anyone so effective," he said. "They're spread pretty thin."

"Good. Good. Well, we're ahead of the game at least. A good place to be. So tell me, General Stone, tell me about this SPEAR team."

"Since they popped up in London I've been digging deep. It seemed as good a way as any to test the resources we have . . . procured. It's the same team that found the tombs of the gods, if you remember? All that Odin stuff too. They also untangled a Korean plot to plant brainwashed super-assassins among the population." Stone proceeded to name and describe every known member of the team.

"Not all were present at Knightsbridge." Webb stared down at a sheet of paper before him where names had been matched to quickly snapped photographs. "Yorgi the thief. Alicia Myles, I believe. Lauren Fox—the escort."

Stone appeared to wince. For a moment, lost for words, he said nothing. Then Nicholas Bell stepped into the breach.

"I guess we don't really know how big the team is."

But Webb barely heard him, concentrating on Stone. The general looked like he'd just swallowed a really, *really* big pill. "Is there a problem, Stone?"

"Ah, we don't know the exact location of every single member. Even our resources can't encircle the globe."

"Accepted. But still, we are nothing if we're not a proactive group. The curve of destiny is always before us but we must now strive to remain ahead of it. If SPEAR is causing us problems we should take steps to stamp them out."

"I suggest you stay on track," Stone said quickly. "Nothing can be gained by deviating here. Look what happened to everyone else that stood up to them, even the Shadow Elite. We have schemes and plans to see us through the next two years. We should concentrate on those."

Webb thought about that. Stone was usually his most staunch ally, his hardest rock. Today, something was off with the man. Perhaps it was the influence of that damn builder, the uncouth Nicholas Bell. Perhaps it was something else entirely.

Time to test the general.

"This is your plan, Stone. We allowed you to take first strike. I must insist now that you man up and face a most thorny issue."

Stone's eyes bulged at the slur, face suddenly flushing beetroot red. "Man up!" he blustered. "Man up. Me? I've seen more action than any man here. I'll have you know—"

Webb tapped the desk. "Calm yourself, General. Your reaction is the one I was searching for. But the basic issue remains. Drake and his colleagues need to hit the proverbial brick wall."

Stone's face scrolled through a medley of emotions, finally settling on deceitful. "There is a way," he said. "Maybe."

Webb sat back, happy to see Stone back to his normal self. Clifford Bay-Dale jumped in with a stiff elitist comment, "Hurry up, man. We don't have all day."

Stone continued as if the interruptions hadn't happened. "Some time ago, across in the Czech Republic I understand, Drake and his team pretty much destroyed a terrorist arms bazaar—"

"When they found the *third* tomb of the gods?" Webb, by now, was familiar with their exploits.

"Yes, in Germany. Now, through the ears of the NSA and the eyes of ground-based assets I do know that this arms bazaar was attended by men who are normally ghosts. They pull the strings of the puppets we know. Terrorist royalty if you like, with a long reach and an even longer memory. The SPEAR team were marked that day, etched in the memories of these powerful men, though so far their constant exploits have kept them untouchable."

"How's that?" Robert Norris wondered.

"It's hard to track and plan to kill a team always at war," Stone said. "A team that doesn't even know itself where it will be the next day, or even the next hour. Drake's team has been on the move for over a year and situated in all parts of the globe. But now," he mused aloud. "Now we might have a chance."

"Go on," Webb said, reading through a dossier as he listened, a dossier compiled on that very team and its every member.

"The terrorists don't know where Drake is right now but *I* do. *He* doesn't know his team have been marked. If we do this right we could have every terrorist in London burning his house down."

"Removing him from the game," Webb said. "And adding a rich depth of confusion to it."

"You got it. Now, give me some time. I have a little event to plan."

Webb agreed to the general's signing off. Within ten minutes he had said his goodbyes to the rest of the Pythians, effectively cutting their meeting short but hearing no complaints. Tyler Webb had started this group, the vision was his to enjoy, the game his to abuse and manipulate. He would have everything go his way or not at all.

General Stone had slipped up somewhere, he was sure. There were no clues in his latest dossier. Perhaps Nicholas Bell knew something—the outspoken builder had been atypically quiet throughout the meeting.

Webb's sense for trouble, as practiced and shrewd as a Shaolin master's, unfolded inside, its edges jagged, sharp like thorns. Even among the superior ranks of the world, he mused, death's heavy hand could strike at any time.

CHAPTER TWENTY TWO

Alicia Myles checked her watch for the hundredth time. "How come we ain't getting no bloody action?" she complained. "Drake and those blokes in LA got plenty. How 'bout little ole me?"

Russo, crouched beside her behind a hedgerow, grunted. "Coming from you the term 'action' could mean half a dozen different things."

"Quit speaking, before I break that mountain you call a face with my boots."

Russo frowned, his crag-like face shifting like sliding rock. "I accepted you, Myles. Doesn't mean you can insult me."

"Believe me that was no insult. And besides what's wrong with being a game girl?"

"Nothing. So long as you don't bring that 'game' near me. I get the feeling that the term 'safe sex' isn't even close to your playbook."

Alicia licked her lips. "No such thing."

At that moment, Michael Crouch, the leader of their little team, spoke up. "I realize watching a cemetery through the night is a little boring, chaps, but try to keep the noise down."

Alicia heard Healey snigger, the young man's emotions getting the better of him. "Hey Zack," she said. "You ask Caitlyn out on that date yet?"

Caitlyn, knelt next to Healey in the ditch, turned her head

away. Healey immediately crimsoned. "Umm, well, do ya think I've had bloody time?"

"Nope."

Healey shook his head, muttering a word.

Alicia's ears caught it. "Don't call me a bitch, Zacky. You know that kinda talk just turns me on."

Crouch gesticulated. "Look!"

Alicia studied the flat open-plan graveyard they had found in the heart of Paris early that morning. Arriving in the fog of 4 a.m. they had located a hiding place and settled down to watch. The Church of the Three Holy Innocents bordered the Rue St Dennis and immediately called to Alicia as a truly gruesome place. The mausoleums were dirty, old and broken, their doorways like jagged teeth. Snarled weeds grew everywhere. A mural of the danse macabre patterned one large wall whilst rumors of charnel houses blighted the place. History spoke not only of terrible charnel pits but also of the dreaded plague pits, bodies being tipped into deeply dug holes in the ground like endless toppling heads of corn, their arms and legs entangled, their dignity in death destroyed. Several mercenaries known to be on the Pythians' payroll had been identified visiting the cemetery over the last two days. Armand Argento at Interpol had fed the information back to Crouch.

"At first the Paris police weren't interested," Crouch said, matter-of-factly. "Nothing ever changes. But after the events in London and LA, my bet is they will suddenly *get* interested. Especially . . ."

Alicia watched a dark-clad group of men thread a path through the broken-down graves on their route to the center of the cemetery. She decided they had been right not to send someone into the graveyard to snoop around. The mercs were here and they were totally exposed. Ripe for the plucking.

"Ready?" She shifted tensed-up muscles, ironing out the knots of the last few hours.

Crouch signaled a go. Under a crisp, brightening dawn sky they moved off. Stars and the moon still twinkled in the frosty heavens; a brisk wind snapped around them. Moving with a low center of gravity and absolute silence, Alicia and Russo led the team out of hiding. Guns were prepped; in the case of Caitlyn tracking devices, information-gathering tools and communications systems were tuned and monitored. She ran at the back, armed and flak-jacketed, but with orders not to engage until Healey had made good on his promise and trained her up.

As she ran, Alicia fixed the ragtag group of mercenaries in her sights. They were closing now, only one of them seemed even half-observant and he was studying a patch of darkness in the other direction. The front four men suddenly dropped out of sight, giving Alicia a moment's pause, but then their heads reappeared and she realized they had jumped into a previously excavated hole.

"On point," she whispered into her comms. "All good. They're bringing up the samples now. We'll catch them red-handed."

Still, an air of unease trickled across the back of her neck. After what had transpired over in London and Los Angeles this campaign almost felt inadequate. Could this actually be the Parisian cops trumping the mercs? Or perhaps they didn't have much of a crew?

"Underestimate me at your peril," Alicia breathed as she

came upon one of the mercenaries with his back turned. "I may look like a fantasy but I'm your worst fucking nightmare."

Her knife made sure he didn't even squeak. As Russo descended like an avalanche the rest of the mercs spun. Healey and Crouch were already on one knee, taking aim, and picked two off without wasting a moment. Alicia danced around her falling man and engaged the next. This was too easy.

All four mercs were climbing out of the hole. Crouch fired again, sending one writhing back down. Alicia thought fast and sprinted to reach the hole first, leaving the rest of the mercs to her team. Those emerging from the hole would have the desperately needed samples.

As she ran, a figure dropped out of the sky, landing eight feet in front of her. A figure wrapped in a skintight black bodysuit. Somebody who snagged her attention so violently she tripped and fell.

"Beauregard!"

Alicia covered her fall with a roll and a leap. The assassin, Beauregard Alain, hadn't moved, but stood with a feline grace, muscles bulging.

Alicia hesitated. "You may have beaten the SPEAR team once," she said. "You won't beat *me* again."

Beauregard's lips turned upward. "You tripped over when your eyes met mine." His French accent was music to her ears.

"Is that why you zip that stacked body of yours into a skintight suit?" She allowed her gaze to drift down to what she considered to be Beauregard's biggest asset. "To keep that monster from tripping *you* up?"

"Maybe one day," Beauregard leaped at her, "you'll find out!"

Alicia sprang to the left, head still intact by an inch as Beauregard's heel snapped at thin air. "Promises, promises."

Spinning fast she jabbed an elbow into the small of his back. Again Beauregard stood motionless, studying her. Alicia changed tack. "Why are you fighting for these people? And aren't you supposed to be locked up, for God's sake?"

Beauregard couldn't resist a little sneer. "Aha, your silly team allowed the *authorities* to handle my interrogation." He stressed the word in a disdainful way. "They were not a match for me."

Alicia felt a sudden urge to take this man down, teach him his place in the world. "If you challenge me that way," she said, "you'll end up crawling at my feet."

Beauregard arched an eyebrow. "I believe I might enjoy that."

"So why are you here?"

The Frenchman struck fast, clearly trying to make an impression; if not in her mind at least on her body. "Money," he said. "Always the money."

"You're on the wrong bloody team." Alicia fended him off and took a second to review the rest of the team. Three mercs still fought Russo and Healey, whilst Crouch had his hands full with another. Through the earpieces Caitlyn shouted excitedly about a merc with a backpack standing quietly behind Beauregard. Alicia noticed him for the first time.

"Who's your boyfriend?"

"We have what we came for," Beauregard said. "Stop me if you can, Alicia Myles. We're so far ahead of schedule we may even be stopping over for the night."

Alicia paused even as she fell into a well-practiced move. *Was that . . . ? Did he just . . . ?*

Russo's clamorous voice brayed through the morning like a claxon. "Myles, stop chatting the bloody man up and take him down!"

Alicia eyed the assassin. "You planning to switch sides?"

"Le Grand Hyatt," he said without moving a muscle. "But be careful of monsters there."

"I'd better encounter at least one." Alicia didn't know how to explain it but, flirting aside, she *trusted* Beauregard. Their world of shadows and death, one-night encounters and paid wet work was far from reality. Alicia had been there—done it. She knew the ropes and how to test the character of the people that stood among them. Perhaps it was familiar souls, comrades in arms; perhaps it was that he'd gone easy on them and surrendered back in England in a knocked-unconscious kind of way; perhaps it was some kind of new desperation. *Always look forward,* she thought. *Never back.*

Russo brayed again. Alicia sensed him pounding up behind her. She nodded quickly at Beauregard and performed a weak attack. The Frenchman skipped away, bruised her ribs and sent her sprawling. Then he twisted Russo despite the big man's strength and threw him onto Alicia.

"Fuck!" she yelled as the tremendous weight sprawled atop her.

Beauregard grabbed the man with the backpack, relieved him of the burden, and ran straight into the brightening dawn. The remaining man drew a pistol but was taken down almost immediately by a sniper's shot from Crouch.

"Get the hell off me, you daft lummox!" Alicia shouted.

"I'm bloody trying." Russo struggled to roll his body off her. "Last place I wanna be, believe me."

"*Ow!*"

"And if you hadn't spent so much time trying to get shagged maybe we would have taken him down."

"Hey, Russo, your miniature backup piece is digging into my ass."

"Eh? I don't have a . . ." Russo finally managed to roll clear, groaning. "Oh, I get it."

"Good." Alicia sat up. "Keep it in your pants." She noticed Crouch drawing a bead on the fleeing Beauregard and shouted at him to stop.

Crouch lowered the weapon, calm, regarding her curiously. "What did you do?"

"I talked us into a chance," she said, giving Russo the eye. "Using my distinctive charm, of course. We're sitting ducks out here but the mercs don't know *we* know where they're staying. The Le Grand."

"You mean to steal the sample back from under their noses?" Crouch caught on quickly. "What makes you trust Beauregard?"

Russo snorted. "I can think of one thing—"

"I bet you can, Robster, but Michael knows what I mean, don't you? You were there at Sunnyvale. You know Beauregard could have seriously hurt us. And now . . . chances are he could have escaped with the samples anyway."

Crouch chewed his lower lip. "Tricky operation, Alicia.

Even with a fully trustworthy soldier on the inside. And a hotel is not exactly perfect for a team raid."

Alicia nodded. "Agreed, sir. But if I can get hold of Drake straight away, I believe we have just the man."

CHAPTER TWENTY THREE

At 7 a.m. on a cold and windy London morning, Matt Drake and his team regrouped in a local hotel. This was no longer a single entity discussion—by necessity it had to include all the cooperating teams and more. Karin handled the heady logistics, helped by Caitlyn Nash on the Paris side and Dan Radford in LA. Armand Argento also tuned in from Interpol.

Drake reclined in an easy chair, facing a work desk where Karin had placed two laptops. Arranged around him were his teammates. The atmosphere was a little despondent, but despite their loss they still showed good spirits. With all the governments around the world searching for the samples it was only a matter of time before they showed up. In addition, with most of the Pythians' mercenaries identified and being tracked it would be relatively easy to anticipate their next move.

Drake put an arm around Mai, receiving a slight smile in response. Grace, perched on the soft arm beside her, kicked her legs to and fro and stared into space. Most everyone else studied the laptop screens as they began to fill with images.

Alicia's face popped up suddenly. "Hey!"

Drake laughed. "Damn, I've seen some things in my time but that's scary."

Alicia pouted. "An insult means you're missing me. I get it."

Hayden stepped in front of the screens. "Everyone is

online? That's good. We can start. I'd like to get a feel for what has happened so far. Mr. Crouch, if you can start."

Drake listened without giving his full attention. In the end, all their stories were pretty much the same. They had lost the samples. The bubonic plague, or a form of it, was on its way to be weaponized at some secret factory.

Then Alicia's voice cut through his deliberations. "I have a plan to steal our sample back."

Dahl was first to jump in. "You know where they're taking it?"

"Not quite like you mean," Alicia said. "I simply know where it will be *today*. Perhaps even tonight." She went on to describe her meeting with Beauregard and its favorable outcome.

Drake thought about the master assassin's conduct during Coyote's recent tournament. The reward was worth the risk. He nodded as Hayden turned toward him with questioning eyes.

"Yorgi," he said. "Time to be useful."

The Russian thief smiled widely. "For too long," he said. "I have sat on your sidelines. Now, I prove my worth."

Kinimaka checked his watch. "You'd better leave immediately, bud. It's an hour's flight and then some to Paris."

Yorgi rose. Hayden took him into a corner, explaining the details and handing him cash and a phone. Alicia asked about any special equipment he might need and then the thief was ready.

Agent Claire Collins spoke up from Los Angeles. "We're on full standby out here, but now we also have an agenda of our own—"

Trent cut in. "A man called the Moose. Contract killer. Threatened or killed some of our friends a few months ago during the Blanka Davic takedown. Now he appears to be working with the Pythians—"

"We want this man," Silk broke in. "Badly."

"Understood," Drake said. "If it comes to it, and you haven't caught him by the time all this is over, we'll fly over there and help you take the bastard out."

Collins smiled. "All right. So what's next?"

"Following our loss," Crouch began. "It may be time to start pursuing a different angle. I mean, what of the Pandora myth? How does it connect with all this? Are we missing something?"

Dahl and Kinimaka both nodded at the same time. The Swede spoke up. "I've been wondering that myself." In answer to Drake's smile he said, "Yes, Swedish men can multitask, unlike the English. My feeling is that they named this dreadful creation the Pandora Plague for a reason."

Drake's smile grew wider. "I just love how you change nationalities when it suits. Anyway . . . Michael? What do you know about Pandora?"

"First woman on earth," Crouch recapped. The ex-leader of the Ninth Division had always been a lover of archaeological mystery, of fabled history and dusty old legends that just might turn out to be true. It was why he had created the new Gold Team and how they had recently discovered two caves full of Aztec treasure.

"Created at the command of Zeus. Given a box and told not to open it. What would anyone do? She set loose all the sins of the world. Now the gods, feeling a little sorry for her, had also placed inside the box a good creature whose task it was to heal the body and soul. And so was born hope. Hope managed to escape the box at the last minute, just before Pandora closed it, and flew around the world, healing the wounds that the sins and plagues had already made. But, as she escaped last, she is always the last to arrive. That's why, when people are beset with worry, it is hope that always helps see them through."

"Wait a goddamn minute," Smyth barked from his protective place alongside Lauren. "If I'm hearing this correctly, the gods wanted to punish mankind? So they sent woman. Am I right?"

Lauren swatted his arm, not kindly. Smyth grumped and checked the perimeter of the room. He was nothing if not always prepared. Immediately after his impromptu outburst he whipped his cellphone out of a back pocket.

"What about the box?" Karin asked. "It's always Pandora's *Box.* Maybe it's an important artefact or something."

"A box that once held all known sins would be considered the greatest find in history. The stories say it could actually have been a *pithos*, a jar, made of clay or bronze metal. The actual story of Pandora is a theodicy—an attempt to address the question of why there is evil in the world. From the paintings of Lefebvre to the Soprano Nilsson she is always depicted holding the box, about to unleash the plagues."

"So the naming by the Pythians could be nothing more than another message saying they're evil?" Dahl stated. "And about to unleash a pandemic."

"Possibly." Crouch shrugged on screen. "Does anyone have a take on the story?"

Alicia, always one to have an opinion, spoke first. "Personally, I enjoy most of the sins of the world," she said. "But not these. Plague. Famine. The sins released by Pandora relate to what the Pythians are creating—a new plague."

Drake coughed. "Wow, what have you been feeding her, Crouch? Brain food?"

"Piss off, Drakey."

Crouch was thinking hard, missing the exchange. "The Pandora story is so very ancient. Her daughter, Pyrrah, was said to have survived the great deluge along with Noah. Yet when she first appeared on the slopes of Mount Olympus, in the same vein as Eve, she signaled a change in the world from happiness and contentment to suffering and death. This can also be put down to a sign of technological advancement, for her coming was punishment for Prometheus giving mankind the stolen gift of fire."

"Technological advancement," Trent said from another screen. "Just one more angle."

Hayden returned from briefing Yorgi. "And another thing, guys, probably as important. The Pythians are not ghosts operating on an astral plane. We *have* to find their HQ. Judging by what we know this Pandora plague is merely a beginning. More lives will be lost unless we locate them."

"Footprints, digital or otherwise," Caitlyn said. "Some must exist."

"What news of Stone and Bell?" Dahl asked.

As Hayden reported their total lack of developments, Drake watched Yorgi prepare to leave the room. His mind recalled when he'd first met the young Russian thief, back in that hellhole of a prison where Zanko played god of war. They had helped each other back then, and Drake had seen the man's potential and realized his skillset might come in handy someday.

Today.

Quickly, he scooted off the sofa and intercepted Yorgi by the door. "Leaving without a word?"

"I speak English not too well." Yorgi shrugged with a slight smile. "I not want to embarrass."

"Ah, bloody hell, you speak English just fine." Drake pulled the Russian into a bear hug. "Stay safe out there, my friend, and think fast. Just do your job, nothing else."

Yorgi nodded. "It has been a while but I am happy to be helping."

Drake opened the door and watched Yorgi head out. It didn't seem right letting him walk off alone but he knew that members of Crouch's team would meet him straight off the jet. Yorgi would be stalking the street of Paris by lunchtime.

"It's a three-way hunt then," Crouch was saying. "The Pythians. The Pandora angle. And the secret facility. Let's get to it."

As Drake wandered further into the main room he passed Mai on the way out. The look on her face set his angst into overdrive. Without asking he made a decision to follow her out of the room and into the empty corridor. Mai met his eyes.

"Hibiki," she said, gesturing with her cell. "He has news on the family of the man I killed over in Tokyo."

Drake winced, but stopped himself from talking. Mai appeared to be more hooked up on this than she had been on the search for her parents. The only help for her was to let her see it through.

Dai Hibiki, Mai's Japanese police contact and old friend, spoke fast. "After you killed the husband the Yakuza killed the rest of the family, just to be sure. The daughter escaped. We don't know where she is now."

Mai crumbled so fast Drake thought that her very soul must have collapsed. Her face went slack, her legs shook. Drake moved in to support her. For a moment there was utter silence.

"We will keep trying to find Emiko, the daughter, Mai. We'll never stop. All reports says she's a good girl. She'll turn up soon, I guarantee it."

Mai opened her mouth but nothing came out except a grating far back in her throat. Drake gently took the phone from her hands.

"Cheers, Hibiki. Mai needs to digest all that and you need to monitor international chatter for any sign of the Pythians or their bases. They're a world threat now."

"Understood. There has been intelligence lately to suggest several groups of men employed by these Pythians have moved across borders in southeast Asia, along with whisperings of a lost kingdom on an Atlantis level. We are investigating."

"Good. Keep us informed." Drake ended the call and then held Mai. When her head fell across his shoulder and her body began to shake he knew they were in desperate trouble. Knowing better than to speak he thought of all that they had been through since that wonderful, fateful day back in '98 when Mai and he had teamed up to take down a Chechen warlord. The years had been more than rough—

they had ravaged the life out of both of them. But here they were—together, fragile but happy in their relationship, destined for a better life. Drake's personal battles and losses had pushed him closer to Mai, but now hers were pulling her away. He had made his peace and moved on, finding contentment even after Ben's death and the murder of others, in this unlikely family he had discovered, this improbable team that loved and lived and fought for each other every hour of every day of the week.

He urged Mai back into the hotel room, seeking that companionship. In an uncanny moment the only person that noticed them was Alicia, eyes flicking his way from the TV screen and registering a glint of concern. Drake dropped Mai into a chair and stood beside her, hoping the turmoil would break her emotional miasma.

Strangely, he noticed that Lauren Fox had risen to her feet, about to address the room. Maybe it had something to do with General Stone.

"I have an idea," she said. "Totally off the wall. I mean so far off the wall," she pointed to the small partition beside her, "it's on the other side of the room . . ."

All eyes turned to her. From Los Angeles, Agent Collins said, "Oh, thinking with diversity. I like this girl already."

Lauren gathered her thoughts. "It occurred to me at the beginning of all this when Stone first invited Bell to participate in our trysts. I could check with my friends in the *trade*. We're a very close-knit group. We have to be to warn each other about bad punters, dangerous *johns*, as we call them in the States. Our warning network is first class. Has to be. Now, if Stone and Bell frequent escort girls in DC, do they also frequent them somewhere else?"

A moment passed, then Crouch said, "That's a bloody good idea. A habit is a habit and you're right. Both men will have used escort girls elsewhere. You just need recent or coincident occurrences."

Lauren flushed at the compliment, clearly not the jaded individual she appeared to be. Being useful, being a part of the team, evidently placed high on her needs list.

Grace, so far very quiet, came over to stand by Mai as she realized the Japanese woman wasn't herself. To her credit she remained silent, offering only companionship. The young woman had enough problems of her own as memory loss gradually gave way to an emerging past of slavery and abuse. The complications of letting such a past go were huge as that past now felt like her present. Drake wondered if their world was about to unravel.

And then the call came in. Hayden snatched up her cell first, listening and turning parchment white as someone shouted in her ear.

Fifteen seconds later she was pocketing her phone and running for her jacket. "Meeting over!" she cried. "Just heard James Ronson has been attacked by mercenaries. We have to go!"

"Ronson?" Crouch repeated. "You mean *Prime Minister* Ronson? Oh, my God. My God. What the hell is happening?"

"We'll be secondary, but we have to be there." Hayden checked her weapons, already heading for the door.

Drake rose, shaking his head as he met Dahl's eyes.

"Compared to this," he muttered, "Kovalenko's DC attack was minor. This is big fucking league."

The Swede released a deep breath. "Like comparing evil

Barbie to Maleficent. Our planet's screaming," he said, striding past. "Broken down by the unspeakable dreams of small men who would be kings."

CHAPTER TWENTY FOUR

Whitehall was a tide of humanity at 9 a.m., a feeding ground for all players from the oldest profession in the world to the nastiest, right up to Admiralty House. Here, a line of policemen stretched across the road, stopping passers-by and office workers, halting traffic. Horns blared amid the hubbub. Uniformed officers sporting guns could be seen situated on every corner and on rooftops. As they made their way slowly against the flow Drake questioned Hayden as to the seriousness of the attack.

"Shots fired in the vicinity of the Prime Minister is always considered serious," she said. "It's the way it was done that raises questions. Mercs matching the descriptions of those we encountered in Knightsbridge fired shots in the air as Prime Minister Ronson descended the steps from the Department of Energy. He escaped unhurt and three men were cornered. Now they're trapped in the Clarence pub, one of those quaint, tight, narrow-corridor establishments you Brits love."

Drake slowed as the crowds began to thin, relieved that they had left their non-combatants back at the hotel. As they approached the cordon he was impressed by the action of the police and their calm demeanor. What could have been a volatile situation was being defused by self-confidence and composure.

"So why us?" he wondered. "Don't we have more important things to do?"

Hayden tugged at the sleeves of her jacket. "You'd think. But these mercs are more interested in us than giving up."

"I don't understand."

"They've been tweeting about us from inside the Clarence. Our names. Comments on the SPEAR team. Abuse. Challenges. The usual macho bullshit."

"So we're here to shut them down?" Dahl rumbled. "Let's get it done quickly."

"We're here to see if we can figure out what the hell's going on. Mercs don't fire into the air and then trap themselves so easily. They don't tweet like idiots—most of them."

"So something's up." Drake waited as they were shown through the cordon. He moved ahead, eyeing the buildings on both sides of the normally busy road. "Have all these offices and shops been searched?"

"You kidding?" Hayden looked incredulous. "That would take days."

As if in response to Drake's words small coffee shops and cafes to both sides of the street emitted a stream of men. Drake, trained to have some of the best perceptions on the planet, paused at the cordon, sniffing trouble; Dahl did the same. The others walked ahead momentarily. Even Mai, though her awareness was tragically elsewhere of late.

"Wait," Drake hissed. "Something's not right."

The police cordon was snaking as men turned, whispering to each other. Eyes shot up, to the left and right. Drake narrowed his vision. Pedestrians to both sides suddenly shifted away, heading back into shops or hurrying up the street.

Komodo was alongside them now. "What I'm thinking,"

he said. "Can't be right."

The stream of men fanned out. Cops stared in disbelief and denial. Radios squawked. A woman screamed.

Drake saw no advantage in waiting. The men staring him down weren't mercenaries, they were terrorists, and they had been waiting in coffee shops and cafes outside the cordon, already prepped before Prime Minister Ronson was fired upon. No way could these men have drifted here afterward in such numbers. Drake ran even as guns appeared from underneath coats, as a grenade bounced toward the middle of the road, and as a tall, swarthy malnourished man revealed what was strapped to his body.

"A present from Ramses," he said and released the dead-man's trigger.

The central London street turned into a battleground. Drake dropped and rolled. The man exploded a moment after the grenade. Body parts and shrapnel burst everywhere. Drake held a hand across his head and rose the second he felt the shockwaves pass. Luckily the terrorists were running forward, closing a gap they shouldn't have. In their hands were a number of traded and bought weapons. Clearly, the weapons black market, always strong in London, was flourishing. Drake swiveled on his back and kicked out the legs of the nearest man, sending him sprawling. He caught a glimpse of the police line behind him, breaking up as some reached for weapons and others parted to let armed forces race through. Shots came from above—snipers positioned on the roofs. Dahl ducked as he was about to run smack-bang into a scrawny man, sending him ten feet into the air and catching his weapon on the way down. Komodo fought hand to hand with another terrorist.

Drake fired twice and took two out. Hayden came up to him. "They're here for us," she breathed. "Look at them."

Drake already knew. The terrorists, fourteen strong, were converging on the SPEAR team and ignoring the cops, the specialists and everything else. Sensing he was pinned he immediately leaped up onto the front end of a car, rifle steady, aimed and pressed snugly to his shoulder, squeezing off shot after shot. He then ran hard, jumping from the hood of one car to another, firing without let up.

Dahl flung one terrorist against the other, starting a pile. A third pointed a gun at him, found it wrenched from his hands, and was added to the heap. Komodo ducked behind it. Hayden stayed back, maybe still a little sore from her gunshot wound in their battle through the nightmare streets of Washington DC during the Blood King's blood vengeance, a time when so many had died. Though fully healed, she had yet to see full combat. Kinimaka stood beside her.

Mai and Smyth found themselves ducking and diving, more target practice and distraction for the terrorists than anything else. But the contrived tactic was working. Faced by capable operatives and with men dying every second the terrorists were starting to wilt. They were not military or even militia, just a bunch of men hardened by oppression and bullying and three months' training.

Cops joined the uproar. Special Forces slid through. Drake rolled across the roof of a car, down onto its trunk and then slithered to the road as bullets stitched a ragged line after his boot heels. He thought about sliding under the car but decided it was a bad idea. One rolled grenade and he was in bits. He nipped out around the side and fell to the sidewalk, catching a glimpse of a terrorist being thrown into the air, arms and legs flapping, and knew instantly where the mad Swede was. Hayden and Kinimaka were further down the row of cars, taking cover. Drake inched up until he could see through the side window.

Eight terrorists were dead or incapacitated. Of the six remaining one was losing to Komodo, one to Mai and three others were fleeing from the cops. That left . . .

Booted feet smashed onto the front end of the car Drake was hiding behind. A figure came into view, already firing. Drake rolled onto his back, gaining half a second, but the weapon was swiveling too fast. He squeezed the trigger, unable to aim fast enough but hoping the shots would make his assailant flinch back.

No luck. The man was hell bent on dying anyway and came on. The bullets from his gun blasted a line across the sidewalk, along a brick wall, through a glass window and then back toward the sidewalk again as he crabbed forward. Drake shuffled backwards but nowhere near fast enough.

Bullets mowed concrete as they churned around his boots. Firing, he rolled one last time. The shot went wild. There was no satisfaction on the terrorist's face, just an anesthetized, dazed expression.

Then his chest exploded and he fell face first, weapon silenced and clattering to the floor.

Drake took a breath, then saw who stood behind the fallen man. Hayden Jaye crouched and trained her gun to the left as Kinimaka offered Drake his right hand. "Up ya come, bud. Won't do to get shot before lunch."

Drake jumped up, nodding at Hayden. In the road the scene was now quite different. The terrorists were down, cops standing around looking shell-shocked, officers shouting into radios that every establishment should be checked.

Hayden bit her lip. "Did that guy say 'Ramses'?"

"Aye," Drake's accent thickened. "Who the bloody hell is he?"

Kinimaka was staring between them. "Why do I get the feeling the terrorists and the mercs are working for different bosses?" He kicked away the dead terrorist's gun, stumbling over the curb and sitting down hard on the wing of a car in the process.

"Mainly?" Drake said in response. "Because terrorists and mercs don't mix. Not generally. Their ideals are poles apart." He shook his head, thinking fast. "Look, we don't have time to sort through all this. There's more than just Whitehall at stake."

"Message from Karin." Hayden pecked at her cellphone. "Yorgi has landed. The op in Paris is a go."

Drake stared around at the chaos. "Let's hope they have better luck than we did."

CHAPTER TWENTY FIVE

As she assessed Le Grand Hyatt, Alicia found her thoughts wandering. Recently it had become increasingly clear to her that the course of her life had to change. Running would only take her so far and, by its very nature, would only end up taking her full circle. Nobody could run for their entire life. A reckoning was coming, she knew, when she would have to take some time and face the demons of her life—the very real devils that had shaped it.

But not now and not today.

She stood in a window with Yorgi at her side, opposite the fancy looking but timeworn French hotel. Caitlyn had already downloaded blueprints and was trying to isolate their targets' rooms. The other three present members of their team, Crouch, Healey and Russo, were checking weapons, comms systems and other crucial equipment, a practice drummed into every soldier even in initial training.

Alicia ignored the mission and started drilling Yorgi for information. "So, what the hell's up with Mai?"

The Russian looked uneasy. "I speak poor English," he said. "Sorry."

Alicia took hold of an ear. "Bollocks to that. You forget I was there when we rescued you, Yorgi. Now, the little Sprite's got a big problem. Spill."

"In truth I don't know much." Yorgi spread his hands wide. "It is a problem she brought back from Tokyo. I heard she killed man, a low Yakuza employee, and then they kill his family just to tie . . . what you say? Tie up . . . ?"

"Loose ends," Alicia said reflectively. "Damn."

"Only the daughter lives," Yorgi finished.

Alicia whistled, showing no emotion. Inwardly, her heart was with Mai and the family. Such things could never be laid to rest.

"And how's Drake coping?"

It was one question too many and Alicia knew it. Quickly, she turned away, freeing Yorgi from the answer and glaring toward Caitlyn.

"We ready yet?"

The dark-haired girl scrunched her nose. "Second floor," she said. "And check out is at 1 p.m." She checked her watch. "If they're checking out today it won't be long."

Crouch came over. "Despite what Beauregard told Alicia I'm inclined to act first rather than wait and see. Yorgi, you're up."

The young thief inclined his head, showing no real emotion. He double-checked the blueprint and compared it to the row of rooms Caitlyn had isolated. "We know which one has sample?"

Caitlyn shook her head. "You have a choice of three double rooms. Three names they're using are known aliases, yes, but nobody stands out as a leader. I couldn't speculate."

"I'd prefer to avoid open battle." Crouch knew about events in Los Angeles and London.

"It won't be necessary," Yorgi said. "I will take samples from under noses of men."

Alicia grabbed hold of his arm as he started to move out. "You do know I'm coming with you, right?"

"No, no. I work best alone. You will make me worse."

Alicia's brows shot up as one. "*Excuse me?*"

"Always alone. Always. I have . . . trade secret."

Alicia laughed. "If you die alone in there, Yorgi, you're gonna be on my shit list."

"You come so far," Yorgi granted. "Will help. But I finish alone."

"I can live with that."

Alicia strode alongside Yorgi as the thief threaded a knot of back streets on his way to the hotel. Standing almost a head taller, blond and as muscular as a world-class athlete, she immediately looked conspicuous but a padded coat and woolly hat diluted most of her eye-catching assets. Linking arms with Yorgi, the pair strolled around like a couple in love. When at last the hotel's rear entrance appeared ahead Yorgi stopped.

"Why not the front door?" Alicia wondered. "We can take the elevators to *their* front door."

"This way we can take service elevators," Yorgi said. "Not made to be noticed." He gesticulated widely as was his habit. "Rear entrances are watched, yes, but not as carefully as lobby and corridors. Service staff always come and go." He pointed out a waiter sneaking out of a door and lighting a cigarette. "Many chances."

"We're not appropriately dressed."

Yorgi shrugged. "This is true. If it was I, Yorgi, planning this it would take a week or more. We have less than one hour."

Alicia slowed as Yorgi waited for the smoker to leave. At the first appropriate doorway he leaned in and Alicia folded her arms around his neck. "Oh."

"I am sorry. It is necessary," he whispered into her ear.

"I know. But it's still the closest thing to a shag I've had in months." She remembered the open comms. "Except when Russo jumped on top of me."

The man's angry snort was a wasp in her ear. "I was thrown."

Alicia held Yorgi tighter. "Likely story. You're the size of a bloody Sasquatch."

"Beauregard—" Russo began.

"Oh don't mention his name when I'm all cuddled up," Alicia moaned. "Makes me so—"

Yorgi pulled away. Luckily, the smoker had returned to work. The couple made their way to a pair of grungy doors which worked on a push-bar from the inside. Fixed to one side was a bell but there were no door handles. The single door to the left, however, was as standard as they came. Alicia grunted happily, reaching for the handle. Yorgi pushed in front of her.

"Follow me."

A narrow, well-lit corridor ran away, cleaved on both sides by several single and double doors. The noise of a kitchen swelled from the right, doors wide open, and steam and the smell of garlic, tomato and baked bread drifting out. Yorgi moved fast, surprising Alicia, scurrying past the opening as if his heels were on fire. He paused at the next door, glanced in and moved on. Alicia hurried to catch up.

At the end of the corridor a pair of modest steel doors denoted one of the service elevators. Yorgi pressed a button and waited, head down.

Alicia saw the chef first. Emerging from the kitchen he stared straight at them, a look of irritation twisting his features. Alicia read the look in an instant, suddenly understanding that guests tried this on more frequently than she imagined.

"Hey, you're not supposed to—"

His English accent was pure cockney. Alicia fed the man's own conclusions, grabbed Yorgi and swung him into the just-arrived elevator, giggling all the time. With a loud "*Byeeee!*" she jabbed the second floor button and watched the doors close.

Yorgi untangled himself. "From blueprint we go left out doors, count five rooms and enter. Then, it is up to me."

Alicia nodded and watched the Russian assemble the 'special' goods he had asked the Gold Team to procure as he made the London to Paris flight. Nothing spectacular, just a mini wrecking bar, some leather gloves with the fingers cut out and a reserve backpack. Alicia took a moment to hand him a small caliber pistol.

"I not use gun."

"This time you do, Yogi."

"It's Yorgi."

"I know, but I like Yogi better. Get used to it. If it's a choice of kill or be killed I'd rather you shot first. The mercs these Pythians hired won't lose a moment's sleep over killing you."

"But . . ."

"This is *my* world now." Alicia pressed the weapon into his hands, holding it there. "Trust what I tell you and take the bloody gun."

"All right."

The doors whooshed open and again the couple drifted arm in arm toward their goal. Using the service elevator had meant they didn't have to bypass the mercs' rooms and risk discovery. It also meant their target room was closer. Yorgi slipped out a programmed keycard microcontroller and pushed it into the slot on the door of the hotel room they had booked over the Internet but had not had sufficient time to check into. Alicia shielded his body, leaning in and laughing. This time, nobody saw them. The hotel corridors were empty at midday and the maids had already cleaned the second floor.

Yorgi entered the room and stripped down to a tight black bodysuit that covered every inch of his flesh. Pulling on the gloves and placing the wrecking bar into a zip pocket, he shrugged into the backpack. "Simple but effective," he said. "Now, you stay here."

Alicia nodded but followed him anyway.

"Curiosity killed the cat." Yorgi took deep breaths. "You know where that came from and what happened."

Alicia could have responded with a number of comments but, not wanting to disrupt the little guy's focus, she settled upon a moment of silence. Yorgi used the respite to break the window lock and slide the sash upward.

Alicia couldn't refrain from commenting. "You know there's no balcony out there?"

"Empty wall is better," Yorgi said with a smile and disappeared.

Alicia ran to the window, believing she knew the thief's trade secret. Sure enough he was clinging to the sheer brick wall, fingers and shoe tips inserted into tiny depressions, searching around for the next.

Buildering, she thought. If someone of Yorgi's reputation used the illegal sport as a primary means of progress then he had to be world class. She herself had learned the art of buildering as a Special Forces technique, though not at his level. Of course, he would only normally employ it at night, in darkness, and after thoroughly researching every aspect of his intended target. Today, he didn't have such luxury. Finding the samples and stopping the Pythians was paramount.

She watched him advance, feeling a new surge of respect for the man. Buildering, known as urban climbing, counted on an individual being able to climb any vertical wall, finding the correct foot and handholds to complement the perfect body positioning. The body did not always go forwards, but moved around an axis, gaining ground. The skill, concentration and the strength required was phenomenal, although these days only older buildings could be properly scaled.

Alicia made sure the door was locked and her weapons were ready. By the time she returned to her position, Yorgi had gained the first window and was peering inside. What he saw had to be positive for he took out the wrecking bar and inserted its thin end into the window frame. Then, seconds later, he reached inside and struggled with the window itself. This was potentially the trickiest maneuver, since the window was clearly stuck and required pressure to force it free. Too much pressure would result in Yorgi losing his balance and plunging to certain death. Too little and he wouldn't gain entry.

Alicia found her knuckles had turned white before Yorgi dropped inside the first hotel room. Without delay his voice spoke inside her head, perfectly calm. "Empty room. Messy bed so someone was here. Bottles of whisky and used glasses. No gear though. I move on to next."

Alicia watched his head re-emerge, knowing there was little chance the mercs would have left the precious sample unguarded. Caitlyn's voice came over the comms. "I can see you, Yorgi, and I can see into the second room." She paused. "Seems empty. The problem is the *third* room is jam-packed. Almost as if the lot of them have been called to a meeting before moving out."

"Makes sense," Alicia said. "It's what we would do. Can that scope you're using pick out a number?"

"Hard to say. Five, maybe six. I can't see the whole room."

Yorgi climbed carefully across to the second window. Alicia took a moment to make a plan. "Line 'em up in your sights," she said. "Sorry Michael, your wish for peace and quiet just ain't gonna work out. You fire on my word."

She waited for their thief to gain access to the second room. "Yorgi, I counted eighty four seconds from room to room. You capable of making the third in that time too?"

"I say give me ninety."

"All right. As soon as I see your head I'm starting counting."

"Make sure I can hear you."

A minute later, Yorgi appeared. Alicia began the count, scooping up her weapons and readying herself for war. She wondered briefly why teams she got involved with could never complete a mission discreetly, but then concluded that it was down to the desperate, often time-sensitive operations they became involved with. Her count reached fifty and she exited the room, wedging the door open in case something went wrong. The corridor was eerily quiet, her footfalls softened by the plush carpet and thick paneled walls.

"Seventy five . . . seventy six . . ."

Healey, Russo and Caitlyn appeared out of the elevator bank ahead, both panting slightly. Russo shrugged at her. "Crouch is the sniper," he said. "I thought we'd be more useful alongside you."

Alicia hid a smile. When they first met, Russo had acted more like a hot chili in her bolognese, resentment boiling through every comment and movement. Now, after they had shared battle and even saved each other's lives, there had grown a mutual respect that would only become deeper. She nodded at the three of them.

"Well met. Be ready on eighty five. And Caitlyn, you stay in the corridor. Watch out for escapees."

"Ready."

"Eighty . . . eighty one . . ."

She stopped outside the room in which all the mercs were gathered and knocked loudly. Three more seconds and she motioned toward the comms.

"Fire twice!"

Instantly, windows shattered. Voices roared and yelled out in shock and anger. Alicia told Yorgi to wait and then shot out the lock.

"Go!"

The trio surged through the door in tight formation, guns up, squeezing shots off as targets rose like fairground dummies. As if through telepathy they split in three directions, staying low as they raced for cover. The mercs were in total disarray. Alicia saw three down and three standing. Through a half-open door to a small bathroom she saw a flash of Beauregard, but her vision focused hard on the largest mercenary in the room.

The one with the backpack.

She fired. He ducked, instinct honed. She swept forward, still firing, and slid across a polished coffee table, her feet striking his knees and toppling him over. Bullets struck his chest. Alicia wasted no time or conscience on the man, knowing what he carried, and ripped the backpack away from him. Other mercs started immediately toward her.

"We should get this out of here." She held their ultimate prize in her hands.

She leaped over to the window and handed it to the waiting Yorgi. The backpack had always been imperative to this mission and her plan had always been to utilize Yorgi's skills to escape with it, no matter what happened to the rest of them. The Russian thief immediately made his way down the side of the building, away from the mercs. Alicia protected the window, Crouch the street. Now she turned to find Russo strangling a merc into unconsciousness and Healey heading toward the bathroom. The remaining mercs appeared to be panicking.

No. Her heart leaped into her mouth. *Healey!*

Two mercs blasted past Russo, making no attempt to fight, just heading for the door. Alicia noted the big man engaging in pursuit and trusted him to help Caitlyn take them down. In that moment Healey yelped and Alicia sprinted for the bathroom.

Beauregard slipped around the door frame, as sinuous as smoke and shadow. Alicia came to a sudden stop.

"You tricked us, Frogface."

"Did I? Plans change quickly. And here you are."

"You're saying they accelerated the operation?"

Beauregard glided around her as a limping Healey approached his back. "They do that when they have everything they need."

"Bad sign."

Beauregard inclined his head, creeping toward the door.

Alicia had had enough. "Whose bloody side are you on anyway?"

"Today?" Beauregard shrugged. "Tomorrow?" He smiled craftily.

"Tomorrow, you're gonna be thrown into the Bastille, in chains. Life's about to get real, Beauregard."

"Do you think?"

The Frenchman sprang forward at a low angle, twisting as he came, somehow managing to entangle both her legs in his and jerk them out from under her. Alicia went down, the gun clattering away, and Beauregard danced past. She noticed a knife in his hand, but also noticed that he didn't try to use it.

Healey yelled for him to stop.

"Oh yeah," Alicia rolled to her feet, "that'll work."

She gave chase, stopping at the door to take in the scene. It wasn't all she had hoped. Russo and Caitlyn had nailed one of the mercs, the other was nowhere to be seen but at least her two colleagues were safe.

Relatively speaking.

Russo was sitting on his ass, a look of deep surprise creasing the crags around his eyes, a bruise already forming across his right cheekbone. Caitlyn was far worse off, held in the clutches of Beauregard. He stood behind her, pulling her into him, the knife across her throat.

"Don't you dare," Alicia hissed. "Don't you fucking dare hurt her."

Beauregard pulled her closer. Caitlyn winced. Alicia pulled up short.

"Stand back," the Frenchman said. "And I will let her go. Little minx almost took me down."

Alicia blinked in shock and swelled with pride at the same time. Then she remembered who she was and wondered why these foreign emotions had begun to haunt her of late. Something clearly wasn't right.

"Let her go," Alicia said. "And we'll let you go."

"Your word?"

"My word. Put down your weapons, boys."

Beauregard waited for Healey and Russo to comply and then smiled. "A good day's work, non? You retrieved your sample. You killed some bad men. You even got to tussle with the great Beauregard Alain. Well, until we meet again!"

He shoved Caitlyn into Alicia, making his way like a cat down the corridor. Healey and Russo gave a half-hearted chase but they were never going to catch the man.

"You okay?" Alicia asked Caitlyn.

"I'm good. He didn't hurt me. But it's always me," she said. "Always me that gets bloody caught."

Alicia frowned. "You're referring to your beating, torture and escape during our Aztec adventure? Don't worry. It's all good experience."

"Oh, thanks for that."

Healey and Russo came up then, the former looking at the floor, the latter with a wide grin on his face. "So," Russo said, tapping his ear. "Since the comms are still open and you two are finished nattering shall we call in Yorgi?"

Alicia grimaced. In the heat of the moment both she and

Caitlyn had forgotten about the comms.

"Here I am," a voice whispered over their comms and also sounded out behind them. Yorgi was there, backpack in hand.

"You have the samples?" Alicia asked.

"We do." The Russian thief smiled. "We sure do."

"Are they safe?" Caitlyn looked abruptly concerned.

"I guess. All are locked up in a strong medical box of some sort."

Crouch's voice rang in their ears. "Then stop talking and leave. Now. The Pythians are prepared to destroy cities in order to possess those samples."

Alicia gathered the troops with a sweep of her eyes. "You heard the man. Move it."

CHAPTER TWENTY SIX

Aaron Trent waited for news and stared unknowingly at Agent Claire Collins. The Disavowed had been saddled with this ballbuster a few months ago and had quickly gone from dislike to acceptance to massive respect, and more. At work, she had criticized them all, hauling them well and truly over the coals. At play she had kissed them all, danced with them all, but she had settled on him for something more.

Trent blinked as she met his stare. The smile in her eyes spoke of play but the look on her face was pure work.

"Got a tip," she said. "The Moose has been spotted at a trailer park off Highway 1, toward San Diego."

"Already?" Trent stayed suspicious.

"That man's face was all over the news just a few weeks ago. There's not a good Angelino wouldn't give him up after those terror atrocities. I'm surprised it took this long."

Silk was already at the door. "What are we waiting for?"

A car was waiting, a driver too. The new and improved Razor's Edge took their seats and sat back, bathed in early morning light. At this time, especially in the hills, Los Angeles was a gift from God, the angels' own masterpiece in progress as the rising sun threw brushstrokes across the skies. A ball of fire filled the basin, crept across the hills and dappled the trees, creating wonder in all those who jogged or slid early from their beds to watch, or headed for the long commute. Trent, in the window seat, turned his head toward the rising ball and thought of better times.

"The new dawn always makes it better," Collins said.

"Not always," Trent said. "There are some tragedies a thousand rising dawns could never fix. But if you think your life is over," he turned to her, "always take one last look."

Her eyes sparkled. "You just never know," she said.

"I've heard that said about songs too," Silk said from the other side of the car. "Susie and I have one of our own."

"As do Amanda and I." Radford checked his hair in the mirror. "*Shadows of the Night.* Pat Benatar. Seems fitting."

"*You Shook Me All Night Long.*" Silk grinned. "Very fitting."

Trent basked in the glow from Collins' eyes. "Do we have a song?"

Her gaze drifted. Collins was the social butterfly, the dancer, the singer of the group. Trent realized that something like this would be very important to her.

"When we have one, we'll know," she said. "We'll know."

The vehicle blared its sirens and cut through swathes of traffic. Collins relayed reports as they came in. Trent put his game face on and listened to incoming details as they neared the site.

"They practically emptied an entire precinct," Collins breathed. "Trailer park's surrounded. SWAT will arrive three minutes before us, give them time to set up. FBI response teams are en route, and even the goddamn *Marines* from Camp Pendleton! This is the big one, guys. Ain't nothing been wanted more in Los Angeles than the head of this murdering bastard. Not for a long time."

The car slewed to a halt, dispensing the Razor's Edge who checked their weapons and looked for the man in charge. Collins led them to the staging area and into the presence of a big dark-skinned cop with a gray beard and enormous flak jacket that almost doubled his size.

"Collins. FBI," she said. "What do we have?"

The cop deadpanned her. "You in charge? Who the hell's in charge? All I know is it sure as hell ain't me. Got so many goddamn teams on the way here might as well hold a goddamn party."

Trent almost pitied the cop. Collins never took shit. She was the most driven woman he had ever known. "Stand the fuck down," she growled into the cop's face. "And either help me or get out of my way."

She pushed past, making the cop grunt. Trent followed her. The cop grumbled at her back. "Initial sighting was around that blue van over there. That was . . . thirty minutes ago. Ain't nothin' moved since but trailer folk."

"The Moose won't hang about," Silk said. "He's too clever for that."

Collins looked around, surveying the cluster of metal trailers and dirt track roads, the haphazardly parked vehicles, the makeshift washing lines strung from roof to roof, the still-open doors of people that had been evacuated. "Fuck. We're gonna have to evacuate the entire site, not just around here. And we need more men. Get choppers on the perimeter and CHP at every road. Manpower will draw the bas—"

Radford, who had been closer to the Moose than any of them, face to face, saw him first. A man stood in the road ahead, wearing a leather coat, with a bandanna around his head and a shiny silver belt buckle reflecting the sunlight.

"I've never known the Moose to hide," Radford said

quietly as the others saw the motionless figure. "All I do know is that he'll have a plan."

Trent stared, not moving. The Moose stared back, eyes steady. This was the man that had indirectly killed their mentor Doug the Trout, and Trent's wife; the man that almost killed Mikey before Doug took the boy's place; this was a man that loosed sorrow and a flood of tears over the great, scorching city—and he deserved to end his days screaming.

But Trent remained motionless, eyes never breaking contact. Radford, at his side, breathed raggedly.

"It's the diner all over again," he murmured. "Distract us whilst . . ."

Collins raised both hands to show they were empty. "Let's talk," she shouted. "We can come to some agreement."

"*Murdering piece of shit*," she added under her breath.

Trent made no move. The Moose stood stock-still as the breeze whipped up around his leather coat, making it billow. The man's lips, even from where Trent stood, could be seen to form a sneer, a deep mocking expression.

"I say shoot and ask questions later," Radford, always the impulsive one, breathed. "One less Moose in the world ain't gonna be a problem."

"Don't forget why we're here," Collins hissed. "The samples."

The Moose whirled and his coat surged around him like a giant black bat, engulfing his body. Trent saw his hand for one split second, and the black device there.

"Down!"

But Collins fired. She would not concede defeat so

easily. Bullets blasted from her swiftly drawn gun as trailers to both sides of the road exploded. To the left a bright metallic van, shining with reflected sun, burst into flame and heaved to the side, spitting fire. To the right a Caribbean-blue van shuddered as its windows exploded and then its top blew off, rising up into the sky. Further ahead, deadly debris, a confusion of metal, iron, glass and timber, crisscrossed the road with multiple blasts one after the other. Trent, Silk and Radford hit the dirt, staying low through it all, but Collins remained on her feet, firing hard as lethal wreckage made the air bristle all around her.

Seven, eight shots fired at a fleeing shadow. The first definitely caught his jacket, the second a wooden post at his side. The third, as a shard of metal grazed her cheek, flew through his hair, the fourth grazed his scalp. She saw it all in slow motion, as if witnessing her own death, and maybe she was, but the Moose had to be taken down. Such a man could not be left to walk this earth. The fifth bullet took him in the shoulder, the sixth jarred wide as razor sharp splinters jabbed at the hand that held the gun. The seventh took out his elbow as heavy fragments battered her flak jacket.

The eighth took out his ear, blood exploding.

Trent looked up, unable to believe his eyes. His scream went unheard as Collins fired and fired her weapon, focused on the job like a woman possessed by desire and drive and determination. In the end, as the eighth bullet struck, Trent swept her legs from under her, seeing her head turn as a piece of door frame hit, the movement saving her life as it glanced away.

Collins fell into his arms, barely conscious.

Trent screamed.

Silk and Radford scrambled and ran as fires blazed. They leaped through gouts of flame, hurdling the blasted ruins of trailers and furniture, televisions and microwave ovens. The Moose was on his knees, hand to his head, but he was far from finished. The man hadn't survived decades of bloodshed to go down so easy.

He spun, his gun spitting fire of its own, crying out with the pain of movement. Silk and Radford weaved and ducked behind smoldering wreckage. Then the Moose rose once more. In his right hand he held yet another device.

"Take it," the Moose rasped. "She earned it. Nobody's stood up to me like that in thirty years. Nobody." He threw a backpack toward them.

Radford started to rise, but Silk wrenched him back down, sensing what was about to happen. "No—"

The last explosion rocked the ground around them, but only one person died.

Silk hauled Radford up and headed over to the backpack. With infinite care, but knowing the risk had to be taken, he opened it. Inside sat a square black lockbox.

"I think we're in business."

Radford breathed a sigh of relief and waved back at Trent. "Thanks to her," he said. "All thanks to her."

Silk blinked rapidly. "In all my days," he said. "I have never seen anything like that. Never."

Radford hefted the backpack. "Let's get this thing to safety. And see how the other teams are doing. With a bit of luck," he smiled optimistically, "this will all be over."

CHAPTER TWENTY SEVEN

Tyler Webb tried to suppress his anger. It wouldn't do to act hastily here, not in front of his closest minions. If General Stone's great plan had fallen apart it was still only the first of many, still only the beginning. Any one of their great plans could fail, including his own stunning venture constructed around Saint Germain. His unquestioned leadership had to be maintained at all costs.

Stone appeared poker-faced on the colossal television, one of five split-screens, having just revealed that two of the samples had been retaken by specialist teams. The look on his face would have felled an eagle in mid-flight.

Nicholas Bell had a sympathetic expression plastered across his face. "Don't worry, Bill. We still have Miranda's galleons."

Webb frowned hard. This was the first real sign that voting Bell into the Pythians had been a bad idea. Rulers of their caliber should never express certain emotions. *Sympathy?* The emotion simply should not exist here, at the very heights of power. Sympathy was for weak men and children. There was no compassion among kings.

So we will have to trim the pack a little. It is easy enough to do.

"Perhaps the galleons should come next." Webb suggested, thinking ahead.

"But my lost kingdom," Bay-Dale spewed forth immediately, starting the beginnings of a pounding inside

Webb's head. "Work is already afoot. We are close to the site. Tokyo, Taiwan and even the Beijing teams report progress."

Webb held up a hand to stop his prattle. Seriously, this whole collection of uber-powerful whiners was giving him a migraine. Webb had been prone to horrendous migraines since he was a small boy, debilitating headaches that took him to a different world of pure pain. Until recently only utter darkness and the lack of all stimuli had eventually returned his world to a dull ache and then slow recovery. That, and his own special, personal brand of terrorism— something none of these minions would ever know about.

Stalking. The distraction of the lethal prowl. But he was keeping that beautiful, flourishing concept for later.

First, Stone's apparent failure.

"We still have the sample from the London plague pit, yes?"

Stone nodded dully. "The mercenary, Callan Dudley, obnoxious man though he is, delivered commendably."

"And Bell? Miranda? You are on site, yes?"

Bell nodded. "The factory is fully functioning."

"A little small," Le Brun sniffed. "But mostly adequate."

"I certainly hope the long flight didn't swell your impeccable ankles," Webb snapped before he could stop himself. *Damn. Reel your pride and fury in.* They must not fall apart.

"Sir?" Bell to his credit, gave him a second chance.

"This mercenary, Dudley, is he bringing the sample to you personally?"

"I insisted that he do," Stone put in. "With the remainder of his team."

"Good. Good. Then we will at least have one of the samples. Start production as soon as it arrives. The process will take longer, but will still give us our edge."

"Of course."

"And ramp up security." Webb attempted to stave off the pounding by gazing through his picture window, straight at the impressive torrent of water that fell out there every night and day, eternal, everlasting, undying. The faraway falls, previously, had been his only solace when his life fell to pieces.

"We will draft in other teams."

"Do that. We all underestimated the abilities of our opponents this time. Do not let it happen again. And Stone?"

"Yes?"

"That terrorist stunt in London was beyond stupid. Don't ever think of doing anything like that again. The attention we gained has vastly weakened our position."

Stone frowned. "Just a minute. I thought we *wanted* attention."

Webb scowled at Stone's blatant incompetence and lack of vision. "*Not* from such terrorist royalty as *Ramses*," he spat. "Are you mad? That animal has the power to start a terrorist world war. Do you really think that will help the Pythians?"

"No, sir."

"No, sir," Webb mimicked. "For the Pythians to flourish, the world has to be at least mostly stable. We can then start and end our own wars. Take all that we desire. Now ensure that sample is weaponized as soon as it arrives and keep us informed."

Webb flicked a switch, succumbing to the hammering that threatened to pulverize the back of his neck. He was alone. By flicking another switch he closed the blackout curtains and switched off the lights, leaving him in utter darkness. Then he placed his head into the crook of his arm.

His mind drifted to the SPEAR team and their accomplices. No matter.

I will be inside their lives soon enough.

CHAPTER TWENTY EIGHT

Drake took a step back as new information started to roll in. *Actually,* he thought, *more a trickle of information.* Considering what the other teams had already reaped.

Time was a ravenous monster snapping at their heels. They had recovered two of three samples, but the third was still out there and they had no idea where the Pythians' secret factory was based. It had to be assumed that they could make some kind of weapon from the sample they still possessed. Drake and the team sat in a waiting room inside New Scotland Yard, networking, reviewing and learning as much as they could. The chairs were hard and plastic but the coffee was plentiful and came with packets of biscuits that tasted even better when subjected to that grand old Yorkshire art—dunking.

Dahl made a pained face when he saw what Drake was doing. "Do you really have to go and lower the tone, ya bloody Yorkie muncher?"

Drake dipped again. "Improves the coffee. Improves the biscuit. How is that bad?"

The Americans stared aghast as he continued to dunk, leaving him to wonder if he'd lost an ear in the last battle and not realized.

"What the hell are you all looking at?"

The entire team sat around. Even young Grace was there, fresh from another phone call to Aidan Hardy and still no good news. Mai reminded her again that finding her parents might take months, but Grace couldn't relax. Drake didn't want to broach the subject of her returning memories so instead turned to Karin.

"Anything?"

"This is where we stand right now. There are teams studying the samples, trying to figure out the 'what and why' of it and how bacteria might still be viable after so long underground. What you have to remember is the *durability* of plague, of Black Death. From AD541 to 1350, 1650 and 1855, from China to America, this plague has continually reappeared and wiped out more than half the population. Did you know that in some villages in England there are still the old market crosses that have small depressions at the foot of the stone cross? This depression was filled with vinegar in times of plague as it was believed vinegar would kill the germs on coins and so limit the spread of disease. But I believe it is the presence of *other* known diseases within the plague pits that may be our problem. Not bubonic plague."

Hayden put a hand on the girl's shoulder. "Get Crouch's team online. And Collins'. We need everyone working this. No one leaves until we get a break. You hear me? Between the three teams we have the best goddamn assets in the world. Let's make a difference."

Kinimaka sat his bulk down in the chair next to Drake. The Hawaiian's eyes rolled as the plastic rivets groaned. "Hell, if these things had arms I wouldn't be able to sit down at all."

Drake unwrapped another biscuit. "You hear from Kono, mate?"

"The sister from hell? No. I guess she's waiting to swoop

down when we get back home."

"Home?" Drake looked up. "Is that what DC is to you now?"

The Hawaiian shrugged, an immense movement. "My mother's dead. Sister hates me. I have no family now save for Hayden and you guys."

Drake clapped him on the arm, smiling. "We're there for each other, right?"

"Yeah. And I'm really interested in learning how to do that." He nodded toward Drake's cup. "Dunking. Is it really an old Yorkshire tradition?"

"Course it is." Drake laughed, putting the wrapper aside. "Okay, well first thing is to remember is not to let the biscuit get too soggy, 'cause then you have a major disaster on your hands . . ."

Karin's voice drifted through the room. "Every major government is involved in the search. Crouch and Collins—did anybody in either of your teams overhear anything useful during your battles?"

Collins spoke first. "We pretty much shot first and asked questions later. And the Moose? He was no help at all."

Crouch reported a negative too and then said, "I still believe in what we're doing though. They named this project after Pandora for a reason. Caitlyn has been doing further research."

Drake assessed the rest of the team. Lauren sat in a corner; the New Yorker had made calls to several top-class escort contacts, asking for help in finding two abusive clients. She was still waiting for answers. Smyth sat beside her now as he had the last several days, close but not in her personal space, protective but not overbearing. Drake thought the rascally old Delta boy just wanted a new friend after losing Romero. Nobody thought that a rough, tough soldier like Smyth occasionally needed someone to talk to. Nobody except fellow soldiers.

Dahl lay back with his feet up on a table, impatiently flexing his arms and shoulders. As he laughed with Kinimaka, Drake became aware of another presence at his side.

"Yorgi."

"I want thank you for keeping faith," the small Russian said. "In me. You saved me long ago, but only now I start paying you back."

Drake pulled out a chair. "Sit down, pal. And you owe me nothing. Never have. I'll never promise to keep you safe, Yorgi, but I can promise you will always be part of our team. And what made you race straight back here—Alicia scare your pants off?"

"She is a little scary," Yorgi admitted. "But I belong here. With you. And so does she."

"You think?"

"Yes. Everybody finds their way in end. She no different. She will return to you."

Drake struggled not to frown. "To *me?* You mean to *us.* To the team."

"I know what I mean." Yorgi reached for a biscuit. "Let us dunk together!"

Dahl closed his eyes in frustration.

Drake threw a biscuit at him. "Hey, it's better than slugging vodka."

197

CHAPTER TWENTY NINE

Alicia watched as Michael Crouch worked the problem from his own perspective. A respected and accomplished boss of more years than he cared to reveal, Crouch had more personal, influential contacts than a Saudi oil baron and more clout with the British authorities than the Treasury. But this setback was different; it required another skillset to solve. At heart the man had always been a treasure hunter, a mystery solver, and it was this flair and talent that he sought to utilize now.

With Caitlyn he spoke of the gods, the Pandora angle, and how the Pythians might be trying to fit ancient mysteries together with an old plague and a terrifyingly modern plan. With most of Pandora's story already told, Crouch and Caitlyn focused on the narratives and chronicles that intertwined with it.

Alicia drifted over to what she thought of as the soldiers' table. Healey and Russo were already there, sipping water and listening closely. Russo offered her a seat by kicking out a chair on the other side of the table.

Alicia didn't argue. After everything that all three teams had accomplished the realization that they were still on the verge of facing a man-made super-plague hit them all like a lightning bolt.

"Heard from Lex?" Healey asked quietly.

Alicia shook her head, attention still claimed by Crouch. "Nope. I ain't his mother, Zack. Let Lex do what the hell he wants. It's up to Crouch if he gets back on the team."

Back in Vegas, Laid Back Lex had taken a red Ducati and departed in a hurry, an undisclosed seething anger possessing him, barely able to explain his motives for leaving. Alicia took it to mean he was sorting some issues— maybe one day she would be able to do the same.

"So Zeus ordered Hephaestus to create Pandora and cast her upon the slopes of Mount Olympus. On her wedding day she was given a beautiful gift, a jar or box, and told never to open it. We all know what happened next. But later, even Homer made mention of Pandora in his famous *Iliad*, referencing Zeus's palace where two urns stood, one filled with evil gifts and the other with good ones. Whomever received the mixed gifts would face both good and evil destinies, but whoever received only the evil gifts would be scorned, and quote: *The hand of famine will pursue him to the ends of the world.* That's us. Mankind."

"Homer?" Alicia said. "Can we trust a man named Homer?"

Crouch didn't smile. "We owe Homer so much. It is through his poems that Mount Olympus was first identified as the seat of the gods. If you think about the effect that has had on all kinds of literature, interpretations, essays and theses ever since, you can begin to imagine the regard in which he is held."

Caitlyn flicked through page after page of notes, referencing the Internet and comparing every snippet of information with what they knew of the Pythians. The look on her face was not uplifting.

Alicia turned her head to the laptop to watch the SPEAR team working over in London. Even now being apart from what she considered her key team, her family of actual friends, felt unreal, as if this new life were some kind of alternate dream. It was the most natural thing in the world to assume she would soon be back with them.

But then what of Crouch? What of Russo and Healey and Caitlyn? Were they just to be pit stops along the road? *I have to find a home.* Through the experience of all her travels she was only now starting to realize that someone got it wrong—the road does not go ever on. Somewhere in life, unless you want to die alone, it simply must stop.

Caitlyn turned to Crouch, a strange look on her face. "What if we've been going about this all wrong? I have an idea."

"What do you mean?"

"I mean we're coming at our problem through ancient mysteries when we could do the total opposite."

"Which is?"

"Modern technology."

Alicia saw Karin's head swivel all the way across the English Channel. Komodo stood right behind her, blocking everyone else's view. She couldn't see Drake at all and missed the camaraderie they shared.

"The Pythians we know," Caitlyn said. "General Bill Stone. Miranda Le Brun. Nicholas Bell. Army, heiress, developer."

"We're checking into them all," Karin said. "Known associates, movements, that kind of thing. So far they're nothing short of squeaky. Maybe Interpol will learn something more."

Alicia found her thoughts returning to Beauregard. The man had raised her interest back in the UK, and not only for salacious reasons. A world-class assassin, he was an enigma. Who knew which side he was really on? *Why does he help me?* She had heard about men that could fight like him—as sinuous and deadly as toxic fog—but never come across one before. Indeed she had considered them an urban legend. Even Mai Kitano, herself a trained Ninja, taught by masters, could not move the way Beauregard moved. *Where the hell do these people get their training?*

Yet another mystery.

One that she'd like to uncover.

Alicia felt a spicy smile forming on her lips, noticed Russo staring at her in horror and realized she was staring at him. *Shit!* She was giving that man all the wrong signals and for once, felt apologetic. Russo had her back and there was nothing a soldier like Alicia prized more.

She switched her gaze. Caitlyn was still hypothesizing. The Pythians were public enemy number one and it surprised Alicia that the world's security agencies hadn't learned more by now. Then, of course, the Shadow Elite had operated quietly and with impunity for many years, pulling a string here and there when they had to. The Pythians were a different kettle of fish.

Purposely brutal. Egotistical. Inhuman.

Caitlyn tapped at her keyboard. "General Stone. The FBI had eyes on him until last night, DC time. Now, he's vanished, but they're positive he's still in the States. No plane travel. Stone is the one we know is recognizable."

"Are you saying the Pythian HQ—so to speak—is within America?" Crouch asked.

Caitlyn inclined her head. "I guess so. But that's not where I'm heading."

Crouch took a call from Interpol. Armand Argento was added to the video feed, the screen now split into three. Alicia saw the Italian—who his friends apparently called the Jabbering Venetian—for the first time. Swarthy and dark, he had that lived-in look that characterized older, fitter men who looked after themselves. Well-dressed, well-groomed and highly confident, Alicia could see why most people trusted him.

"I am here for you. I am here," he told Crouch. "What do you need?"

"Hold on." Crouch focused on Caitlyn. "Get to the point."

"So forget Stone. Also, Nicholas Bell has vanished. No sightings within the US and no plane travel. Is this coincidence or are the Pythians gathering? Well, what if there's another explanation?"

Alicia liked Caitlyn's train of thought so far. Although she had known the ex-MI6 girl for only a few weeks, Alicia already believed in her analytical talent. Though leaving MI6 under a blanket of uncertainty and with a recent undisclosed horrendous experience in her personal life, Caitlyn was willing to learn, willing to train hard and had withstood her torture at the hands of a Mexican gang superbly well.

The dark-haired girl continued. "The third Pythian," she said. "Miranda Le Brun."

"She's been seen?" Karin asked.

"Not exactly. But her private plane filed a flight plan several days ago. Maybe if Armand can request closed-circuit footage from Thessaloniki International Airport?"

"I can do better than that," Argento told them. "As

Interpol associates itself closely with the Greek police, its chief of police and the International Police Cooperation Division, I can access the feeds myself. It may take just a little time to allow for protocol."

Caitlyn spent the time double checking her information on Le Brun. Not an awful lot about the woman was known, she was married to a deceased oil billionaire, and rarely attended social functions but her various assets and known wealth was in the public domain. Flight plans were filed regularly as a matter of necessity, and air movement messages sent to the local civil aviation authority, in the case of the States this was the FAA, who kept detailed records. Caitlyn hadn't needed a hacker to acquire the information; she had simply asked the Americans for it using the emergency code word attributed to the Pythian situation.

"I am now in the system," Argento said. "And my, my, *amico mio,* it is excellent quality. Most excellent. With zoom I can count the nose hairs, but never mind that. I am initiating facial recognition software and . . . *bavoom* we have our match. Today is . . . yes, and there we have it. Our Miranda bypassed customs but still went through the VIP desk three days ago . . ." Argento chatted on.

Alicia struggled to keep up, trying to identify relevant information from the rambling. Now she was starting to understand why they called him the Jabbering Venetian.

"And she is with a man," Argento exclaimed. "Who I know. But I will run the software again to be sure."

Crouch leaned forward. "Who do you think it is?"

"Wait, wait. Yes, yes it is Nicholas Bell. The pair arrived together. So there you have it. Argento strikes again! We have a success."

Crouch was even further ahead, and so it seemed was Karin Blake. At the same time they said, "Check Callan Dudley's movements."

Alicia felt a surge of adrenalin. If two Pythians arrived in Greece not three days ago then the motives could be manifold, from concealment to recruitment. If Dudley, the Irish mercenary, arrived around the same time it could only be for one reason.

Delivery of the sample he had escaped with.

Argento circumvented the search by running Dudley through his software. A low whistle underlined his surprise.

"Arrived in Greece very recently," he said. "Flew into Larissa Airport, but that is of no matter since it is only sixty eight miles away. It is too much of a coincidence to be innocent, no?"

"Bloody right," Crouch said. "It's a lead and no mistake."

Alicia watched Karin turn around in her seat, addressing someone in the background. "What do you think?" the young woman said. "We're all played out here in London. Should we go?"

Hayden stepped into view. "We need more," she said. "Why are they there? Where exactly did they go? Armand, try the traffic cams and see if they can be useful. I wonder if they even met at all."

Now Drake appeared in camera shot. "Deeper investigation, love. That's what we need here. We can't all go shooting off to the same place. Who knows where we'll be needed next? It'd take a pretty big goddamn reason to send us all running off to Greece." He stopped, then added, "Even if we weren't at war."

Alicia experienced a trickle of disappointment but knew they were right. Both London and Paris were fairly central cities on a worldwide scale. It wouldn't pay to race off on a fool's errand or, quite possibly, a diversionary wild goose chase.

"I can tell you now that Le Brun and Bell entered a waiting car, alone, and that Dudley and two companions, probably mercenaries, took a rental. Do you see? We don't have to track Dudley's movements, just access the car rental firm's records."

"Eyes everywhere, huh?" Russo said with a little sarcasm.

"Would you rather prevent an average of five large-scale terrorist attacks a year or experience them?"

Russo remained silent, staring at nothing. Crouch busied himself with research whilst Argento worked.

"Why Greece?" he whispered to himself. "This bloody location is too much of a coincidence for me."

Karin's voice cane through the monitor. "Greece is an intersection," she suggested. "Cunningly located at the crossroads of Europe, Asia and Africa." Her voice tailed off.

Crouch whistled. "That would mean it's the perfect staging area for the secret factory."

"And ties in with Pandora," Drake added. "A Pythian jest, no doubt."

"I still think there's more," Crouch mused.

"I have clearance," Argento's Italian tones broke in. "Just checking the records now."

Alicia watched Crouch dip his head and become lost in thought. Caitlyn too, was brainstorming the problem, only she used a keyboard. Put them together and they were the brain of this ancient mystery solving team.

"In Greece you find the origins of democracy, western philosophy and *literature,*" he said, emphasizing the importance of the latter. "Political science and western drama. Alexander the Great conveyed many features of its civilization through his movements to the east as did the Roman Empire to the west. It also gave us the Olympic Games."

"So it's the center of the universe," Alicia said with a little sass. "Or was."

"All roads lead from Greece," Russo intoned unnecessarily and with a dark look on his face. Alicia couldn't help but laugh, only casting the shadow even further.

"You know you could debate this all day," Argento cut in again. "And some do. Scholars. Academics. I used to have a history professor who could talk your ear off for hours. Literally chew it to the bone. But no, no, I digress. Luckily, our mercenaries can be tracked. These days, most agencies install a logger in their fleet of vehicles because it's much cheaper than GPS. This means they aren't manning a real-time view of the car but are logging its movements via an onboard computer that can be accessed at any future time. The car is currently stationary within the Mount Olympus National Park, and has been ever since its initial journey."

"*Inside* the park?" Karin wondered. "Why?"

"It's a huge place," Crouch said. "Impossible to keep track of them out there. Ten thousand acres and that's just the core. And, of course as we know despite a rangers' best efforts, national parks aren't the best policed areas in the world. And that's down to funding, not the rangers."

"So Dudley and pals wandered into the mountains," Drake said. "With the samples. They have to be meeting someone, right? Can you track Le Brun and Bell that far?"

"No," Argento said. "The traffic systems outside the cities are not so sophisticated. Yet."

"What about dwellings, as ridiculous as that sounds?" Dahl spoke up. "Maybe they hiked through the park to some private area—"

"Dwellings?" Drake laughed. "You mean like a tree house?"

"You know what I mean. Don't be a knob."

Alicia found a wide grin stretching across her face as the camaraderie the two men shared lifted the tension in the room. Dahl, of course, pretended nothing had happened and rushed on.

"Houses. Estates. Everything from mansions to caves."

Caitlyn clicked around the Internet. "Officially no mention of large caves has ever been made, which does not rule them out," she said. "And sounds somewhat suspicious."

"The twelve Greek gods lived in the 'folds of Olympus'," Crouch said. "Its many fog-shrouded ravines. According to Homer they have their places there and prehistoric man chose to build dwellings at the foot of this wondrous peak. Pantheon, which today is called Mytikas, was their meeting place." He stopped, thinking. "But surely not . . ."

"While I can see Dudley and his friends making it up there," Drake said. "I can hardly see Miranda Le Brun and half a dozen mad scientists completing the journey."

"Still," Crouch said, "Olympus itself is the 'meeting place'. Even in 1941 the Greek resistance found a hiding place there whilst battling the Germans."

"Trouble is," Caitlyn said, "the whole of Olympus has been made an archaeological and historical place to preserve its general topography."

"Still, towns surround it. Litochoro. Katerini. Dion. My hope is that these towns are more *communities.* Outsiders would be noticed immediately. That sends me back to the idea of a covert place where this factory could have been outfitted. Let's face it, a factory like that, once you know the components you need, can be retrofitted in one trip. Scientists can be installed quickly too. Once invested, they would stay until the job was done . . ." he tailed off.

Alicia stared at him. If it ever could be said a light bulb suddenly lit up someone's eyes this was that moment.

Crouch spun around, excitement surrounding him. "We have to go to Greece," he said. "All of us. My God, of course, Mount Olympus is Pandora's birthplace! It's a given that they would base the factory there!"

Silence followed in which everyone digested his deductions. Karin was the first to speak up. "But that doesn't work inside a national park. I highly doubt you could supply even a small factory without somebody noticing. At the very least, the risk of being spotted would prevent you trying in the first place."

"Corruption," the more experienced Crouch said with a bitter expression. "It's hard to think of a worse sin that flew out of Pandora's Box. I think we're looking for an underground cave somewhere in the vicinity of Mount Olympus. Maybe just outside the national park," he added as a consent to Karin.

"And how would we find such a thing?" Healey asked.

"Oh, I can think of several ways," Dahl said. "It used to be one of my specialties."

Argento cleared his throat. "And I also have ideas. Let me implement those whilst you all get on your flights. Let me handle this. Time is the factor, my friends. Time. Get going. Now."

Alicia rose quickly, spurred on by the prospect of meeting up with the old team as much as finding the secret factory. "Move it, Russo. Healey."

The rugged man heaved his bulk upright. "Ain't you gonna miss the Frenchy?" His eyes narrowed knowingly.

"Beauregard? Ah, don't worry that rock you call a head. I can always . . . grab him later."

Russo groaned as Alicia let out a bawdy laugh.

CHAPTER THIRTY

By the time Drake and the team boarded a fast jet, Armand Argento was almost ready to offer a theory. Karin took her time ensuring the communications were sound and secure, but before the jet hit thirty thousand feet they were ready. Alicia's crew were waiting for a "very important person" to whisk them from Paris to Greece, but wouldn't elaborate beyond that.

Drake completed a weapons' check with Dahl. This was the first mission he could remember where the majority of the world's governments were behind them, supporting them, and their cooperation made a huge difference. The jet was already skimming across the airways, a priority status; Hayden kept the many interested parties apprised whilst Argento mapped out his plan.

"If we imagine this cave as a subterranean bunker, which is essentially what it is, contained, self-sufficient, then it will have no open or easily accessible doors. No windows. But it *must* have air vents, do you see? Exhaust vents. More—it must have power cables and even more topside connections. Otherwise the mad scientists—they would die."

Dahl smiled and caught Drake's eye. Kinimaka grinned at them. "This guy's a real riot, eh?"

Drake ignored them, watching Mai. Seated beside Yorgi for the trip and behind Smyth and Lauren, the Japanese woman was barely in the game, no doubt ruminating on her situation and the welfare of Grace, whom they had left behind in London. The gulf between them had only widened since the Pythians upped the stakes, and now he could see no easy way across until Mai faced and destroyed her newly risen demons. The rest of the team was buoyant, reinvigorated by the emergence of the fresh lead, but anxious as ever that it may have come too late.

Argento went on, "So we have all these telltale indicators, yes? Through satellite navigation we can scan the detail of the area and find them. We are using the satellites as we speak. As you say, Olympus is a large area and we're having to double up because of the surrounding sites, but we will have success. I'm sure of it."

Dahl leaned over to Drake. "Satellites," he said. "We have them now."

"How far out from Greece are we?"

"From landing? Two hours. Alicia's team should get there about the same time if their mystery guest ever turns up. Karin is trying to find a nearby landing strip." He gestured at the blond girl working away on a laptop. "Or at least a long patch of flat ground we can land on." The Swede chortled.

Argento came back on line. "We're searching for suspicious shadows, mesh, imaginary borders. Camouflage netting. Pipes. Trails. Even brief heat signatures if we're lucky, as from a man slipping out for a cigarette. They cannot escape us."

Drake's face turned grim. He was more than ready to bring war to the place where these bastards lived.

*

211

Alicia experienced her second utterly surreal moment in as many weeks at the sight of the famous movie star, Reece Carrera, standing at the top of the steps that led to his private plane. The man's smile shone like a stadium floodlight and his warm, welcoming voice melted away all her concerns. This really was the best way to travel.

"Unfortunately," Crouch commented as they mounted the steps. "We now owe Mr. Carrera, as his last favor was the only one he owed. Still, I can think of no faster or more clandestine way to travel at short notice."

"Lucky he was in the area," Healey said, cinching his jacket tighter.

"Yeah, he has homes in Paris, London, Vegas and LA," Crouch said. "All the trouble hotspots. When I first learned of the targeted cities I put him on standby."

Alicia shook her head at their boss. "Man, you're fuckin' awesome. I'd love to be able to put a movie star on standby."

As they reached the top of the stairs Carrera backed away and allowed them access to the luxurious cabin. The first time she had met this man even Alicia experienced a passable sense of awe. This second time however, she was past all that.

"So Reecey, we got about two hours to Greece. What you wanna do? You ever done it with a soldier girl before?"

Carrera backed away to give her plenty of room. "Ah, I do have a girlfriend, Miss Myles. Otherwise . . ."

Alicia slapped him playfully on the bicep. It was like hitting a punch bag filled with lead. "Ach, naughty. I meant what we gonna cook together? You do like cooking, right? That's pretty much all you ever talk about."

She flounced past, heading to the onboard kitchen as if she owned the place.

Russo came next. "You'll get used to her, Mr. Carrera. Some say she's a bitch. Me? I'm undecided."

Alicia heard Crouch muttering some apology, but once Caitlyn was inside and the door was shut Carrera headed straight to the kitchen.

As she'd expected.

"So, you like cooking?" Carrera grinned.

"I like lots of things, Reecey. Some involve knives, others forks and spoons. I'm a forward thinking kinda girl. Always ready for the next adventure."

Carrera nodded as he washed his hands. Alicia couldn't help but notice their size. The man could do great damage with those things, especially since he worked out at a gym five times a week. *Strong hands, capable hands,* she thought. *Makes a girl feel all secure.* Only one man in her life had accomplished that before, and only for a short time.

"You like linguini?" Carrera asked. "I make a spice medley all of my own. Makes it taste—" he kissed his fingers. "*Fantastico!*"

"Ya got corned beef hash?"

At that moment the pilot's voice came over the intercom, asking for seats to be taken prior to take-off. Carrera's odd look transformed immediately into another smile and he turned away. Alicia followed him, allowing her eyes to travel downward as he walked.

Russo watched her from the nearest window seat. "Having fun?"

Alicia plonked herself down beside him. "Got any ice cubes? I need to cool down."

"You'll have your hands full soon enough," Russo said with a touch of irony. "Soon as we land we're at war."

"Have they found something?"

Russo nodded at Caitlyn. "She's still tuned into the feed between Argento and SPEAR. All that bollocks about steam vents and electrical cables appears to have paid off. There's a hidden underground bunker or cave just on the fringes of the national park."

"Defended?"

"Well, not obviously but I'd say *yeah*. It's close to the only main road in the region. They might also have camouflaged choppers that we can't see and God knows what else. But we have the two best teams in the world, right?"

Alicia shrugged. "Maybe. If we swop you for that Agent Collins in LA, I'd feel better."

"Piss off. Damn, you're a confusing one. You run from one team to the next. Even a biker group. One boss to the next. And there's always a . . . um, *romantic* angle. Somebody to be with. Then there's the question of girls or boys—which is it that you like?"

"You asking for yourself or Caitlyn?" Alicia asked lightly.

"Maybe I'm asking and hoping for a serious answer."

Alicia wasn't ready for this. Not yet. What surprised her though was where the support came from—Russo. Big, strong, able to take the knocks. A support platform she could abuse endlessly when the time came to vent, to take back her life.

If it ever came.

"All right, Russo. You want serious? How about this . . .

now isn't the time. When the time is right and if you're around I'll tell you. I'll use you. How's that?"

"Good enough."

The two sat in stony silence for a while as the jet climbed. In truth, Alicia wasn't sure she even wanted somebody to help divert the course of her life. Maybe she would just die alone and skip all the pain of revelation. She'd made it this far.

Caitlyn turned around then. "They've pinpointed a location," she said. "We'll land in Larissa and then chopper in with the Greek Army and Special Forces. No holds barred, guys. If this is their weaponization factory it has to be wiped off the map."

"No way of planning a stealth attack?" Healey asked.

"We have to assume they have an early warning system. Pressure plates, infra-red, whatever. We know Dudley at least is top-notch. The feeling is that the best assault is a blitz, and with the choppers they should only get five minutes warning."

Alicia noticed as Caitlyn allowed her eyes to lock onto Healey's for a moment, communicating a private message. The pair hadn't yet managed that date and for that matter, Caitlyn herself still struggled to find a way through the pall cast by her recent past. *Damn, our team's even more fucked up than Drake's.*

Then she turned her attention to the job at hand, ignoring Reece Carrera's questioning glance, and prepared her brain for hard battle.

There would be time enough later to set everyone's problems to rights.

CHAPTER THIRTY ONE

Drake cooled his heels on the tarmacked runway as Alicia's jet came in to land. The SPEAR team had only emerged into a fresh morning fifteen minutes ago and thought it beneficial to wait for the world-class backup. Truth be told, he was looking forward to seeing his old sparring partner again. In the past the miles between them could never have been enough, but lately that was far from the case. Even Mai had grown to accept the turbulent, passionate heroine though Drake wouldn't like to test that theory right now.

The SPEAR team were going in fully manned. Yorgi and Lauren would remain aboard the choppers, but were still an active part of the operation. The greater the number of people that monitored a mission's comms the larger the amount of information could be gleaned from them.

The jet taxied around. The pilot barely had time to apply the brakes before Alicia opened the door and bounded down the hastily attached steps, a deadly, playful puppy with blond hair and a penchant for violence. Drake couldn't be sure but he thought her eyes were searching for him, only him, because when they locked on a light illuminated inside them.

"Drakey!"

She came up to him, pushing Kinimaka aside with a mock angry face, and just stood there. "Been a while."

"Not really, love. Three or four weeks, max. Ya missed me?"

"Like the modern age misses Attila the Hun, baby."

Drake snorted. "Oh, so put you together with a wannabe historian and an archaeological treasure hunter for three weeks and you're suddenly a soothsayer? Should have done it years ago."

Hayden pushed by them as Crouch walked up. The pair shook hands, and then both teams were rapidly introduced. Drake had imagined a more momentous meeting place for two of the world's most respected teams, but perhaps their first battle together would be more significant—on the slopes of Mount Olympus.

"We all set?" Crouch's voice broke through the din of soldiers familiarizing themselves with new comrades they would soon fight alongside. "Anything changed?"

Karin broke free from Healey, the young man's exuberance written all over his face. "No adjustments to the plan. We're ready to go."

The large team strode over toward the waiting choppers, squatting like black prehistoric birds on the runway, their rotors already turning. Five in total, two had been reserved for the new arrivals.

Alicia stopped with her foot on the skids. "Damn, two of you are gonna have to join us. Um, Torsty, would you mind?" With a flourish she maneuvered him onto their bird. "Drake?"

Mai was already there, giving Alicia the eye. "Thought I'd get to know your team. Do they know about the Taz moniker?"

Alicia rolled her eyes. Drake grabbed a seat in the other chopper and held on as all five birds rose and then swooped fast toward their destination. He made ready, having lost count of the many times he had done this in the past, never knowing the outcome or even more than basic details of the actual assault plan. But it never fazed him, and it never got old. Times like these were when he felt more alive, closer to death but brimming with vitality and life, sat beside his friends as they attempted to save the world once more.

"Ten minutes to target." The pilot's voice broke his reverie.

"Don't worry," he said in acknowledgement of Lauren and Yorgi's apprehensive faces. "This is where we make the Pythians pay for all their atrocities. This is where we end them."

"Five minutes."

Rolling gusts buffeted the chopper as it pounced out of the skies, swinging down toward the fast-moving landscape below. Hugging tree tops, diving into valleys, twisting left and right through hills and approaching the great mountain, it followed its twin into battle. Drake watched the navigation module flash until they were practically on top of their target but below, he saw nothing.

A moment later, everything changed.

The tell-tale streak of a rocket-propelled grenade shot from the scenery below, straight into the front end of Alicia's chopper. Drake caught his breath, knowing who was aboard in addition to the members of Crouch's team. The bird dipped fast, fire raging from its cockpit. Drake's pilot acted on instinct, following the chopper down. Another RPG flashed upward, this one shooting wide of the mark. As Alicia's chopper neared the ground it leveled slightly, black clad figures crowded the doors and the skids and then leaped off, rolling to the ground below. Flames still covered its front end. Then, as more figures leaped free, the bird lunged back up, still in control.

Nice maneuver, Drake thought. The pilot had used the grenade strike to fool its shooter into thinking that they were out of the game, landing his team safely and then dipping away. *First class.* How would their own pilot fare?

All lights turned green. Men shouted and moved to the doors. Drake watched as another bird hovered beside them, its chain gun hammering bullets into their assailants below. Hayden and Kinimaka jumped, then Smyth, Komodo and Karin. Drake went last, with a final look toward Lauren and Yorgi.

"Stay safe."

"You too."

The ground came up hard. Rolling, he was fast on his feet, gun up. The grenade launcher was down, riddled with bullets. He ducked as a shot whickered by, a bullet from a sniper's rifle. Dahl, several feet ahead, sent a hail of gunfire in his direction, ensuring he wasn't heard from again.

"We got an entrance yet?" Drake asked through the comms.

"Following a trail," Alicia came back. "Where the hell you been?"

"Scenic tour."

Drake followed his companions among the slopes, the green underfoot giving way to jagged rock then turning back to green. Dense bushes blanketed the area. Mountain fissures and small ravines cut to left and right. Ahead, their vision was filled by a gigantic, gray rock face, rising to enormous heights and painted whiter with snow as it climbed. Drake couldn't tell which mountain was the actual

Olympus peak but it was up there somewhere, the seat of the gods.

All those tombs we found. But nothing here? It occurred to him then for the first time that, yes, they had found a chain of three tombs—stretched between Iceland, Hawaii and Germany—but what if there were more? Another chain? A different myth. *Instead of the Vikings, something even older?* Prehistoric man. Whoever lived and breathed and died in all those lost kingdoms. It was said that satellite images proved that the so-called cataclysms which destroyed ancient kingdoms such as Atlantis and Mu had not happened—the earth's crust's tectonic plates revealed no signs of such significant upheavals, but definitive truths and answers rolled like waves and changed like the tides. The world was once believed to be flat. Nobody believed we could walk in space, land a rocket on an asteroid and that there was life on Mars.

Now . . .

Today's definitive truths are tomorrow's sorry mistakes. History proves this. Drake threw the deluge of notions aside as more gunfire broke out ahead.

Alicia threw herself below the rising curve of a deep ravine. Bullets skipped off the top, rocketing toward nowhere. Drake landed near her boots, rolling in. Dahl was behind him and Mai was to their right.

"Four o'clock," the Japanese woman said. "Armed mercs protecting a doorway."

"Use a grenade," Hayden said over the airwaves. "These assholes will have an escape route and no mistake. Time is against us."

Alicia quickly complied. Drake had almost protested,

wondering if the blast might block the entry but then realized such frivolities didn't matter. Moving forward was everything. An explosion brought screams and then a sudden silence. Drake peeked his head out.

"Clear."

They ran, followed closely now by Hayden and Kinimaka, Smyth, Komodo and Karin. Alongside them came Crouch and his team. Drake helped drag the bodies from a small entrance, draped with dark netting. The tunnel inside was dimly lit, a gantry of low wattage spotlights attached to the roof. The team pounded along it as the Greek soldiers crowded at their back. Rock walls narrowed and widened.

"This place will be purely makeshift," Hayden's voice whispered. "Temporary. They haven't had time to establish anything permanent yet, so take it down hard and fast."

A pool of light irradiated the walls ahead, spilling from a wider space. Alicia ducked and dived into a niche as gunfire roared in the confined space. Drake joined her, firing back blindly.

"No grenades down here," Hayden's worried voice whispered through the comms. "We don't know what chemicals they're mixing."

Alicia shook her head. "What does she think, I'm stupid?"

Drake snuck an eye around the corner. "You can't help the way you look, Myles."

"Ah, so you've grown a bit cocky since I left, eh? No one to keep you in check. We'll have to find a way to fix that."

Drake placed a hand on her shoulder and gripped softly. "Truth? I've missed you, Alicia. Who would have guessed it?"

"And how's the lady friend?" The Englishwoman motioned at Mai on the other side of the tunnel. "Seems a bit . . . uptight. More than usual."

"Long bloody story."

"I'll settle for the gag reel."

"Believe me, there ain't no laughs anymore." Drake picked off one of the mercenaries. Dahl stepped into view and peppered the tunnel's far end. Mai ran low, leading the pack as the Swede fired constantly over her head. Within seconds the two had reached the end of the tunnel. Drake and Alicia came next, stepping out into a vast underground chamber.

Drake shot a man in the vest, then capitalized on his stumble, laying him out cold on the dusty rock floor. With a moment to spare he absorbed everything around him, the Pythians' secret factory. As Hayden intimated, the workshop was sparse, rough and ready, but effective. Six long wooden desks stood end to end, their surfaces crowded with all manner of paraphernalia from glass tubes and centrifuges to computer screens. Some of the containers had liquid bubbling over, some smoked. The computers whirred as they crunched numbers. Men in civilian clothes cowered to one side. *Not a bad thing,* Drake thought. Scared men imparted information without too much complaint. As the teams flooded the room, Drake ranged to one side, searching for stragglers or hidden shooters.

"Not buying it," Hayden said through the comms, her words matching his feelings. Her next orders were very loud. "Interrogate those assholes! We need the sample's location and to know if they managed to weaponize anything. After that, we need Dudley and the rest of his pack of reprobates."

Drake continued hugging the walls, finally arriving at a concealed exit. He clicked his earpiece. "Another tunnel right here. Leads deeper into the mountain."

As he spoke several men, hidden guards no doubt, leaped out of the tunnel's deeper murk, striking at him with sharp weapons. Drake blocked two knives at once, then struck into his opponent's body with a clenched fist, twice, three times, each punch a devastating hammer blow to the ribs. Both men went down groaning. Alicia nipped in to his left, grabbing the arm of another man and bending it until he screeched. The knife dropped and the man followed it, rendered unconscious. Drake dragged the next man out into the open, handing him off to Mai. Two more filled the gap, guns drawn. Drake opened fire before they did, ending their lives. He moved inside the tunnel even as he heard the voices of terrified technicians rapidly revealing whatever Hayden demanded of them.

Drake crept along, Alicia closer to him than his own shadow. "If Dudley escaped this way," Dahl said, "I figure he has a good ten minutes' head start on us. Get your flat Yorkshire feet moving or let me lead."

"I'm creeping so I can hear Hayden's outcome," he told the Swede. "Dudley might have slipped out the front for all we know."

"Naw, lad, not bleedin' likely!" A voice cracked from up ahead, "Here. Chew on that while I make me escape!"

Something bounced down the tunnel toward him, something that jumped and bobbled and leaped with each metallic clang. Drake backed up fast, slamming into Alicia and Dahl and having to wait until those at his back squeezed out of the tunnel.

Not fast enough. The grenade exploded into a fiery ball and a whoosh of air sped along the enclosed space. Drake wasn't free and saw the flames and the shrapnel about to destroy his face until, at the last moment, something huge took hold of his jacket and yanked him back into the cavern. Drake gasped, head and legs flying forward, back arched, as he took flight. The heave sent him rolling head over heels and away from the gout of flame.

"Jesus."

Drake glimpsed the immense thighs, the bulky torso and thick neck of Mano Kinimaka. The big Hawaiian held out a meaty paw. "You're welcome, dude."

Drake climbed to his feet, dusting himself off. Hayden paced over to them.

"It's not good. Dudley escaped with the sample and three *aerosolized* prototype boxes containing a derivative of bubonic plague, which is to say the plague mixed with a variety of old and contemporary diseases, weaponized in the form of an aerosol. Luckily, we got here before they could engineer more. This derivative gives them such a range of options . . ." She shook her head in fear.

Alicia and Mai slipped back into the tunnel.

Drake eyed the scientists. "We should wall them up down here."

"Some were coerced, it seems, but yes others did it for the money. We can wall those up if you like."

"Antidote?" Dahl eyed the scientists who regarded him with dread.

Hayden answered. "Dudley took it with him."

"Are you *sure?*" Dahl growled at the boffins, most of whom mouthed silently in abject fear, but half a dozen attested to the evil Irishman's fast getaway with everything they had concocted.

Alicia and Mai reappeared. "Tunnel's still passable," the Englishwoman said. "But barely and some of it looks unstable." She paused. "I'm game if you are."

"Game is hunted and killed by cowardly men with big guns and tiny penises," Mai said quietly. "We are soldiers. We'll hunt *them*."

Russo nodded vehemently and Caitlyn looked like she wanted to applaud.

Drake nodded. "The road," he said. "Or a hidden helicopter. Those are Dudley's only options. Call the birds back."

"Stealth is always an option," Mai said. "We were trained to be ghosts drifting like mist along the terrain for days if need be. Weeks."

"We're not exactly dealing with Ninjas here," Alicia pointed out. "At best they're trained mercs."

The team exited fast. Crouch led his team out first, using Healey and Russo as point men. Hayden fell in next to Drake.

"The geniuses inside told us one more thing," she said with a slight smile. "An older woman and a younger man escaped with Dudley. The woman was complaining."

Drake grinned. "Mint! Le Brun and Bell. That rules out a covert escape. They'll be hightailing it back to Pythian-land."

Dahl, one step behind, shook his head in wonder. "It never fails to stun me—the crazy, lazy mixed-up language that shoots out of your mouth. I mean *mint*? What does that even mean?"

"Good." Drake looked surprised. "Y'know? As opposed to you saying 'oh, dearest darling Johanna, that was such a stupendous movie', us Yorkshire folk go—'that were mint'. Same thing, only we save words and time. Think of all the extra hours we so easily gain."

Outside, four of the choppers had returned and were hovering inches above the ground. The Greek soldiers milled around, directionless. Hayden spoke to their boss and then paged Caitlyn.

"You still have a connection to Argento?"

"I do. What do you need?" Caitlyn had been listening into their comms so would be fully briefed.

"Satellites. Lots of them."

Caitlyn signed off to contact the Italian. Half the Greek soldiers fanned out to search the area, hoping to flush out any marksmen, runners or even people who may be concealed. Drake and the others climbed aboard their helicopters.

Almost immediately Caitlyn came back on the line. "I have Armand. He's . . . a little excited."

Drake flinched as the Italian's loud chatter filled his ears. "I have them! Well, surely it's them! A convoy of three cars, black SUVs, speeding away from you and toward the coast. The *eastern* coast. Damn things weren't there five minutes ago, now they're zooming along in close formation. Go, go, go!"

Hayden waved at the pilot, twirling her finger upward and to the east. "He's nothing if he's not enthusiastic," she commented drily.

Two choppers rose, team SPEAR's and team Gold's, black vultures seeking out prey. As one their noses dipped and they shot forward, skimming the trees. Almost straight away Drake spotted the black tarmac ribbon.

"We've got 'em."

Both helicopters found the road and followed it, swinging with the curves. As they raced through the air Argento spoke up. "Oh no. I'm using a satellite with a built-in redundancy. It's the only one available. There's a ten-minute delay. Our friends, it seems, have a chopper of their own. It just lifted off—and I'm calculating back to *real* time here—about two miles in front of you."

Drake's leaned forward with a serious face. "Don't worry," he said quietly. "We have two choppers and we're about to shoot theirs right out of the bloody sky."

CHAPTER THIRTY TWO

Drake hung on as their pilot picked up the pace, chasing the black tail of the bird ahead. To his right, Hayden was floundering, beset from all sides by agitated parties desperate to know the situation—at least three governments, cooperating teams and ministers, the American military, the British, even Greek Special Forces that had been left behind at the cave. In the end she removed the headphones from her head and held them together.

"Let 'em prattle away to each other."

Their pilot turned his head, staring back into the rear cabin. "They're within range, Miss Jaye."

Hayden winced. Drake knew she would have to send the request up the chain of command and that would only lead to more gibbering. By the time . . .

Hayden fixed Drake with a stare. "Dudley. Two mercs. Le Brun and Bell, right?"

"Right. We believe."

Hayden tapped the separate device in her ear. "Caitlyn, can you get anything tasked to tell us how many are in that chopper?"

"It's not that easy," Caitlyn said after a minute. "Besides, don't you have aerosolized plague on there?"

"The scientists told us all three aerosols were stored inside boxes. I'm damn sure they'll be resilient."

"Still . . ."

Drake chewed on a nail. "You do realize how this all fits

with the Pythians' idea, don't you? The Pandora plague. Engineered in Pandora's birthplace and then transported in a *box.* If you didn't know it before you sure as hell do now— these assholes have more cracks in them than a politician's promise."

"Totally apeshit," Dahl agreed. "Destroy them."

Karin jumped out of her seat, staying low. "Caitlyn's right. You can't risk—"

The pilot cried out and the chopper veered violently at the same time. Karin sprawled head first, smashing her nose against Kinimaka's shin. For as second the world turned on its side and then they were level again.

"Evasive maneuver," the pilot said calmly. "They're firing on us."

Komodo hauled Karin upright and strapped her in. Kinimaka apologized for his clumsiness. Karin laughed. "Sure, Mano, next time I show my inexperience make sure your stupid shin's not attached to your leg."

A second missile separated from the lead chopper. Drake watched as their pilot again dodged the lethal streak.

"Fuck this," he said. "Get alongside so we can fill 'em full of holes. Make them force land."

The pilot threw the cyclic stick at the top speed symbol. The chopper accelerated rapidly and the gap closed. After a minute the lead chopper swung across the landscape, making a sharp turn and Drake saw a gleaming blue expanse ahead.

"The Aegean Sea," Hayden said. "That can't be good."

The reason for the chopper's maneuver soon became clear as a town began to unfold amid the countryside below.

"Larissa," Hayden said. "We can't shoot them down now. Stay close."

Three helicopters blasted across the skies, heading for the bright, shimmering blue. If Drake had needed any reminder as to the madness of their opponents it soon came as Callan Dudley threw open the side doors of his chopper and pointed a machine gun at them. Laughing, he opened fire, strafing the skies with lead. Their pilot dropped down and back, tucking in behind the mercenary's bird.

"That guy's starting to friggin' annoy me," Smyth's voice declared over the comms.

Drake stared at Dahl, then Kinimaka and the entire chopper erupted with laughter. Judging from the noise across their connection the second chopper descended into the same state. Smyth grumped aloud. "What? What the hell you laughing at? Guy's a total dickhead."

Drake enjoyed the moment of levity. Sometimes, it was all you needed to gain total focus. In other ways, it reminded you of what you were fighting for. Men like Callan Dudley would never understand.

All three helicopters shot over the town, Dudley loosing rounds into the sky for sport. Drake noticed red blips following them on the radar and pointed them out to the pilot.

"I saw them. They're the army helicopters."

"Good."

"If they land in Larissa with those aerosols . . ." Mai warned.

Hayden nodded as she listened to her headset. "Already on it. The risk is off the scale. The Greeks . . ." she sighed, "are trying to come to a decision."

But the chopper flew fast and straight, arrow straight, with the Irishman firing recklessly toward the rooftops of

Larissa and the blue expanse only growing larger ahead. Occasionally Dudley would lean out dangerously and take a potshot at their bird. A bullet glanced off a skid, then some framework. Eventually Dahl leaned out and fired back, peppering the chopper's body with holes.

Drake glared. "Stop it."

"Guy's pissing me off. I didn't aim for the engine."

Then Larissa was behind them and a golden coastline opened out. A sandy beach stretched north and south, dotted by leafy parasols and timber-constructed lifeguard stations. Small figures were laid out on sunbeds down there. Children ran through the waves, splashing and brandishing plastic spades and buckets. Life was good for relaxing locals and vacationing travelers.

And then Drake saw it was about to get incredibly, infinitely worse.

"Where the hell are they—" Hayden began and then clammed up in horror. "Oh no."

Dudley's chopper dived toward the deck of the biggest cruise ship Drake had ever seen.

CHAPTER THIRTY THREE

Like an enormous floating hotel it sat in the Aegean, several miles offshore. Pure white, its hull shone against the sparkling blue waters. Idling, at ease, it might be offering its passengers a unique view of Mount Olympus, or about to turn around.

But it had no idea of the horrors plunging out of the skies on rotors of black steel. It had no clue what was coming.

Drake did. Everyone did. And there was only one way to stop it. ˙

"Fire!" Dahl cried. "Shoot them out of the skies!"

The pilot's hand flashed toward the weapons array and then hesitated. "Miss Jaye?"

Hayden spoke rapidly into her mic. Seconds passed. Hayden screwed her eyes up. Their window was closing.

"We're over the sea," Komodo put in helpfully.

Hayden turned on him. "Don't you think I know—" Then she stopped, listened and spoke with harsh determination.

"Fire the missile."

The pilot reacted instantly, flipping open the red safety cover and covering the button with his thumb. A moment to align and then . . .

Dudley's chopper fell hard, perhaps anticipating the missile. Drake heard a hiss and a streak emitted from their undercarriage, marked by white smoke. It shot ahead just as Alicia's chopper came alongside, offering support. The

Englishwoman gave them a thumbs up through the open door.

Dudley's bird dived, nose first. The missile flashed toward it. The cruise ship grew outlandishly big through their cockpit windscreen, the stunned faces of passengers clearly visible. The falling chopper lurched as the missile struck, an explosion ripping chunks of metal free and sending them tumbling to the decks below.

"Of all the goddamn, appalling luck," Dahl breathed, fearful for the ship's occupants.

The enemy chopper slowed and leveled out, visibly reaching for the ship's lido deck, a flat stretch occupied only by sun loungers to the rear. Passengers fled in every direction, leaving belongings and dashing away on bare feet. Ship's crew stared in disbelief. The chopper crashed skids first, bouncing and listing for a moment before losing all momentum. Flames flicked out of its left-side door, the metal framework there hanging torn and ragged.

"Get down there," Drake urged their pilot. "This hell is just beginning!"

Figures jumped out of the stricken chopper. Dudley and one other well-built man. A third dropped through the flames, unmoving. Then a woman jumped to the ship's deck, falling as she landed hard, followed by a more agile man.

Lauren stared but didn't need to try too hard. "That's Nicholas Bell," she said and shook her head. "He seemed a nice guy, you know? Wrong place, wrong time, that kinda thing."

"You're still thinking he could be an ally?" Dahl asked as their helicopter closed in. "Even after this?"

"You're as bad as friggin' Alicia," Russo growled from the other chopper. "And her *Beauregard*. Bastard can't conspire with terrorists if he's dead."

Drake listened but—surprisingly—the moment passed without comment from Alicia and then they hit the deck. Instantly he was out and running, following the route Dudley's crew had taken moments before. A shot cracked. Drake stared grimly, unmoved as plastic splinters burst out of the parasol pole near his head. The shot served to locate Dudley's team, concealed behind a questionable divider, but civilians still crowded the walkway behind them.

Staring. Crying. Filming the scene with their cellphones. Flicking onto Facebook to tell their friends. Slap bang in the line of fire.

"Get the feck outta here!" an Irish brogue colored the air.

They ran, Dudley forcibly dragging Miranda Le Brun back into hiding. The oil baroness's face was blackened, her clothes torn. The last remaining merc fired another shot.

Drake ignored it, Dahl at his side. The decision proved to be a mistake as the bullet slammed into his flak jacket, sending him to his knees with a cry. Dahl stared down at him.

"Stop being such a fucking pussy. It's only a bullet."

Drake struggled to his feet, still gasping. The Mad Swede was already halfway across the lido deck and now Smyth and Komodo were at his side. Karin hung back, but held her weapon and analyzed the scene with growing skill. Behind her Alicia's helicopter slammed onto the deck.

The blond woman leaped out like an avenging Valkyrie. "You all right, Drakester? Saw you go down when you took a hit."

"I'm fine." Face reddening he wondered if the entire goddamn world had seen him stagger when he got shot.

"Don't be so embarrassed." Alicia ran up to him. "We all have our off days."

Soldiers streamed across the deck. Drake slipped out toward the rail, keeping their enemy in sight. As they closed in, civilians ran in the opposite direction until the walkway behind Dudley was empty.

The Irishman stepped into view, one hand held high and clasping a polished wooden box with a gold lock and hinges. "One av tree!" he cried in his thick accent. Drake struggled to understand it as "one of three".

"Tree boxes, tree aerosols. Stand down, yer arse bandits, before I open Pandora's feckin' juicy Box on yer!"

Hayden hissed a warning through the comms. "Do it! We don't know what capabilities he has."

As one, guns were pointed toward deck. Dudley grinned, almost capering in his delight. "Better! That's better. Now jump yer feckin' arses over that rail. Yeah, that's right. Swim, yer bastards."

Nobody moved. Crouch, Healey and Russo were in Dudley's blind spot and inching closer. Yorgi moved to join them, eyeing the route up to the deck above as if he might be considering a climb.

Hayden recognized the thief's signature tactic at the same moment Drake did. "Can you get above him, Yorgi? Distract him."

"Da. Yes, I can."

"Then do it."

Yorgi scooted forward, leaping at the higher deck and finding handholds in the smooth-looking shell that shouldn't exist. They didn't have to hold him for long as his feet found purchase and then launched him even higher. In mid-air he caught hold of the next deck's handrails and supported the rest of his body. Another lunge and he was over, crouched at the foot of the rail.

Crouch stared up after him. "I doubt I could have done that even in my heyday."

Dudley pulled out a gun. "So. Yer fixin' ter jump or do I have to shoot yer where yer stand? And yer goin' first." He motioned at Drake. "I remember yer."

"The ship's filled with soldiers," he said. "The Greek Army is ten minutes out. Give it up, help us, and you might get to rot in jail for the rest of your crazy life."

"Feck it," the Irishman bellowed, sprayed a hail of bullets, then turned away. "We'll see how yer like me when I grab some passengers."

Drake was down, again, but this time so was everyone else. The lead flurry had been nothing more than a wild diversion. By the time Drake gained his feet, Dudley was gone.

"I have him," Yorgi said. "It is jogging track up here with glass bottom. A nice feature. I can follow mercenaries for short way."

Drake slammed through the nearest door. "Report!"

"Ah, heading straight back to stern. Passing sporting equipment—gym. Dudley has one box in his hand and a small backpack. He's dragging woman but other Pythian is helping her. She not happy. Other mercenary is falling back, probably waiting for you."

Dahl slipped past Drake. "Good."

Bloody hell! The man's unstoppable. Drake was forced to

fall back a little as the paneled corridor they were traversing narrowed. Soon it opened out into a typical gym, rows of cross-trainers, treadmills, bicycles and rowers laid out in a bland, uninspiring, uniform array. Drake glared in every direction, constantly moving his gun. Then Alicia slipped past. *What is this? First to bag a terrorist day?*

Yorgi got in on the action. "Past gym and crossing sports deck, I think. Other man stayed behind power plate."

Drake shifted. There was only one. A flash, the faintest glimmer of movement and he opened fire. There was a low grunt and the merc collapsed, his weapon clattering away. Dahl was already on the other side of the gym. Drake caught up to Alicia, signaling for Kinimaka to check the body.

"We have problem," Yorgi said. "Dudley and others are among passengers. And the glass deck has ended. I am climbing back down."

"Do not approach," Hayden ordered. "Observe only."

"It is no problem. I have no weapon."

Drake frowned. *A damn stupid oversight.* The deck disappeared above their heads to reveal the skies for a short period whilst they negotiated the sports deck, then another door appeared ahead.

"He's in there," Drake whispered. "Careful."

Dahl smashed through the door, calling for quiet. Passengers squealed and huddled in a corner. Drake fully expected to see Dudley standing over them, box held at arm's length, maybe even open with the aerosol mechanism exposed, but the Pythian team were nowhere to be seen.

Drake slowed. Crouch and Russo spread out to the sides. Hayden paused alongside, thumbing through her tablet computer. "Next is a pizzeria, then a set of staterooms, and finally a way up to the sky deck, the highest deck. Up there is mini-golf and the entrance to the big water chute. But there are three ways out of the pizzeria."

She reverted to comms. They had teams exploring the outer walkways who would spot Dudley if he emerged from the main hub of the ship. Komodo, Karin and Mai were on one side, Healey, Lauren and Smyth on the other.

All hands on deck, Drake thought, *never had a truer meaning.* They didn't want to put their non-military assets at risk but today they had no choice. Caitlyn was still aboard one of the choppers, streamlining and maintaining the complicated communications system in addition to working with Argento's satellites.

They entered the pizzeria, overturned tables and frightened passengers revealing that Dudley had already stormed through. One of the cooks, wiping his hands on a towel, pointed toward the far door. Dahl was the first to reach the exit with Alicia right behind him. Drake moved to back them up.

"Watch out for traps," Hayden's voice came softly through the comms. "Dudley is one sneaky asshole."

Drake saw Dahl pause then move ahead. They entered a plush lined hallway, doors to each side. As they penetrated the stateroom section all sound faded away and when Dahl stopped to listen, he couldn't hear even the faintest of whispers.

Beyond the staterooms was a sliding door that led to the ship's prow, or stairs and elevators up to the sky deck. Drake knew the exterior teams would be heading for the prow, which left the stairs to them.

"Front end's clear," Smyth's short, sharp snap whipped between Drake's ears. He could also hear Lauren talking in the background.

"Look up to the sky deck," Hayden told him. "See anything?"

"If that's the bit at the top then no. No movement."

A scream rang out. Drake clicked the comms but Smyth's voice beat him to it. "That *definitely* came from up there. Hurry!"

Drake pounded at the stairs, almost clipping Alicia's heels. Yorgi said, "I can make it up outside quicker. Half a minute."

Drake cursed. "No. You have no weapon. You're not—"

"I'll live."

Shit. Despite Yorgi's assurances Drake was more than skeptical. Even discounting Dudley's obvious irrationalities there were also the aerosols to worry about. The entire team ran hard. The chance of an ambush was slim, all of Dudley's paid colleagues having perished. The sky deck soon appeared above, accessed through another sliding door. Dahl ducked as soon as the door came into view, assessing the scene.

"Dudley and the Pythians," he said. "With several passengers. Where does he expect to go?"

Drake stayed low. "Man's a loon but he ain't dumb. Le Brun and Bell have endless contacts."

"What are you saying?" Crouch asked.

"Just . . . be ready for anything."

Through the door they could see Dudley manhandling a woman in a bikini whilst Bell tried not to watch. Le Brun held a gun which almost pointed toward three other passengers, two men and a woman, its barrel wavering between their heads and a view of the sea. Thankfully, when nerves made her accidentally pull the trigger, the bullet flew wide.

"We have to end this. Now." Hayden made a move toward the door, but Dahl held her back.

"Wait."

Drake agreed but didn't say so. Instead, he whispered, "We need a fix on the aerosols first. Nothing's more important."

All hell let loose. Yorgi appeared on the deck to the side, jumping from the bulkhead above. Le Brun whirled, gun barking. One of her hostages chose that moment to be a hero, leaping at her. Healey and Smyth and Lauren appeared over to the left, heads rising above a balcony as if they'd climbed the set of spiral-shaped stairs that clung to the outside.

"Damn it, Healey," Crouch hissed. "Stay put."

He was too late. Le Brun's bullet shattered the door in front of Drake, showering them all with glass. Yorgi leaped at her throat just as the hero-hostage struck her from the other side. Dudley, face set as hard as a tombstone, lifted the woman he'd been accosting high above his shoulders as if she were the weights in a lifting contest.

"Shit, shoot that bastard!" Kinimaka growled.

Dudley stepped toward the edge of the ship, still hefting the woman high. Drake spotted the small rucksack on his back.

Head shot.

But before he could even begin to lift his gun Lauren, breaking free of Smyth, sprinted for the deadly Irishman.

Drake saw in an instant what was happening. Lauren saw only a woman in trouble, her reactions were instinctive.

From out of the clouds on the horizon came two midnight-black birds.

Drake ran past Dahl, passing the scuffle where Le Brun fought to maintain a hold on her gun, knowing Dudley would immediately catch sight of him and move his attention away from Lauren. The Irishman reacted in a moment, throwing the unlucky woman straight at Drake and bowling him over, then springing across the deck. His moment of opportunity was rapidly closing as Healey and Smyth converged from one side and Dahl, Hayden and Kinimaka from the other. Drake untangled himself from the woman, forehead pounding where she had struck. He saw Mai join from the right and Alicia stood by him.

Dudley would have to be a magician to get outta this . . .

Then the Irishman grabbed at Lauren, took a blow to the throat and staggered. Buoyed by her victory, Lauren struck again.

"Not twice, wee minx."

Dudley caught her wrist and twisted, causing her to cry out. Smyth yelled protectively at the top of his own voice, threatening barbarity, but Dudley only cackled. In a deft move he shrugged off the backpack and held it in his free hand, spreading the drawstring mouth. By now the black birds had come close enough to see that they were military issue, unmarked and old, probably bought from one of hundreds of black-market arms bazaars held monthly around the world. Machine guns hung inside their open doors.

Dudley lifted the backpack in signal. Drake saw the

choppers swoop toward their target. Time to make a fast decision. The Greek military choppers had all disgorged their occupants and returned to the mainland. If Dudley and the Pythians escaped this way they would have an almost unassailable head start.

He moved forward. "Let her go. You have more than a dozen guns aimed at you."

Dudley sneered. "Ah, the best of the best, no? Your crew ain't gonna give me any trouble, fella. Do yer know why?"

Drake did.

Dudley allowed the backpack to fall, leaving three small black boxes clutched in his left hand. "Y'see this wee silver button here? I press that an' . . ."

"Fucking madman!" Lauren struggled in his grip.

"Quit it, pretty. Afore I stuff Pandora's sweet wee Box down yer throat."

Alicia stepped up, pushing Drake aside and closing the gap to Dudley. "Hey dude, did you mean to make that sound so dirty? 'Cause, man, I'm all for some girl-on-girl action."

Dudley blinked, surprised. It was the instant they all needed. A dozen fingers stroked triggers, aims were double checked, and then a shot rang out too quickly, too soon, and Miranda Le Brun jumped to her feet, wailing.

Right in front of Dudley, the Pythian woman clutched her chest as blood bubbled around her fingers. She ducked and weaved, screaming, dying, still holding the gun that had been turned on her and firing off rounds erratically into the air. A bullet struck Nicholas Bell, but only snagged his jacket and sent him spinning to the ground. Another blasted into the arm of the hostage-hero, sending Yorgi sprawling on top of him.

Le Brun's reign came to an abrupt end as Dahl calmly executed a head shot.

By then the choppers were hovering overhead and machine guns were trained on the sky deck, masked men poised behind them.

Dudley grinned at his audience. "What is it they say? 'Til feckin next time? Git yer skinny arse over here, Bell."

Drake didn't back down. "We can still take you out, mate."

"Aye, and die doin' it. But I guess that don't matter to heroes like yerselves, eh? Well, how about this?"

Dudley pushed the silver button on one of the boxes, dispensing the aerosol inside and releasing the weaponized gas—straight into Lauren's face.

The SPEAR team, to a man, cried out. Machine gunfire smashed into the deck from above as Lauren fell. Dudley sprinted hard and leaped over the side of the ship toward a swinging harness, two boxes still in one hand, and swaying back to offer a powerful arm to Bell's outstretched hands.

"Look at it this way," he yelled. "Now yer feckers have a test subject!"

Drake found cover as the deck disintegrated under fire.

CHAPTER THIRTY FOUR

Mayhem and chaos ruled in Greece. Dudley proved his madness by refusing to flee and forcing his saviors to pepper the cruise ship with round after round. His screeches of laughter were audible even above the clamor. Drake crawled hand over fist to grab Lauren and pull her out of the line of fire. Dahl took hold of the screaming bikini-wearing girl and Alicia took hold of Yorgi's ankle and hauled him off the wounded hero.

"Get inside, Yogi."

She scooped up the injured man and carried him inside as bullets chewed the deck around her ankles. Not wanting to appear too hasty she used her free hand to return fire at both black choppers. Drake grabbed her and heaved her to safety.

Hayden immediately took charge of Lauren and flew down the stairs, Kinimaka at her heels. Smyth and Crouch followed closely, then Karin, screaming into her comms to alert Caitlyn.

Drake knew they could scream all they wanted. Without an antidote Lauren was dead.

He stayed put with Dahl, Alicia and Mai. The old soldiers. Waiting for any chance they might get. Russo joined them. Everyone expected Dudley to order his escape at any moment but the irrational Irishman hung around.

Drake eyed Dahl. "He's madder than you."

"I'm not entirely sure I approve of that statement."

"Oh, yeah, now I remember. You dropped out of private

school because it was too . . . what? Cliquey? Snobbish?"

"I dropped out of *a* private school. They're not all like that. And I don't really want to talk about it, particularly not now."

"When this is over then. Over a pint?"

"Ah, Drake, I have to say sitting in a bar with a glass of milk just doesn't do it for me."

Drake stared through wreckage as bullets smashed into the sky deck again, a spotlight for Dudley's riotous fury.

"Next time it's beers all around. Believe me."

"Is that wise?"

"Mai isn't dead, Dahl, not like Kennedy, and I'm not an alcy. I can handle it."

"Of course you can. I was just . . . um, are the two of you okay?"

Drake smiled a little at the big soldier's clumsy attempt at sympathy. Truth be told it had come out a hundred times better than anything Drake could have tried. Soldiers like them never became all warm-hearted, most showed their respect and love for their adopted families through time-honored traditions such as cutting sarcasm and caustic wit.

"Tell you later," he said at last. "We'll get drunk together, you and I, Alicia and Mai. And right the world. Who wouldn't want to be at that table, involved in that conversation with us?"

Dahl pointed to the skies. "It's a deal, my friend. So long as we survive *this.*"

His last word was accentuated as a Greek military chopper joined the fray. Dudley must have seen it coming, but still chose to remain. As the chopper flew over the ship's deck Dudley's men fired on it. The chopper swooped and evaded, men hanging on inside. Its front end rose a little and a missile flew from its underbelly. Drake heard an explosion and then a rain of metal and fire spilled onto the deck. Men crawled through the debris, screaming.

"Jesus Christ!" Russo yelled.

"Keep your knickers on, Robster." Alicia patted his arm.

"The laws of damnation and luck tell me that wasn't Dudley's helicopter," Dahl said just as the Greek chopper swung hard left, raked by a volley of lead. Metal pings raked its entire right side. Drake saw a skid strike the side of the deck and the huge vehicle bucked forward, nose-diving hard. More bullets shattered its back end. Men leaped clear of the rearing vehicle, slamming into the deck and rolling, some instantly peppered by bullets.

In another moment the helicopter dropped over the side of the deck, smashing into the sea. Dahl was on his feet and sprinting the moment it was out of sight, four comrades at his heels.

"We have to save those soldiers."

Outside, the fires burned bright and pure chaos slammed into Drake's every sense, almost overwhelming.

But he did notice one thing as he stooped to help the nearest soldier.

Dudley's chopper was already a speck in the sky. The madman had escaped and he'd taken two aerosolized boxes with him.

CHAPTER THIRTY FIVE

Drake and Dahl had had enough. The Pythians had left nothing but death and crisis, heartbreak and devastation in their wake. The world was reeling. Since day one his team had been on the back foot, always playing catch up, but now, after all that had happened this day, the Yorkshireman and the Swede were about to take the bull literally by the balls.

They were going to squeeze until they got answers. And then there was Smyth, distraught over Lauren; Alicia always up for the destruction of a madman's dream; Hayden and Kinimaka, ever the professionals, but like coiled vipers when backed into a corner; Mai, having taken a back seat until now, starting to wonder if she could have helped prevent what had happened to Lauren. And Crouch's team too—Caitlyn, distressed at the news and moving mountains with her investigative knowledge; Russo and Healey, barely able to holster their guns, and Michael Crouch—the man with the wherewithal and the contacts to get anything done.

A fully fuelled jet. A shower on board. A quick, energy-laced meal and they were well on their way back to Washington. Drake wished he could have joined Mai in the shower, if only to liberate a little tension, but the Japanese woman remained distant. Alicia offered to join him, but since she'd already offered to join Russo and Caitlyn too he decided to completely ignore her, not even offering a rejoinder.

But he remembered the good times. Perhaps long ago now, but they had been great together once. Drake and Myles. Their stories, their exploits, their wild times together in and out of war would fill a book. Several books.

Christ it was so long ago. Far away now, like most of the best memories of his life. Of course, as he'd learned over time, you only realized you were living the best times of your life when you lost them. *Never go back.* The idea rang true for Alicia Myles, but not necessarily for him. He had returned to Mai, returned to England and to the place where Alyson died, returned to Coyote.

Has it helped?

Truth be told, he didn't know. But one absolute remained unexplored. Before all that, before everything, there was the SAS, the Ninth Division and Alicia Myles. *Looking back,* he thought, *you usually romance your memories. You remember them better than they actually were.*

But not always. Sometimes they really were as good as you remembered them.

He watched out the window as Washington DC unrolled below and geared himself up for what was soon to come. Now wasn't the time to vacillate, now was the time to storm across their enemies' field of play, decimating their forces.

The moment the wheels bounced and squealed on American asphalt he rose to start doing exactly that.

"Do you have a location?" Hayden used a black walkie-talkie, holding the case to her lips.

A man's voice came back, clipped tones conveying a no-nonsense attitude. "We have eyes on. Founding Farmers. Been there forty minutes, looks set for the night."

Drake was listening in. "Hope he bloody well gets gut-rot from his last meal as a free man."

The team, with Alicia's new crew as crucial backup, hastened through DCs clogged arteries, updated constantly by the team on site. Drake experienced a little déjà vu. The last time he'd driven along these streets, a time that now seemed a long time ago, was when he'd chased the Blood King to the Foggy Bottom metro and saved President Coburn's life. By the time they pulled up close to the restaurant known as the Founding Farmers, only a block away from one of their previous HQs, he felt totally lost. That started up a longing for the old streets of York where he'd started anew and met Ben, and that brought him full circle to the fact that they were here now, fighting hard, whilst most people in these parts basked in a healthy spring; forced to put an end to yet one more murderous son of a bitch's apocalyptic plans.

Quickly they moved into position. When they were ready Hayden took a glance around the now admittedly overlarge team. "So who doesn't he know?"

"Don't worry," Dahl growled. "It'll take me just a minute to shove a gun down his throat and march him right out the back."

"No. There's innocent people in there. Kids."

Dahl stepped down.

"Every second counts," Smyth said, not only now for the good of the world, but also for a dying Lauren Fox.

Komodo said. "I'll go in with Yorgi, Healey and Caitlyn. Mismatched colleagues grabbing a drink after work. We'll find a way and fast."

Quickly, the four were prepped and given civilian

jackets. Alicia put a hand on both Healey and Caitlyn's shoulders, leaning in to give advice.

"Now remember, we're in a hurry. No slinking off to the restroom for a shag."

Healey took a deep breath but then almost squeaked as Alicia gave them both a slap on the behind for good luck. "Now you're both jealous of me." She grinned and slipped back into hiding.

Drake watched the foursome enter the Founding Farmers. "Do you ever let up, Miss Myles?"

"Not in this life, Drakey. Just keeping my mojo train on the right track and moving forward. Life's too short for repentance."

"You have none then? No regrets?"

"Fuck, yeah. I have a ton. Just leave 'em all behind."

"Can't do that forever."

"Who says so? *You?* No way you hang on to yours, Drake, not without lugging a dump truck behind you."

"Gee, thanks."

They moved over to Hayden. A surveillance team had been watching their target for over an hour – after he finally reappeared on the radar – through a series of scopes they had assembled inside a neighboring office block. Drake took a peek through one of the glasses, carefully following Komodo's progress as he meandered through several occupied tables. Yorgi, Healey and Caitlyn kept pace. Of course there were no free tables near the target, but the man, sat with his head bowed, didn't know that. Komodo quickly took the seat next to him and leaned in, grabbing his arms and locking them to his sides. The maneuver looked like someone giving a greeting to an old friend. Drake imagined

Komodo laughing out loud. The others took the remaining spare seats and also leaned in—perhaps secreting weapons that Komodo had already found, maybe imparting advice, but always covering their real intentions.

Within minutes, Komodo was leading the tall figure out of the restaurant. Healey left money on the table and Caitlyn and Yorgi were ready to field any questions. None arose.

Drake left his place of concealment to face the man whom the Pythians believed was probably the one most unlikely to betray them.

"General Stone," he said. "You're gonna tell us everything you know."

CHAPTER THIRTY SIX

"Starting with," Hayden said, "where is your friend Dudley taking those samples?"

Under strictest security they had taken the General to a safe location. Now he sat handcuffed to a spartan desk inside a spartan room, a man alone in more ways than one. With the ongoing crisis Hayden had taken it upon herself to keep Stone isolated from standard protocol. She figured they had a few hours before questions were asked.

And anyway, time was hardly their ally today.

Stone glared impassively. "I am a United States general. This isn't Afghanistan, young lady. I demand access to my representatives."

"I have two representatives for him." Alicia held up her fists. "Morgue," she nodded to her left. "Hospital." She indicated the right. "Let him choose."

Smyth was dangerously close to breaking the door down. Drake dragged them both away and back behind the two-way mirror. "Give Hayden a chance, guys."

Hayden took a moment to reveal to the general the severity of his situation, citing first Lauren and her revelations and then the Nicholas Bell sightings and several intelligence leaks including one where Washington DC came under attack by a drone, involving access codes which were stolen from Stone's office. Even the general's face melted a little at the charges being leveled against him.

"You think I'm a member of the Pythians? Are you insane?"

This time the bluster was gone, replaced by a lackluster rhetoric. Hayden slammed a clenched fist on the table, making its legs bounce. "None of that matters! Callan Dudley is in the wind with *two* mass-casualty aerosolized weapons. I'm not sure yet if we're classing them as WMDs but do you really want that on your fucking résumé too?"

"You think I'm crazy," Stone said quietly. "A monster of circumstance. But I see what happens in our government, I see the corruption and the games that are played, and I see the need for a higher authority. That's what the Pythians will give you. Real leadership. Not power plays and six-figure bribes and intimidation. You will know where you stand with the Pythians."

"Where has Callan Dudley taken the aerosols?"

"We are the Pythians," Stone said. "We are everywhere and we will start a very real war. Through China and Taiwan we will find the lost kingdom. Then to the pirate galleons of America. And Saint Germain—the most important, shocking and amazing discoveries of our . . ."

"Shit, I wish we had chance to squeeze him for everything." Drake saw how this was going. "But right now—" he looked at Smyth and paged Hayden.

"Time to send in the dogs?"

"Last chance, General." Hayden said. "Speak freely whilst you still can."

"You think we don't know you? Ever since London the Pythians have been working you through their intelligence network. And it's exhaustive, believe me. Text. Pictures. *Video.* Hayden Jaye, once liaison to the now very dead Secretary of Defense, Gates. Father—dead. Boyfriends—who knows how many, but at least one is dead. How many,

Jaye? Pretty piece of ass like you—I bet those thighs have seen plenty of two-way traffic—"

Now it was Kinimaka who reached for the door, but he needn't have bothered. Hayden was professional enough to keep her cool under such weak taunting, but chose this moment not to.

"I realize from surveillance of our own that if I try to bust your balls, General, you're actually gonna enjoy it. So I'll stay clear of that area. Instead—"

She delivered a fast strike to his face, breaking his nose at the bridge. When his hands came up in reaction she looped the chain of his handcuffs around his neck and pulled. Drake kept an eye on her face, impressed with the composure he saw there.

"She's almost there," he said to the big Hawaiian. "Give her a sec, matey."

Hayden tightened the makeshift noose until the general could barely breathe. "All right, motherfucker," she whispered into his ear. "This is now one very real world, where lonely, persecuted and misunderstood government agents use any and all means to save the men, women and children of their country and preserve their way of life. Even if some of those men, women and children protest that they don't want or need this kind of help. Do you think they'd change their mind if a terrorist cell entered their kids' school or the shopping mall? The airport or train station they commute from? How quickly past atrocities are forgotten."

Hayden squeezed as she spoke, finally relenting and allowing Stone a little room to talk. The general struggled in her grip to no avail.

"Love . . . loving the sexual asphyxiation technique. Your hot breath. Your hands on my neck—"

Hayden wrenched the chains once again, catching some of Stone's hanging folds of skin between them and earning a yelp. This time the general's face was turning purple before she let go.

"I can keep it up all night," she breathed close to his ear. "Can you?"

Smyth turned to Kinimaka with characteristic belligerence. "Shit, your girlfriend's hot."

Stone's gasping filled the room. "Bitch, damn bitch. You'll get nothing from me."

Alicia stepped up. "I think it's time your, um, 'off-the-books' associates sorted this out. We were never here, right?"

Drake was about to agree when Hayden thrust her gun into the general's mouth. Unable to gulp air he began to breathe through his nose.

Until Hayden pinched his nostrils shut.

Stone kicked at the table and threw his head from side to side. Hayden clamped his body down. Still close to his ear she whispered once more.

"Ready to talk, General?"

Stone slapped his hands on the table, the freak inside possibly even excited by the pain. In the end Hayden's determination chipped away all his resolve.

"Callan Dudley," he said when she removed the gun, "left Greece with two boxes. Small aerosols. Once he reaches the *second* facility he will be able to incorporate them into anything we want. A mid-air bomb. A direct rocket. Street-level aerosols. Shit, we can even replicate a Typhoid Mary."

Drake's heart fell. *Second* facility. *Oh no . . .*

"Where?" Hayden pressed.

"At the Canadian north." Stone gave her a location. "Hudson Bay."

Hayden stepped back. "You mean the mountain? The *ski resort?"*

Stone flashed her an evil grin. "Yeah. Whatever."

Hayden's lips tightened. "You lying bastard."

"Try Manitoba," Stone said. "You might even be safe there."

"And all the innocent people you're about to kill. What about them?"

Stone shrugged emotionlessly. "In any war there are unintended casualties. Just ask your *new* Secretary of Defense."

Drake narrowed his eyes as Hayden ignored the odd jibe. "But this is a war *of your own making.*"

"Every new world order must first make its mark," Stone said coolly. "True respect only comes with a well-measured mix of fear and pain."

Hayden shook her head and turned to the window. "That's not respect, you asshole," she murmured. "It's *hatred.*"

Hayden used the gun and pushed harder. She pushed until tears ran down Stone's cheeks. But in the short term, they had nothing that could break him further. The man turned into a gibbering idiot, but always there was that smug, aloof light of superiority in his eyes.

"We'll get no more from him." Hayden walked back into the outer office. "Whatever else he is, he's US military, trained to withstand pressure at the highest level. If I'm being honest I believe he thinks the Pythians will come for him. Save him. What do we have?"

Drake nodded toward a computer screen where the inimitable Alicia Myles had already clicked onto a Superdry website to best illustrate the style of clothes she'd prefer to be wearing when they crashed the Canadian pole.

"So we're nowhere with Lauren's cure?" Smyth rasped. "Dudley's capture? Give me a crack at that piece of—"

"Have you heard from Lauren's doctors?" Hayden interrupted.

Dahl nodded. "She's deteriorating quickly."

"Just as important for Lauren," Smyth said. "Is there any more news on this new version of the plague?"

"Only that it's derived from a concoction of old diseases. They say that the virus dies quickly when buried, right? Well, what if sometimes they're wrong? Check out these scientific absolutes we found. I quote, 'the degree of preservation of a cadaver cannot be predicted by the type of coffin used or the location of the internment. Completely preserved bodies have been found in both wooden and lead coffins. Some contain dry bones but others occasionally contain a viscous black liquid, known as coffin liquor. This can include soft tissues'. You following me so far? Now *regardless of age soft tissue is recognized as a potential hazard. If present, expert medical advice should be obtained from the CDDC before proceeding'.* This is particularly important with well-preserved bodies. My guess, the Pythians found the best preserved old gravesites in the world."

Alicia leaned her head against the glass window. "Y'know, guys. Moving on, Stone could be right.

Remember when we had Beauregard in custody and then his . . . whoops I mean *the* slippery snake turned up in Paris? The Pythians won't let Stone rot."

Drake stared at her. "So you're saying we should let Stone escape? And then what? Follow him? Don't be bloody daft."

"Do you have a better idea? Or are you too busy falling over every time you get shot?"

"Piss off, Myles."

"Seriously," Kinimaka said. "Every second we stand here means the aerosols, Dudley and the Pythians get further away."

"I'll do this." Dahl flexed his arms and fingers. "We have to be well above an executive rationale now. Stone will break . . . one way or the other."

Hayden put a hand on his arm. "Let me call Secretary Price first."

"Call him while I'm working." Dahl opened the door. "Shit."

Drake was about to remind the room of Stone's reference to Secretary Price when the opening chords of Foreigner's *Hot Blooded* shook the room. Smyth fished his cell out of a pocket. "What the—"

Drake frowned at the shock on Smyth's face. Hayden paused in mid-dial. Even Dahl halted for a second.

Smyth answered the phone. "Lauren?"

CHAPTER THIRTY SEVEN

Smyth jabbed at the handset, putting the call on speaker.

Lauren's voice was frail, faint. Drake felt spears of empathy and rage pierce his heart as she spoke.

"How are you talking in your condition? Which asshole made you call me? Tell me his name. I'll—" Smyth's ire waned when Hayden jabbed his ribs.

"Shut the fuck up. She's trying to tell us something!"

Lauren coughed and wheezed. Eventually her voice came again, weaker this time. "Remember the calls I made? Before . . ." More coughing.

Drake thought back to the beginning of this mission. Lauren had been their way in to the Pythians and the only reason they were so close to stopping Pandora's Box. She had paid for that bravery by getting a face-full of plague. But he couldn't remember any calls . . .

"I do," Smyth said in the most subdued voice Drake had ever heard the man produce. "I was sitting beside you at the time."

Karin snapped her fingers. "Yes. You called the escort network on the assumption that both Stone and Bell, being what they are, would have used their services elsewhere."

"We are a tight-knit group. We . . . we have . . . to be."

"You watch each other's backs," Smyth said. "I get that."

"They came back to me. And yes . . . Stone and Bell they—" Lauren's voice broke as a series of wracking spasms shook her body. Drake heard either an intern or a nurse begging the woman to sit down, to hang up the phone, to rest, but Lauren croaked at her to be quiet.

Both respect and sadness swelled inside him at the same time. Lauren Fox didn't have long to live but here she was, still fighting for the team and the world at large.

"You guys still there? I have . . . have a little cough."

Hayden smiled with a mixture of severity and sorrow. "We're right here, Lauren."

"Both of them . . . Stone and Bell . . . separately and together have ordered ladies in the city of Niagara Falls. Canada side."

Drake felt a jolt of electricity. "Recently?"

"Over a couple of months."

"What a fucking network!" Smyth cried. "*What* a brilliant network! Are you sure?"

"They keep very detailed records of high rollers."

"So what are we waiting for?" Drake was surprised to hear Mai's voice, strong and sure. "Let's go get the aerosols and wipe these goddamn Pythians off the map in one go."

Now he understood, or thought he did. She was anxious for this mission to be over so she could pursue the Grace angle. The best quality he could glean from that was her upstanding faith that everything would end well.

"Let's go save Lauren too," he said. "And bring an antidote back to her."

"Fuck that," Smyth said. "We're taking her with us. I'll carry her all the way if I have to."

Nobody questioned him. Nobody thought about gloating in Stone's face. No time was lost. The two teams, SPEAR and Gold, were professionals to the end and prepared to move out.

"You might want to call the Razor's Edge guys," Drake said to Kinimaka. "They deserve to be in on the end of this. And the help sure won't go amiss."

The big Hawaiian nodded and tapped his phone. Hayden was already talking to Secretary Price in an effort to smooth their entry as Crouch informed Armand Argento at Interpol. Drake knew why. Despite Argento's distance it was sometimes crucial what such deeply rooted agencies could accomplish.

Alicia looked around at all the activity and gave Drake a mixed smile. "God help Niagara Falls."

"It's what we're trained for."

"Yeah, I know. But with all our firepower and *their* army we're gonna destroy the place."

"We'll find a way, Alicia. We always do. In any case won't you be mega-happy we're moving on? Maybe you'll even get to see Beauregard again."

Alicia's expected witticism didn't come. Instead she eyed Drake very closely. "Is that a hint of jealousy I hear?"

Drake effected an idiotic grin. "After all we've been through together why would I suddenly feel jealous?"

"Dunno. Maybe because I'm me and you're human?"

"Bollocks. You got me."

"It sure looks that way." Alicia flounced off, a satisfied smile on her face.

Drake turned a little wearily toward Mai. The Japanese woman sent him a troubled grimace but made no move to come over. In the end it was Dahl who appeared at his left elbow.

"Quite a team, huh?"

Drake stared around at the bustle of activity. Hayden and

Kinimaka on their cells, gaining ground with every word; Karin and Komodo, Yorgi and Smyth trying to ward off their anxieties about Lauren and the aerosols by familiarizing themselves with Niagara Falls; Crouch's team joining in. A jet was ordered to be made ready in a few hours, weapons prearranged, authorities battled with. The problem was, no matter the severity of the threat or the reputation of the team involved, there was always at least one man in authority looking to make a name for himself.

Drake nodded slowly. "It sure is, my friend. I can't think of a better one I'd rather be going into battle with."

"Aerosols. Antidote. Pythians. Dudley." Dahl ticked the boxes with his fingers. "In that order."

"And then that pint?" Drake stared into the middle-distance.

"Sure. We'll set the world to rights."

"Someone needs to."

"Correct. The way it's going our children or our children's children are heading for . . ." He tailed off, unable to finish the sentence. "Y'know, Drake. There's one thing people never tell you about having kids. One thing you can never truly understand until you're a parent. *You never stop worrying.* Not for a second."

"They'll be fine, mate."

"Oh, I can sure tell you're not a parent, Drake. I don't simply mean worrying *now.* Or next week or over the next few years. I mean *ever.* With such evil in the world, I even worry that my daughters will experience some terrible anguish over *their* sons or daughters."

Drake looked into the bigger picture, the unending unease. It only reminded him that Alyson had died with their unborn child still growing inside her.

"Some people would still like to have the chance," he said softly.

Dahl flinched a little, as if realizing what he'd said. For a second both men stared at nothing, shoulders together, soldiers together, envisaging all that they fought for.

Then Drake turned away. "C'mon dickhead, let's go grab some guns and maybe a bacon sarni."

Dahl shoved Drake in the back. "Typical Yorkshireman. Always thinking about food. No doubt they sell fish and chips wrapped in newspaper in Niagara Falls."

"Yeah, but I'm not sure how much of Niagara Falls is gonna be left after we're done taking down the Pythians."

CHAPTER THIRTY EIGHT

A monumental meeting took place inside the first floor conference room of the Maple Lake hotel, based on Dunn Street, Niagara Falls, behind the lofty Tower Hotel. This little place, with its C-shaped design, attention to cleanliness and detail, and adjacent wedding chapel, was massively overlooked and overshadowed by the towering award-winning hotel that stood over five hundred feet above the Niagara gorge and provided restaurant and room views of the stunning cascade. For that reason it was the perfect meeting place for three of the most capable, deadly and determined teams in the world.

Drake had never seen so many dangerous people in one room before. These men and women fought for peace, for a way of life they believed in, often without recognition or thanks. They were true heroes, and here they were about to put everything on the line once again.

He stood at the back, near the buffet table, sipping water and working through a plateful of nibbles. Mingling with his own team was Alicia's new crew, who were actually Crouch's unit. *Damn, that's gonna get confusing.* It was easy to picture them as Alicia's team because the woman was a pure force of nature. If she followed it was simply because the person leading was heading in the same direction that she was. Crouch, he guessed, was the one of the only bosses she would trust completely.

Russo seemed solid, a man he could accept. Both Healey

and Caitlyn were young but dedicated and bright. They mingled well with the SPEAR team. The newcomers from California were an odd bunch, older than Drake had imagined, and somewhat of a misfit. Trent, their undeclared boss, was a grim-faced individual, slow to smile but with drive and purpose fuelling his every move. The concentration level with this man was huge and, to some, probably quite intimidating. Still, when he did occasionally direct a smile toward the woman in their group it was deep and genuine.

The woman, Claire Collins, was a force to be reckoned with, a multitasker, absorbing everything around her and commenting or acting with a leader's confidence. Drake saw she wore the new bruises and cuts on her face without emotion; perhaps they would heal, perhaps not, but either way it wouldn't matter to her. She had withstood a firestorm whilst taking down the Moose—*that* was what counted.

Radford and Silk were different again. The first a good-looking, scrawny individual who tried hard not to stare at all the ladies in the room; sporting an intellectual look that might well fool most people into underestimating him, and put them at his mercy. Drake wasn't sure if the look was purposeful or just coincidental, but it no doubt worked for him. Silk, the roughest looking member of the Razor's Edge, was an easy man to read—brought up hard he played hard and fought hard. Accustomed to nothing he took what he had to. Silk was Drake's kind of man and the first the Yorkshireman naturally gravitated to.

"Drake," he said, holding out a hand. "Matt Drake."

"Adam Silk."

"Great job over in LA. I hear you guys kicked major ass."

"LA is personal for us, man, and especially me. I grew up on those shitty streets. Ain't no criminal organization gonna use some kinda bioweapon there."

"The Pythians are more than just a one-hit wonder." Drake took a sip from his bottle. "We will have to destroy them totally to beat them: head, body, tail. And when they're dead it's immolation. Crushing. Burial. No mercy."

"If I had my way it'd be the same for all criminals and terrorists."

"Are you ex-military, Silk?"

"Not exactly. I was recruited into the CIA at a very early age. Trained. Sent to black spots. I guess I earned my stripes in the field."

Drake nodded, saying nothing. Silk had been a CIA black-ops specialist. Those guys were ghosts, slick, lethal and smart. He nodded toward the other three members of the Razor's Edge.

"They all as good as you?"

"Nah, but they think they are." Silk grinned. "Trent comes across as remote, stand-offish, but that's just because he's always been a leader and shouldered all the responsibility. I couldn't ask for a better man to guard my back. Radford—childish, makes every mistake in the book at a personal level, but in the field? He's top dog. And Collins?" Silk smiled fondly. "A few months ago I wanted to shoot and bury her. Now . . . I'd have her babies if she asked. She's diamond-cut, man. Hard, reliable, trustworthy. And more fun than Johnny Depp on a mad bender. Believe me, I've been there."

Drake raised an eyebrow. "Isn't that what all Angelinos say? That they know some kind of famous star?"

"Nope. Not really. But when Collins has done chewing you out, busting your balls for an afternoon, she'll take you out to the Sunset Strip and dance with you till dawn. Viper Room. Skybar. We've done 'em all. And the next working day she'll come right back and take your head off again."

Drake couldn't help but stare at the baby-faced, black-haired FBI agent. "Maybe we could trade her for Dahl."

"The big Englishman over there? He looks tough."

"Ah, he's Swedish. And not too bright. Our weakest link. Make sure you tell him I said that."

Silk gave Drake a knowing look. "Yeah, I'll get right on it. So, what's the plan, action man?"

Drake laughed. "I think Hayden and Crouch over there are laying something out. We'll have tech support from Caitlyn Nash—" Drake pointed the blond girl out, "And Karin Blake. Both based in the field."

"Isn't that a little risky?"

"Normally, yes, but with this super-plague about to hit hard we're guessing that there's no longer any 'normal'. We're up to the whacked-out, do-or-die leagues now, mate, and the risk is . . ." Drake paused. He'd been about to say "acceptable", but memories of friends that had died along the way hit him abruptly, and hard.

He turned away.

Silk, a soldier in arms, knew the look and placed a hand on his shoulder. "I'm right with you, bud. Right with you."

Hayden walked to the front of the conference room and called the meeting to order. "Hey guys, thanks for being here. This will have to be quick so we'll save introductions for the celebration party later. For now, let's focus on survival. The Buffalo FBI and Niagara Falls DOJ have been running CCTV operations and physical black-and-white sweeps for about twelve hours now. Nothing relating to Nicholas Bell has come up, but Callan Dudley was spotted by a traffic camera about twenty minutes ago." She tapped an extending pointer against the wall where a large map of the city had been projected. "Here. Kister Road. It's a tree-lined, open-plan industrial area with several large warehouses and businesses. Wide roads. Big junctions. Hard to approach without being seen. My guess is the Pythians have rented a plot there for their second facility."

"Could he just have been passing through?" Trent asked quickly.

"Doubtful. He passed the traffic cam both ways in a matter of minutes. There's a small strip mall in the direction he went."

"Still . . ."

"We're watching the area in unmarked cars and through civilian walk-bys. We have guys on industrial lawn mowers, that kind of thing. There aren't any sidewalks as such, but it's still a popular area for locals to get a good deal," Hayden said. "Techs are scrolling back through the last few days of camera footage. In truth, Aaron, we have little else."

"Any word on the Pythian HQ?" Collins asked.

"All we have are the testimonials from Lauren Fox's associates and this sighting of Dudley. We also know that General Stone made several visits to Niagara Falls in the last few months, overnight stays each time. Facts like this appear much clearer when you have something concrete to back them up. My guess? If we take out the second facility the Pythians will burst out of the woodwork."

"It would be helpful to know the identities of the rest of

the Pythians," Dahl said. "We know Le Brun is dead, but how many more are there?"

"Not many," Drake said. "Webb is one, whoever he is. They'd want to keep it exclusive."

"Maybe," Hayden acknowledged. "But this is the new breed of secret regime. Who knows how screwed up their agenda is? Or even if they have an ultimate goal."

Saint Germain, Drake thought, but said nothing. That was a conversation for another day.

"We go in one group?" Trent questioned. "That's going to be hard to manage."

"Blitz them," Hayden said as Kinimaka nodded at her side. "Caitlyn and Karin can handle the operational logistics."

"Speaking of which," Karin spoke up. "Our vehicles are fifteen minutes out along with an ensemble of Canadian authorities. We might wanna wrap this up."

Drake noticed the soldiers in the extreme gathering starting to assess their clothes and belongings, taking an inventory of what they needed and checking the status of what they had. Alicia, quiet since their last little exchange, meandered over just as Mai came up.

"Good luck, you two."

Drake saw a fire in Alicia's eyes, a reminder of the days when she and Mai had been enemies. Was Alicia challenging Mai? Or was she merely urging the Japanese woman to get a fucking grip and see what was right in front of her?

Mai didn't hesitate. "Now isn't the time, bitch. Test me later if you want to stay upright."

Alicia just smiled, content in the knowledge that she'd

ruffled Mai's composure. Again. Drake ignored them both and began a weapons check of his own. In front of him, Smyth had whipped out his cell, firing off another text.

"Lauren?" Drake asked.

"Yeah. The, um, nurses are having to text for her now." Smyth's glum face held its downward position.

"She's safe here at least," Drake said. "And close to the antidote."

Hayden stopped next to them. "C'mon guys, we gotta get moving. They say Lauren has about an hour before she's beyond help."

Drake flinched. "Bollocks. Maybe we should—"

He later thought the attack succeeded merely because the three teams were so intent on absorbing information and making ready to move out. It was certainly true that they hadn't deemed it essential to place a guard around their perimeter, rather every member of their group would function better if fully briefed.

And besides, no one knew they were there.

The mercs hit at air and ground level, a devastatingly huge two-pronged assault. Reactions were instant and effective within the room, every man and woman organizing their efforts into decisive action. Drake ran to the windows as cars squealed into the car park and choppers thundered overhead. Kevlar-clad men leaped out of the still-running vehicles, machine guns panning left and right. He counted twenty in three seconds.

Looking up, he saw a flock of helicopters gathering overhead. All bore civilian markings and could probably even produce tourist licenses, but no doubt belonged to the Pythians. Could this be part of their exfil plan?

Quickly he headed for the rear-facing door. Dahl was already there. "Clear for now but they'll be coming."

"Go."

The company rushed out onto the concrete balcony that ran around the outside of the hotel's first and only floor. Bright yellow rails stood before them with featureless doors stretching to either side. A tattered seat stood outside every room.

"Up!" Dahl made the decision, jumping so that his boots hit the top of the narrow rail, balancing with his arm against a tinny upright. Flinging his gun over his head he sprang upward, catching the lip of the roof. With one easy maneuver he was over. Drake quickly followed, Mai at his side.

Mercs were abseiling out of open helicopter doors, the machines' flamboyant colors and cheerful appearance undermined by the falling men and their wicked-looking guns. Dahl opened fire as he began to sprint, catching the men as they touched down. Those he hit twisted and fell, screaming. Others jumped from above, riding their luck. Still more leaned out of the open doors and returned fire.

Drake sensed Alicia at his back. He saw Trent out of the corner of one eye. The Disavowed man looked grim. "The others are racing both ways along the balcony. Shots from below. We're split three ways now."

"Have faith," Drake yelled. "We'll not be apart for too long. And we'll run all the way from this rooftop right to the goddamn facility if we have to!"

Men struck the ground inches to his left.

Alicia fired upward, forcing the choppers to veer and sway. Dahl was already approaching the edge of the roof.

Mai darted into a merc who had somehow escaped a bullet, making him wish he hadn't as she crushed his windpipe and cheekbone at the same time.

With a deft movement she stole his gun.

Drake ducked a hail of fire and shot a man leaping toward him straight off a rope that swung in the air.

For better or worse, good and evil, they were all fully committed now.

CHAPTER THIRTY NINE

Drake saw eight rope lines dangling from the assembled choppers. The combined thunder from their rotors was more than deafening; it was a sheer onslaught to the senses. Keeping his sense of balance as low as possible he ran hard, following Dahl, hoping the mad Swede had some kind of plan.

Dahl skidded to a stop at the edge of the roof. "Whoa, didn't expect that."

Balls.

Drake tackled a merc around the waist, forcing him to the ground. Alicia's weapon barked. Mai peppered pilots with devastating ammo. Two choppers jerked violently as their pilots reacted, sending men tumbling from their ropes.

But still more men landed than the five could deal with.

Trent smashed his stern visage into a merc that landed just in front of him, then faced three more. A wild shot skimmed his midriff. Mai vaulted in gracefully from the side, using hands and feet to raise bruises and break bones. Trent joined her in the melee, battering his opponents with heavy strikes.

Dahl stared over the edge of the roof. Alicia skidded up to him. "What the fuck's up, Torsty?"

Drake ground his teeth. "That's a long drop, mate."

"No!" the Swede said. "There!"

He sidestepped several times to a new position, right above a bright red soft drinks machine.

"Ya thirsty?" Alicia wondered. "Or in need of caffeine?"

Dahl jumped three feet to a lower thin brick ledge, then to the top of the drinks machine and, without pause, leaped off and landed with a roll across the grass. Then he was up, gun raised.

Drake shook his head. "It better be as easy as it goddamn looks."

Alicia turned, opening fire as several men converged on their position. Mai and Trent were steps away, the west coast man flinging a struggling merc face-first to the floor. Even Alicia almost winced as the man bounced.

"Nice move."

"Where to?"

"Ah, down . . ."

Drake jumped, landing briefly on the ledge and using it to spring forward so that he landed atop the drinks machine. From there he bounced and rolled just as Dahl had, becoming slightly tangled in his weapon's strap but still retaining dignity.

Alicia covered Trent as he jumped down. Then she waved Mai forward but the Japanese woman smiled sadly.

"You first, Taz. This is part of my burden, I believe."

Alicia shot a looming merc. "You looking to die, Little Sprite?"

"My own fate is out of my hands now."

Mai sprayed the mercs, giving them much to consider as Alicia made the jump. As she fired she plucked a smoke bomb from her vest and flung it. Mercs shouted and dived for cover, not knowing the type of grenade she'd used. Mai used the distraction to skip stylishly to the floor.

"A tad better than Yorkshire style," Dahl observed.

"One thing I've thankfully never been accused of," Drake said, "is having too much style."

The Swede moved to the side of the building just as men approached from the front parking lot. Before they could blink, the team were under fire again.

Sirens wailed in the distance.

Crouch sprinted the length of the balcony as men shot at them from below. Caitlyn ran behind him, sheltered by Healey and Russo, both returning fire. Behind them raced Silk, Radford and Yorgi. The remainder of the company jogged in the opposite direction, splitting the enemy forces.

Crouch reached a door and yanked it open, herding the others through. Healey headed straight for the stairs.

"Move it," Crouch told Yorgi, the last through. "There are civilians here. We have to vacate asap."

The Russian made eyes at him, probably wondering "Ya think?" and slipped one leg over the staircase handrail, passing their frontrunners as he slid down. Not the best of decisions, since he was a non-soldier and that put him first in the firing line, but one he couldn't now change. Yorgi flew off the end of the handrail and landed face-first onto the carpet of the hotel lobby. Crouch flew down after him but Russo, seeing the danger, leaped three steps at a time and hit ground level almost simultaneously.

Mercs were entering the front doors, spilling into the lobby. Russo saw a side door, yanked Yorgi up with one hand and headed right for it. They were halfway across the lobby before they were spotted.

A shout went up. Guns swiveled. By that time Crouch and the others were behind Russo and already firing.

The hotel lobby erupted in a hail of gunfire. Potted palms disintegrated and turned into dust motes flitting through the air. Plaster exploded from the walls in large white chunks. Glass shattered, raining to the floor. Crouch and his team dived and rolled and crawled through it all, covered in debris, faces turned away from the worst of the flying wreckage. Most of the mercs remained upright and paid the price, struck by jagged pieces and razor-sharp shards, badly aimed bullets and falling candy-bar dispensers. Others fell back through the doors they had just entered, sprawling outside. Crouch hit Healey's scrambling feet but rolled on, falling through a fragmented hell, blood trickling from a dozen cuts and gashes. Russo lumbered through the side door without even thinking of stopping to open it, the man-mountain tearing the hinges right off. Staggering outside, he still held the entire door as mercs descended on him. Russo swung it to and fro, knocking assailants aside like bowling pins.

Crouch was the last to enter the parking lot as his team covered their flanks. Some way off to his right he had already spotted Drake's impromptu team, keeping pace with them. His mind turned to thoughts of the others.

Hayden led the team that ran across the balcony in the other direction, followed mostly by SPEAR members with the addition of Special Agent Claire Collins. Kinimaka was beside her as always, positioned between her and the exposed railing. Hayden pushed her body hard, wondering if she'd feel any discomfort from the now relatively old gunshot wound, but felt nothing. Great news, considering the position they were in. Hayden slammed open the door, ducked as a stray bullet shattered the glass, and slipped through. Karin came next, pushed by Komodo. Smyth and Collins brought up the rear, untroubled by the mercenaries below.

"Bastards are aiming at the other guys," Collins barked. "Even after I wounded two of them."

"I know one way to help." Hayden hastened down the staircase, finding it led to the rear of the property. On cracking the door she had a side view of the enemy. Quickly she turned back.

"Ready?"

Many weapons were raised in answer. Then Komodo said: "Wait. Where's Smyth?"

The irascible Delta soldier muttered only three words in repetition as he pulled up in the line of fire.

"Comin' for ya. Comin' for ya."

The room number jumped out at him, the sight of her lying so vulnerable, so drained it would be forever seared into his mind. Bullets sprayed the wall above, stitching a new line there. He smashed in the door with a kick as his comrades sprinted out of sight.

"Comin' for ya."

Lauren lay helpless, connected to tubes, with nurses hovering and looking scared out of their wits.

"Does she have a chance, any chance at all, without these damn tubes?"

"Not long," one of them responded. "But then she doesn't have long anyway. Take this." She held out a long syringe filled with a clear mixture.

"What the hell is it?"

"A little something to slow her metabolic rate. Drastically. It should give you a few extra minutes."

"Why not give it to her now?"

"Because if you do, when she wakes, everything will speed up and she'll die faster."

Smyth understood. "I'm all for Hail Mary passes," he said. *Damn,* he knew exactly where all this was coming from.

Romero. That ass!

Goddamn Romero had gone and got himself killed whilst running from the Blood King's men. Smyth had loved that overgrown ass and would gladly have taken the bullet. Now—Lauren had gone down under his watch—not in actual *fact* but since when did that matter?—and now he would give everything to save her.

Smyth scooped her up, the lifelessness of her body causing his mouth to draw into a thin white line, and pocketed the syringe. "Lie low," he said. "They're not here for you. We'll be luring them away soon."

Outside, he sprinted after his group.

Hayden moved out soundlessly, slowly, not wanting to draw any attention. The first merc to see her died with a shot to the forehead. As the rest turned her team opened fire, sending them cartwheeling and dropping desperately to the ground.

"No time to waste." Hayden swiveled and raced for the side of the building, the parking lot ahead. To her right, Crouch's team were already in fast motion and far beyond them Drake's team.

Choppers lifted off the roof above, their guns rattling,

and dozens of mercs surged from the hotel behind Crouch. Hayden dropped to one knee.

"Cover them!" she cried.

Her team knelt beside her.

"Fire!"

Mercs collapsed as they converged on Crouch's team.

Behind her, Smyth placed Lauren in the center of their defensive guard and faced the other way. "Rear guard," he barked. "Fire!"

More assailants dropped behind the hotel.

Hayden dropped a raised fist. "Fire!"

CHAPTER FORTY

Drake darted ahead with Dahl a step behind. He saw Hayden's team drop and cover Crouch's escape with bursts of gunfire, then watched the choppers lift off the roof. Now beyond the hotel's property, he skidded to a halt on the gravel drive that led to the front door of a wedding chapel. Further down the wide road he spotted a large TGI Friday's and, beyond that, the soaring Tower Hotel, wider at the top and bristling with windows that gave as good a view of the city as they gave of the falls themselves.

With no access to comms or a radio—the raid had happened before they could be deployed—he signaled to Crouch that he should continue. Then he shrugged at the others. "Let's make it tough for those choppers."

As the birds swooped down, Drake and Dahl with Trent alongside filled the air they flew through with lead. Alicia and Mai deterred the mercs atop the hotel roof from trying any potshots. Crouch's team ran ahead, spilling out onto the road and then stopping and turning. The chopper veered up and away, then came down in the hotel's parking lot, finally grudgingly accepting they offered no advantage and disgorging the rest of their men onto the ground.

Drake and the others ran hard toward Crouch. His old boss met them in the middle of the road.

"Keep running!" he cried. "Hayden needs your help. We'll head toward that restaurant. We need transport fast."

Drake accepted the orders without question. He sprinted

on, arcing around Crouch's position and swinging toward Hayden's. She was already in motion, sensing the backup, and urging her comrades onward. Drake stopped at the side of the road and fired at the mercs behind and to the side of Hayden's position, making the already traumatized mercs lurch away in surprise.

Hayden and her team raced past them. Drake covered their run, then he turned to Dahl. "Our turn. Let's go."

The five whirled and ran hard. Ahead, Crouch and Russo, Healey, Silk and Radford stood in the center of the road, picking any mercs off who tried moving forward. Three more times they swept as separate teams in rough semi-circles, each team covering another as they opened up space between themselves and their enemies, following a curve to left and right, kneeling and standing, firing in ranks to keep up a steady hail of bullets.

The lesser force pinned their enemy down.

"Who says there ain't safety in numbers?" Alicia grinned as they all finally merged with their comrades.

With soldiers guarding their flanks, the sirens wailing ever closer and flashing lights now almost upon them, the company's leaders came together. Hayden took point as Caitlyn and Karin handed out working comms.

"We need two teams. One to hold these assholes off and stop them destroying any more of the city. The other to hit the facility before they move the friggin' aerosols again."

"And the antidote," Smyth said, still with Lauren over his shoulder. Komodo had already volunteered to take her for a while but Smyth held on as if she were the Holy Grail. Hayden gave him a wan smile.

"Yes. The antidote. It must be at the facility, Smyth. Where else would it be?"

"Those fuckin' Pythians would keep it all for themselves. Make no mistake."

"You're probably right." Hayden glanced toward Drake. "Soon as we get a locale let's split into a third team."

Drake nodded. "Let's make this quick. Those wankers are regrouping."

Hayden fielded a call. "All right," she said when she'd finished. "We have some sort of major activity at one of the warehouses where Dudley was spotted. Could be that this ongoing failure here has sparked something over there."

"Panic." Alicia rubbed her hands. "Oh, let's hope so."

"Failure?" Dahl breathed toward the now moving choppers. "Not exactly."

"I have the FBI and the Canadians patched into my comms now," Hayden said, then glanced at Collins. "One of the station chiefs says hi."

Collins all but blushed and looked anywhere except at Trent.

Radford leaned in. "Another *dance* partner?"

Collins shoved him. "Shut your goddamn face."

Drake set off at a sprint. "Move it!"

Crouch eyed those choppers still sat near the hotel's parking lot, many of which had lost crew and pilots. "I have an idea," he said thoughtfully.

Russo and Healey grinned at the same time. "Yes, sir."

Drake headed for the shadowy first-floor level of the TGI Friday's multi-story parking lot, seeing several patrons hovering around their cars. Knowing it would be traumatic for them and hating himself for it, but still putting the safety of the greater world first, he waved his gun at the sky.

"Keys," Alicia said, dashing past and commandeering a vehicle.

Drake leaped onto the back of a midnight-black MV Augusta, opening the throttle even as he landed on the seat. Alicia, already climbing into the car—an old Alfa Romeo—shot him an irate look.

"Bastard."

Dahl altered his run at the last moment, jumping up behind Drake. "Nice idea, Yorkie."

"Thanks, Ikea. You're only on here to piss Alicia off."

"Of course!"

Drake peeled out of the parking area, threading a line through parked and exiting vehicles, swerving around the side of a black-and-white police cruiser. Alicia, Mai and Trent were in the Alfa, struggling to keep up. The huge yellow TGI's writing set against a long, curving wall and red-and-white livery flashed by to their left as they hit Fallsview Boulevard at speed.

Hayden stayed in their ears. "We're a minute behind you. See the Tower Hotel to your left, white fascia?"

"Aye, and the Marriott," Drake drawled.

"Forget it. Head back down Dunn Street and then left on to Ailanthus. Then it's the 49 to Stanley. Got it?"

"Yup."

Drake gunned the Augusta, feeling Dahl wrenched back in surprise behind him. The Swede's scrabbling hands tugged at the front of his jacket for a moment.

"Careful, Dahl," Drake breathed. "If I were Alicia you'd be dead by now."

Alicia's voice came over the comms. "He just grab your tits?"

Drake chuckled. "Yeah."

"He's right, Torsty. I don't stand for that groping crap."

Dahl took hold of his seat and exhaled with gusto. "Just drive."

Drake took the hint, unleashing the Augusta's power as they leaned into the corner that led to Ailanthus.

Hayden's voice came over the comms. "A truck is preparing to leave the facility. Hurry!"

*

Crouch ran for the nearest chopper, sprinting across Dunn Street in full view now that their enemies had regrouped a little further away, preparing to utilize the helicopters nearer the hotel and still on the roof. At first they ran unseen, cutting the gap in half, but then the call went up.

"Damn!"

Crouch herded Caitlyn behind him and ordered Russo and Healey out front. When he looked around he also noted the presence of Silk, Radford and Yorgi.

Two birds then, he thought. *Bloody hell we're going to cause mayhem.*

Was there an easier way to guard Hayden's and Drake's back and complete this takedown?

Right then the question was rendered moot as four mercenary helicopters took off from the grounds of the Maple Lake Hotel, their innards bristling with paid, corrupt men toting machine guns, rocket-propelled grenades and much more.

"Let's take this battle to the skies," Crouch shouted as he reached the first unmanned chopper and waved Russo into the second.

The mercenaries swooped into attack formation.

*

Drake followed Hayden's instructions, leaving the tourist areas of Niagara Falls behind and proceeding into an open-plan industrial area. Drake marveled at the wide roads, huge intersections and appealing tree-lined avenues.

"If this were back 'ome," he grumbled. "There'd be a multiplex, a supermarket, three bathroom outlets and a bowling alley on one road, two gyms, a police station and a nightclub on another, one bus route and some knobhead counsellor who doesn't drive sitting in an office, looking at ways to make it even harder for cars to get around."

Dahl pointed ahead. "There!" he shouted. "Coming toward us. That's the truck!"

Drake gunned the bike, swerving around the front of the white van and laying the bike into a short arc as he passed around the back. For one moment his eyes met those of the men in the front.

"Ain't gonna be no mercy shown here, guys."

Three hundred yards from the secret facility, Drake chased the escaping van along the wide road, using the Augusta's speed and dexterity to bring him close to its rear. Dahl unstrapped his gun from around his shoulders.

"Force it off the road?"

"Oh, yeah. And Hayden, Alicia, when you guys do finally get here, head straight to the facility."

"Copy that," Hayden's reply was as expected.

"Don't be a twat, Drake." As was Alicia's.

Dahl aimed at one of the truck's rear tires. The rattling noise of the truck's rear tailgate interrupted him.

"Bollocks!"

Drake turned sharply, leaning the bike over. Four men stood inside the back of the van, pointing weapons at them.

They fired immediately, the bullets passing over Drake's head as he tilted the bike over, only one sparking off and denting the fairing.

Dahl sputtered, hanging on for dear life.

Drake steadied the Augusta as an enormous truck loaded with wrapped plastic tubing appeared ahead, lumbering along at low speed. The furniture-van sized truck they were following didn't hesitate, just pulled out and overtook, causing oncoming traffic to veer across the sidewalks and the road verges. Drake blipped the throttle and closed the gap once more.

"Shoot those bastards, Dahl."

"Get closer!"

Dahl peppered the rear of the truck with a hail of bullets, sending their enemies scuttling.

"You sure? They—"

"Closer! Now!" And the mad Swede lived up to his name as he began to climb. Drake shrugged off utter disbelief, realizing he shouldn't be shocked where Dahl was concerned. The Swede maneuvered his body so that he crouched in his seat before quickly firing again. Then, with his enemy distracted, he urged Drake right up to the tailgate of the truck and climbed onto his shoulders, using the Yorkshireman's head to balance. The Augusta raced hard in pursuit of their enemies, trees and buildings whipping by. Dahl kept his balance easily for a moment before leaping off Drake's shoulders, rolling through mid-air, and landing *inside* the truck, allowing his body another two rotations before planting his feet and looking up.

Eight pairs of eyes stared back in utter shock.

Dahl sprayed them with lead, tackling the nearest with

one arm, smashing an elbow to his throat and then hurling him from the truck. The Swede took a bullet to the chest and staggered. Drake took out a pistol and joined in the battle. Dahl came up hard, head first, sending a second merc tumbling into space. A third was down, incapacitated by bullet wounds, the fourth injured. Even so he came hard at Dahl. The Swede slipped aside with more grace than a man of his size ought to possess, caught the merc's head under an arm and flipped the man onto his back. Drake knew when he was superfluous, opened the bike rapidly, employing its swift acceleration, and surged right up to the front cab. Without warning he shot out the windscreen and then took out the passengers. In another moment the truck was shuddering and freewheeling to a halt.

Drake spun the Augusta hard, laying rubber onto the asphalt, billowing smoke from the spinning tires. Dahl jumped down from the back of the truck and waited for him.

"Nothing in back," the Swede said calmly through the comms. "Possibly a diversion."

Drake saw police cars converging. "Relay a message to the cops, Hayden. Tell them to check the men in the cab. We're about to hit the facility."

Hayden's affirmation came back instantly. "And we're right with you."

Two cars shot by. Drake picked up Dahl. The second facility was one minute away.

Crouch employed great skill in making his helicopter take flight. It had been many years—so many he didn't like to calculate—since he'd taken a bird into the air and especially under such pressure. Not that his passengers, Caitlyn,

David Leadbeater

Healey and Yorgi noticed, they were too busy gearing up and certainly didn't need to be made aware of their extra peril. With the cyclic stick and collective gripped hard, his feet operated the foot pedals and worked each component simultaneously. He opened the throttle, increasing the speed of the tail rotor, realizing just how rusty he was as the chopper juddered a little. He pulled on the collective and pressed the left foot pedal, painfully aware of the mercs' own choppers now within shooting range. Luckily, to his right Russo was already in the air.

Shoulda kept up my fieldwork instead of sitting in cafes drinking Frappuccinos all day.

At last he felt the cyclic become sensitive and nudged the chopper forward. Healey had stationed himself at the right door, Yorgi the left. Crouch felt his heart lurch as he saw them.

"Strap yourselves in, for God's sake. This ain't no scenic flight."

Russo banked to the right, drawing two enemy helos. Leaning out of his nearest door was Adam Silk, already drawing a bead on their assailants. Crouch pitched in the opposite direction, turning underneath the other two. Over the top of the hotel he gained altitude, bringing his bird around in a wide arc.

Healey opened fire, aiming broadside and sliding forward at the same time, adjusting his aim.

Below, Crouch saw a midnight-black bike racing around a corner followed by a speeding Alfa Romeo. That could only be Drake and his pals, heading for the secret facility at breakneck speed, desperate to find the antidote. His mind flicked momentarily to Smyth—the tough, snappish solider

288

laid low by a fellow team member's struggle against death. Before he could think again he saw an enemy helicopter swerve after them. Instantly, he blocked its path, inclining the helo and turning so Healey grabbed its attention.

Bullet holes stitched across its side.

Crouch used a deft touch to lift them higher into the sky, thankful that the old skills were returning. The second merc chopper blasted straight at them. Behind it he saw Russo taking on two more, swerving and pitching out of the skies as Silk and Radford loosed automatic firepower from its open doors. Bullets trailed through the air. Crouch flinched as he felt impact, a line of lead travelling across his own hull, and sent the chopper into a dive. Healey moved superbly with the maneuver, twisting so he could stay focused on their attacker. His own fusillade smashed a side window and sent their attacker tilting away, sideways through the skies.

"Go!" Caitlyn cried at his side. "They drove down Ailanthus. Let's lead the mercs in another direction."

Crouch allowed Healey and Yorgi to loose another barrage before lining the chopper's nose up with the Tower Hotel and darting forward. Caitlyn's advice was justified as both enemy 'copters swung around in pursuit. Russo, listening closely to the comms, performed a similar maneuver. Dunn Street fell behind and a clear blue sky momentarily opened up ahead. The chase was on.

Six civilian choppers loaded with mercenaries and soldiers, guns and grenades, flew over the tops of some of the most famous hotels in Niagara Falls—the Fallsview Marriott, the Oakes and the Hilton—before banking right, each blasted by bullets and veering from side to side in evasive maneuvers, to come up against a sight that shocked even them.

"Jesus Christ!" Crouch exclaimed. "We're heading straight into the falls!"

CHAPTER FORTY ONE

Drake roared the black Augusta up the curb, taking flight over the sidewalk, touching down inside the warehouse's grounds and almost clipping the back of the braking Alfa Romeo. Before the car stopped Alicia was out of the driver's seat and already in her stride, Mai doing the same from the passenger side. Drake let the Augusta fall, jumping to the side. Trent swung out of the rear of the Alfa.

The second car dispersed the rest of their team as engines roared from the rear of the lengthy, blue-panel corrugated structure. Drake headed toward a half-open roller-shutter front door, then hesitated.

"Shit, if the truck was a diversion that could be—"

"The real thing?" Smyth was white with worry, standing over Lauren who rested in the back of the second car.

Hayden paused, caught between two impossible choices. "*Damn!*" Her gaze snapped to Lauren, then the warehouse. "I don't . . . I don't . . ."

It was the first time Drake had ever seen her stumble.

Kinimaka placed an enormous hand on her shoulder. "We have the manpower for both."

Hayden nodded, snapping back to routine. "Drake's team, since you're already practically inside, take the warehouse. We'll stop whatever comes around this goddamn corner!"

"Hope it's not a tank," Alicia wisecracked from near the roller-shutter door.

"Doesn't matter *what* comes around," Smyth snarled. "Party's over for these motherfuckers."

Drake urged his team into the dim innards of the warehouse. Instantly, they were beset. The place itself was outfitted much the same way as the first facility back in Greece, half a dozen tables stretched down the middle of the space, each one equipped with laboratory supplies and computers. No chairs were in evidence. Glass phials and test tubes, jugs and juice containers, deep freezers and lighted display cabinets were everywhere. Drake came to a sudden halt when he was faced by a dozen men in white lab coats.

To a man they looked terrified.

Somewhere, a gun was cocked.

And a voice roared out, "Yer again, may the devil choke yer and yer feckin' mother's offspring. This time yer feckin' dead, yer hear? Dead!"

The blood-crazed mercenary, Callan Dudley, opened fire, blasting apart the laboratory workers who, moments ago, had been helping him with the Pandora's Box plague samples. The first thing Drake knew was the red spots appearing on the white coats, then the stumbling figures and shattered midriffs.

"Down!" he screamed. "Get down!"

Hayden raced to the side of the warehouse just as three black Jaguar XFs came into sight. Engines roaring, windows totally blacked out so that they appeared to be low-slung monsters, enormous grilles like bared teeth, they were speeding down the narrow driveway toward her.

She jerked back, Kinimaka at her side. "They mean business, guys! I'd be guessing if I said this was the antidote on its way to the Pythians but, either way, they need stopping."

"Any news from the white truck?" Karin asked.

"Yes. The police are there now, examining the dead mercenaries. Nothing has been found either on them or inside the truck."

"So it *was* a diversion."

"Who knows? We can only deal with what's in front of us."

Her words became immediately prophetic as the three powerful black cars shot past toward the road, the last in line slewing across the gravel before its driver managed to get it under control. Hayden jumped into the discarded Alfa with Kinimaka and Karin and urged Collins, Smyth and Komodo back into the vehicle they'd arrived in—a bright red, four-door Lexus.

Together, they peeled out in pursuit.

"Get up close!" Smyth had strapped Lauren in as tightly as he could and was leaning across the back seat now, rifle in hand. "Give me a terrorist to shoot."

Collins bounced around the passenger seat. "Almost there, man. You gonna fight me for the privilege of wasting these assholes?"

"Damn right I am."

As the three Jaguars snarled down Kister Road, heading hard toward the north, the Alfa and the Lexus coaxed enough speed and power out of their engines to pull alongside. Suddenly it was a five-vehicle chase without a car's length between them, the antidote to a deadly aerosolized plague being the prize.

Smyth powered down his own window just as all three

Jaguars powered down theirs.

Guns bristled through the openings.

"Now we're fucking talking," the Delta soldier rasped.

Crouch's vision was filled by a tremendous, all-encompassing cascade of furious white water. This was the Horseshoe Falls, one of three that made up the great cataract and by far the most powerful. One hundred and sixty five feet straight down, the raging torrent dropped in freefall, sending spray blooming into the atmosphere and colorful rainbows arcing over the landscape. Crouch had read somewhere that over four million cubic feet of water traveled over the falls every single minute, a figure that was almost impossible to comprehend. From this position, however, it wasn't difficult at all.

"Pull up!" Caitlyn cried.

Crouch saw the large white ship below them, famously known as the *Maid of the Mist*. And in spectacular fashion a vast wall of mist was even now pluming upward. The chopper almost skimmed waves as it dropped low, then shot up before the great falls. Water spray enshrouded it, billowing past. One of the mercenary helos paced them, almost alongside, its occupants leaning out and trying to shoot him down.

Then Russo's machine was barreling in from the side, Silk and Radford locked on with their weapons. Their shots smacked home on target, puncturing metal skin and glass windows and then the bodies inside. The chopper groaned and went into freefall, plunging through the mists and the turmoil of water to the harsh rocks below.

An explosion rocked the base of the falls, fire competing

with water for a few brief seconds before the deluge consumed all.

Crouch swept up over the top of the falls, attention fragmented by the beauty of the sweeping horseshoe and the nearby Bridal Veil Falls, the colossal width of the river, and the stretch of railing to his right where hundreds of people stood watching.

No time for niceties, Michael.

He swung the bird around, sprayed by water, momentarily lining up with Russo's own deadly whirlybird, before shooting off in a different direction. This time he swooped down vertically with the water, almost matching the falls' deluge foot for foot, watching as the drifting ship below grew closer and closer. Faint flashes sparkled from down there; tourists taking photos. Crouch leaned his bird over, allowing Healey to fire out of what was now effectively the "top". Ignoring the engine's groaning complaints he saw Healey fire into the undercarriage of another merc chopper, making the whole frame judder. As he righted his own machine he saw Russo dipping down under fire, following the great curve of the Horseshoe Falls, blasted by water and mist.

Healey fired once more, sending another merc chopper into the hungry waters below. Now they were two on two and Crouch didn't expect their good fortune to last much longer. A moment later he cursed himself, realizing he'd tempted fate as his own windscreen cracked under fire. Not only that, as he evaded and swung away he was faced by a different bird, this one with a man leaning out of the door and an RPG in hand.

"Evade!" Caitlyn screamed.

Crouch shoved the stick almost through the floor as Healey yelled and the weapon discharged. Yorgi smashed his skull against the door's metal frame, drawing blood and almost losing his grip on his weapon. The RPG skimmed them with a whistle, passing through the white cascade and detonating soundlessly against the wall of the falls. Crouch veered around as their enemy prepped another rocket.

"Healey!" he cried.

The soldier turned but he was on the wrong side. Yorgi, holding his weapon clumsily and wiping blood across his cheeks, sighted their adversary.

"I may not be good shot. But you, my friend, are worth whole clip."

He kept his finger depressed until the man with the RPG fell from the chopper, swallowed by churning waters. Unfortunately he dropped the grenade launcher inside the chopper and it was picked up by another man.

Crouch blasted forward again, crisscrossing Russo's own path but fifty feet below. His route took him up and over the concrete viewing deck which sent uncountable tourists and locals scrambling to safety.

Russo thundered above the falls once more, the sound of his rotors scything through the air muted but not lost under the overwhelming noise of flowing water.

Crouch touched his comms. "Remember your training, Russo. Get on their tails. Let's finish this."

Drake rolled and tucked, escaping any stray bullets as the twelve lab rats went down screaming. To either side he saw Alicia and Mai, Dahl and Trent jumping for cover but also carefully watching their rear to gauge what was going to happen next.

As the scientists went down Callan Dudley was revealed, tall, brawny and sneering, eyes wild with promised violence. Alongside him were six men, all toting weapons.

"Ain't no cures here, arsehole. Yer bitch is as good as dead! The antidote, as they say, just left the building."

Drake relayed the information through his comms.

Alicia glanced from behind a low-standing freezer. "Do you ever stop talking? You're louder than a friggin' space shuttle launch."

"Oh aye? Well come out here, bitch, and we'll do more than blather."

"If that means 'talk' then all right."

Drake wasn't caught unawares by Alicia's sudden move. He knew her well enough by now to be expecting it. When she popped up from behind the freezer he rose too. Mai fell to the floor to their right, already firing. Bullets formed a lattice network in the air, a lethal grid of death. Alicia took a hit to the chest, Trent to the arm. By design, both wore Kevlar and neither faltered. Drake didn't fail to notice that Alicia stayed on her feet when hit but hoped the intense situation would make her forget.

Dudley paced forward with all the arrogance and rolling shoulders of a prize fighter. He wore a white vest that showed off brawny arm muscles and faded tattoos, tight blue jeans and highly polished Doc Martens. He flung his gun at Alicia as she shrugged off the bullet.

"Yer goin' on yer back, bitch."

Alicia's smile was as sweet as honey. "You clearly don't know me very well."

Dudley punched hard like a boxer, keeping his right fist at his cheek as his left probed with exploratory jabs. Alicia palmed the hits away, light on her feet, always moving. Drake snaked around the side of the large space, coming up on a mercenary about to take a shot at Alicia.

"Ey up!"

Confusion was his final expression before a bullet ended his contract with the Pythians.

Drake pushed on. Dahl was a bulldozer barging down the middle, leaping from table to table onto intimidated mercs. Mai swept up behind him, rendering his wounded victims unconscious before they could rise and cause further problems.

Trent crouched at Drake's side. "Alicia Myles," he said. "I've heard stories about her. The real thing is a little different. More . . . rousing."

Drake moved through a tangled network of what appeared to be oil barrels, tracking two more mercs. "Oh aye. We keep hoping she'll settle down. Take up PlayStation or something."

"That may not help. My kid, Mikey, has one. Even makes him crazy."

"Shit. We'll keep video games behind a childproof lock then."

Drake tackled a barrel like an American footballer, hitting hard, forcing it back and then over . . . right on top of the man sheltering behind it. The rim of the barrel struck just above the man's eyes, leaving him bloody and unconscious. Drake sprawled atop him.

In full view of the second merc's raised rifle.

Trent vaulted his own barrel, both feet connecting heavily with the merc's skull. His shot, a reaction, went wild as his body slumped to the ground.

Drake spun, intent on the others. Alicia was still circling Dudley, a bruise on her cheek revealing that he'd made it past her defenses at least once. The arrival of more mercs took Drake's attention.

Alicia had had enough of letting Dudley take the lead. It wasn't her way. She'd already purposely given him a way through her defenses. When he tried a second time she was ready, feinting at the last moment and ducking in.

Up close.

She delivered a flurry of punches. Ribs, solar plexus and gut. The Irishman's muscles absorbed the worst of it, but Alicia was no soft touch and she drove him back. Suddenly his onslaught was forgotten as he tried to cover up.

Alicia used her feet. A strike to the knee made Dudley stagger. As he went down Alicia stepped in, only to walk straight onto a powerful rising uppercut. If the blow had connected under her chin it would have been lights out at the very least. As it was, the blow smashed into her sternum and clipped her chin, making her bend double and then fall to one knee.

She couldn't remember ever being hit so hard.

Dudley danced away, skipping his feet from side to side. "Ah, yeah! Gotcha! Yer won't beat ole Callan Dudley in a bout o' boxin', little love. Champ o' the Irish underground I was, and then some. Now let's put yer on yer back."

He kicked out, aiming for her face. Alicia rolled backwards, coming up on her feet and trying to mask her pain. Dudley wasted another minute of his advantage rapping at her and then advanced again in a boxer's stance. Alicia saw she was going to have to break this bastard out of his comfort zone.

Drake finished the mercs off with a low grenade, ducking as explosive debris saturated the air. Trent caught a loner by the neck and fought hard for a few moments before the man collapsed. Mai caught the attention of two more.

Their decision to take her on directly proved to be a bad one.

Drake paused at the side of one of the lengthy tables. A computer screen flickered alongside him. Comms chatter had been crackling along quite efficiently throughout the battle. He already knew that Crouch and team were engaged above Niagara Falls and Hayden's team were involved in a road-warrior battle with three Jags.

Dudley's voice brought him back to the moment. "Stand still while I hit ya. Yer like a feckin' meerkat popping up and down like that!"

Alicia jabbed at his throat, shutting him up. Drake moved toward her from her left, Dahl from her right, but the Englishwoman stepped back and held up a hand.

"No," she said. "Sometimes you just gotta fight crazy with crazy. This one's mine."

Drake didn't like it, but knew better than to ignore her. Dahl pulled up too, but kept his gun handy.

Alicia took a blow to the forehead, feinted right and again dived in. Dudley was a pure boxer, he didn't like his legs messed with. Alicia kicked his knees, his thighs and then clasped him tight, bringing a knee up to the groin. When his eyes bulged she pushed him away, hard.

Dudley gasped. Alicia leaped in again, nose to nose, chest to chest. "A hit to the plums and you're suddenly a jelly? Pathetic!"

She repeated the move. Dudley caught his breath without

making more than a brief shriek, threw another cross-jab at her, but the attempt was unfocused, weak. Alicia stepped in once more.

Dudley rose, all power and lethal ability, again faking the hurt in an effort to draw his quarry in.

Alicia saw the about-turn too late, saw it in his eyes a moment after she was totally committed. *This is it then,* she thought. *The killing blow.* Dudley had engineered this opening by sacrificing his nuts and would be putting all of his homicidal strength into this move.

But only as Alicia had anticipated. Yes it was risky, but she wagered that an Irish brawler of Dudley's obvious prowess wouldn't balk too much at a blow to the gonads. Probably even enjoyed it. So she faked it, faked the final step in so he would at last show his hand.

And Dudley did. He swung upward and with every ounce of strength, missing Alicia by a whisker and exposing his entire body below the chin.

Alicia had been trained to take a man out with a single blow. Now, with every inch of Dudley unprotected she delivered more than half a dozen to his vital areas. The sack of meat that hit the ground a moment later was fully incapacitated, unable even to crawl.

Drake leaped over with a set of plastic ties.

"Aw." Alicia tried not to show her pain. "My trusty, obedient bunny."

Dahl approached, one hand touching the comms set fastened to his ear. "About bloody time!" he shouted. "Hurry it up. We have a lead on the Pythians' HQ!"

"And the antidote?" Mai asked.

"They're fighting for it," Trent replied, stern face looking worried. "They're sure fighting for it."

CHAPTER FORTY TWO

Crouch swerved their 'copter into the path of an oncoming enemy machine at the last minute, preventing a broadside gun battle, and making them pull up swiftly. This caused one man to fall, plunging straight down into the turbulent, frigid waters below. Crouch came around in a wide, ascending circle, finishing on the tail of his would-be assailant. Healey leaned out and fired a volley, young face set rigid with concentration.

Crouch noticed Caitlyn watching him with fear and was reminded that the two were trying to set up a date.

"Don't worry. He'll be fine."

"God I hope so. He's too young and virile to end up as fish-food down there."

The comms crackled. Alicia's voice, predictably dry. "And that arse is so terrific and instantly slappable . . ."

Caitlyn blushed, having forgotten about the comms in the heat of battle. "I guess you're never going to let me forget that one. We're gonna have to find a way to mask personal observations," she commented. "Maybe keywords or something."

"Where's the fun in that?" Alicia laughed.

Crouch finessed his machine in the other's wake, allowing Healey to fire off a well-directed volley. The tail rotor of the other shredded after a moment and the craft swerved hard and fell away, searching desperately for a place to land. Crouch saw it crash nose-first into the cliff wall underneath one of the observation decks, plumes of fire rolling up toward the guard rails.

"Get out of the goddamn way," he muttered as people leaped safely to all sides.

"Three down," Caitlyn observed. "One to go."

Crouch nodded. Russo's bird was tracking the final mercenary 'copter high above, following the curve of the falls around the Horseshoe bend and all the way to the American side. An arch bridge spanned the river there, called the Rainbow Bridge, which separated the Canadian side from the American side, tall and gray, eye-catching. Crouch saw the final chopper heading toward it.

A plethora of worries invaded his heart. Everything from a rocket attack against the bridge to a landing in one of the many featureless parking lots. Quickly he hauled on the collective and gave chase from below as Russo pursued from above. The last chopper swooped low and shot through the great arch of the Rainbow Bridge, closely followed by Russo and Crouch, pushing for even more speed. Shots were fired from the fleeing machine but seemed rather half-hearted now.

"So now they have another agenda?" Crouch realized. "It has to be the Pythians! What else could it be? Who else could turn this chopper around? Listen everyone, I'm guessing that the Pythians have a pretty much foolproof evacuation plan and a whole army of men to execute it. They've called in the reinforcements now. Follow our lead."

Affirmations snapped in through the comms, most of them implying grim relief. The Pythians were on the run. At last. It was a capture or kill mission now.

*

Hayden felt like she'd been sidelined for years. Truth be told, since she'd been shot, she hadn't really missed the field. The break had given her time to think, to adjust, to recuperate whilst reflecting on her life. From FBI agent and then liaison to Secretary Gates to leader of SPEAR in so short a time; through her chaotic relationships until she finally let Mano Kinimaka be the person he'd always wanted to be. For most of her life she'd felt as if she'd been waiting for something to happen.

Treading water.

Always the person on the fringes, looking in. But since she met Matt Drake the adventure, the whirlwind, had never stopped.

She hoped to God it would never end.

Fired up, she let Kinimaka drive whilst she took the Alfa's passenger seat. The Hawaiian, big behind the small wheel, nevertheless drove with dexterity and brilliance, shooting the mid-size, lime-green car to within a hair's breadth of the third Jag's black rear fender. With all the windows open the snarl emitting from the car's twin tailpipe was a noisy, powerful, mechanical howl.

Kinimaka held the Alfa at top speed, seeing a clear stretch ahead.

Karin shook her head. "They're gonna pull away from us."

"Not if I can help it." Hayden watched as all the Jag's windows came down and black barrels were poked out. The other car, the red Lexus, powered past to her left, its own windows down and Smyth's head sticking out: a pissed-off, vengeful Alsatian. The Jaguar slowed slightly, and came up alongside.

Hayden threw her door open, clung with one hand to the top side of the door frame and leaned across the roof, steadying her gun by lying on the smooth metal. Gusts of wind ripped at her. Tiny motes of debris blasted her clothing. She took aim on the array of gun barrels and didn't waste a moment.

She opened fire. One . . . two . . . three shots pumped into the back seat and then the front. Blood splashed the side of the car, red against pitch black. A gun slithered out, bounced against the asphalt. Shots were fired wildly into the air. The last Jaguar veered and then righted itself as Smyth's Lexus swerved in on the second in line. Hayden fired more shots in the driver's direction. A bout of return fire sent her ducking behind the frame, knowing how futile the gesture was but accepting it as a normal reaction. Her own window shattered but no bullet struck her.

Kinimaka's face was distorted by worry and anger. "Get in!"

Hayden fired one more time, sighting carefully and taking a deep breath. Her bullet took out the driver. The black Jag bumped across a concrete verge, spun a one-eighty and then motored up the first hill of a verdant golf course, chewing grass and snapping off a lonely flag. Men in white T-shirts and checkered pants ran screaming.

Hayden climbed back inside. "One down."

"I hate it when you do that!" Kinimaka nevertheless floored the gas pedal to come up behind Smyth's Lexus.

"Been a while," Hayden said. "Missed it."

She watched ahead as the second Jag in line suddenly spouted an excess of gun barrels through its side windows. Smyth, being the closest, flung his own door open and stepped onto the door sill, hanging with one hand on the frame. Unlike Hayden, he was on the *right* side of the car, next to the Jag. Screaming at the top of his voice he reached out and wrenched a gun away from its owner, then another. As his driver inched even closer Smyth reached inside the other car's window and grabbed a man's throat, pulling him half out the window.

Stuck as they were outside the window, the gun barrels couldn't properly reposition to fire at him. Then the Lexus swerved, striking a pothole, and Smyth lost his grip. Thinking fast he pushed off the side of the Jag and landed back inside his own car, almost sprawling onto Lauren.

The New Yorker's eyes were open, lackluster, almost lifeless, but she still managed a wan smile. "Still playing the clown, huh?"

Smyth had never played the clown and both of them knew it. Even now she was teasing him. He held out a calloused, bloody hand and placed it so gently on her knee she could barely feel the pressure.

"Hang in there, beautiful. We're close."

Through his comms he heard Hayden explaining that the third Jaguar had been seized and searched by following police and nothing resembling an antidote had been found. She also confirmed that the road ahead was relatively clear. The authorities, using police choppers and commandeering others, had sealed off most of the off and on ramps.

He sat up. Bullets pinged through the car, smashing windows. In a moment he realized Agent Collins had been far from idle; seated in the front passenger seat she had replicated Hayden's earlier movements and was holding the door frame and leaning away from their car, out over the asphalt at ninety miles an hour, to evade enemy fire.

Smyth growled, jumped back onto the door sill and wrestled another gun away from its owner. Then, without a split second's pause, he launched his torso across the deadly gap and through the Jag's open window.

Inside the rear, it was an instant melee. Two bodies already crowded the footwell. Smyth punched hard into the chest of the man he'd landed upon, the one he'd disarmed a second ago. As he did that a final merc, shuffling around in the far seat, took a bead on his face with a handgun.

"Say bye bye, soldier boy."

The finger pressed. Smyth couldn't get out of the way, but continued punching his own adversary right into the last instant of his life. Anything . . . anything to save Lauren and take these mercs and their evil bosses all the way down to a place where they could only drink brimstone.

The merc fired.

Smyth jerked his head back, expecting pain and death. Instead he saw the merc lurch sideways as a bullet took *him* in the side of the face. His shot twitched wide.

Smyth, still punching, glanced back. Collins lay prone on the top of the Lexus, entire body outside the car, sighting along her outstretched arms.

Smyth stared. "Jesus Christ." *Is she for real?*

Her business-like grin said that she was.

Turning back he realized that the merc he was punching had succumbed long ago. Now only the man in the driver's seat was still moving.

"Get out! Get out!" Smyth heard Collins' scream barely through the ringing in his ears. *What the . . . ?*

Looking ahead he saw that the Jag was out of control, the

driver now slumped, the car veering slowly toward a Shell gas station and a dozen empty pumps. Faster than he could think he scissored his body around and opened the rear door, letting it swing wide.

Komodo guided the Lexus to within a foot of the speeding, drifting Jag.

Smyth leaped over as Collins rolled off the roof and distorted her body to fit back through the open window. The movement took its toll, wrenching her handgun away, scraping her spine and elbows and making her scream, but the result was worth it.

Panting, she rolled toward Smyth.

"You okay, buddy?"

His vision was momentarily blinded as the second Jaguar careened into the gas station, smashing through upstanding pumps and rebounding off a metal stanchion, then spinning several revolutions before hurtling into the kiosk. Bricks and mortar rained down on it.

His thoughts were only for Lauren. "I just hope the antidote wasn't in that car," he said as the first licks of flame surrounded it.

Lauren Fox reached out a shaking hand to comfort him. "Don't . . . worry. Don't. Thank you for trying." A breath rattled through her frame. It sounded like her last.

Smyth had to turn away. As he did he felt the covered syringe move in one of his pockets. *The drug that would slow her metabolic rate!* Heart surging with hope he withdrew the hard plastic tube and prepped the liquid.

Please. Please work.

Quickly, he uncovered Lauren's arm and injected the fluid. Now they were working on hope and luck and good will. He smiled as her eyes fluttered open.

Collins nodded, grim-faced, at the lead Jag.

"Now we end this. And them."

Hayden ordered Kinimaka to plant his foot through the floor. Their Alfa spurted forward just as the Lexus sped up. If these Jaguars had initially been heading for the Pythian HQ, delivering an antidote that the second facility had just formulated, then they were now fleeing for their freedom, their lives. It wouldn't have surprised Hayden to find that the Pythians had ordered the second driver to smash into the gas station. Hopefully, the lead driver wouldn't do anything quite so foolish.

As their cars swept up to the side of the last remaining Jaguar, the men inside started shooting. The Lexus took a peppering to the front fender, the Alfa a stippling around the front wheel arch. Still, nobody backed down. Engines roared in protest, shuddering the very air they dispersed. Ahead now, the two-lane carriageway was about to run out, the road curving into a built-up area. Hayden realized they had seconds to act.

"Again!"

She flung her door wide, but it was already too late. The Jag roared ahead as its driver decided to utilize its own firepower rather than its occupants'. At the last moment Komodo, driving the Lexus, tried to swing over into its slipstream but turned an instant too soon.

The Lexus impacted against the rear of the Jag hard enough to make the driver lose control. The results were terrifying, sending the huge black car into an eighty-miles-per-hour spin and its occupants into a fortunate oblivion. At first the Jaguar swerved within the limits of the road but then it hit the high curb and flipped, spinning slowly lengthways as all its wheels left the ground. Rolling helplessly, it smashed into a wide glass restaurant frontage, destroying the window, its frames and the brick wall above it. Wreckage exploded inside and outside the restaurant. Tables scattered.

Hayden leaped out the moment Kinimaka squealed to a halt but she was a step behind Smyth. Like a bulldozer the soldier smashed aside hanging clumps of brick and mortar and reinforcement bars. Like a maniac he tore open the front driver's door and took hold of the merc positioned there.

Smyth shook him wildly. "Antidote!"

Then, beyond him, clasped in the trembling hands of the passenger, Smyth saw a clear transparent cylinder, about the size of a tin can, jammed full with small phials.

"Is that it?"

"Save me," the mercenary whispered. "I don't want to die like this."

Smyth reached out and took hold of the cylinder. The moment he did so his heart began to quake, his pulse raced like never before. *Are we too late? Is Lauren already too far gone?*

Gritting his teeth, he ran like hell.

CHAPTER FORTY THREE

Holding the cylinder as carefully as if it held his own soul, Smyth jumped into the Lexus' back seat. Within moments he sensed everyone gathering around him. Hayden, at his shoulder, whispered, "This is for all of us."

He quickly detached the accompanying bags of syringes and upended a phial, drawing clear liquid inside. A squirt to dispel air bubbles and he leaned toward the motionless, white-faced woman that had been robbed of her great vitality, so unbelievably depleted.

"This is from me," he said and jabbed the needle through her skin.

"How long?" he heard somebody ask. Karin's voice.

"How is she? Has anything happened?" Collins' voice.

Smyth discarded the empty syringe, leaning over Lauren's mouth. He didn't care that he might contract or have already contracted the disease. A serious, more aloof head might have, but Smyth was incautious and fiery and, above all, a soldier. He would see this through to the bitter end, for good or bad, and he would not leave any person down.

No breath came from Lauren's mouth, no life crossed her lips.

Drake's voice came through the comms. "We're following a chopper to what we believe is the Pythian HQ. They seem to be panicking and on the run. Or it could be some other kind of misdirection. Anyhow, we have both aerosols and the last sample now. How's Lauren? Did you get the antidote?"

Smyth hung his head, unable to speak.

Hayden's voice was less than whisper. "We're waiting."

Kinimaka added, "Smyth administered it. But it may be too . . ."

Smyth placed a hand on Lauren's cheek, as gentle as a feather landing. "Please," he whispered. "Don't die on us."

Hayden took a deep, juddering breath. Though intense noise and activity surrounded them not an iota penetrated their team's cocoon. It was only when Lauren's face twitched under Smyth's touch that anyone thought to take a breath.

"Lauren?"

Her eyes fluttered, her body gasped air. Her whole frame shuddered. Far too weak to move she nonetheless forced breath through her lungs and opened her eyes.

Smyth leaned in so close he couldn't focus. Relief flooded him, a liberating fountain. For the first time he could remember, he didn't feel anger in his heart.

The others crowded around, congratulating and rejoicing.

Smyth stayed put. No way was he going to let them see the tears in his eyes.

Drake joined Alicia, Dahl, Mai and Trent in the race to catch up to Crouch's choppers. The Augusta had developed a fault after his mistreatment back at the warehouse so they were now crammed into a military Humvee, following Crouch's directions. The roads of Niagara Falls were filled with the noise of wailing sirens, K-rail barriers and rows of police. Drake already knew the Canadian authorities were cooperating fully with the international effort, and was grateful for it; no way would they want to be the ones that dropped the ball on something of this magnitude.

"There!" Drake pointed at the skies. "Two o'clock!"

Dahl approximated their position on a map. "They're following the Niagara River. Can you make this thing go any faster?"

"We're trying, sir. We're trying."

The vehicle roared onto the Niagara Parkway and then River Road, racing past a colorful place called Daredevil's that promised ice cream, pizza, popcorn and fries. Alicia moaned as she went past.

"God, I'm hungry."

"Here." Drake broke out a Mars bar. "You remember? The SAS used to swear by them. A sugar rush before battle. Trouble is, nowadays they're so small you need two."

Alicia sat back in fond memory. "I do remember, Drakey. I remember much more than you think."

The Humvee blasted on, following the curve of the river, a low stone wall to their right and thick clumps of trees hiding real estate to their left. River Road was a prime location, its properties large and mostly hidden by the treeline. Crouch's voice crackled across the comms.

"We're hanging back now. Yes, I know they've already seen us but we're not going to fly right into a trap. The Pythian chopper is slowing, banking, going down! It appears to be a house right here on River Road. We're kind of level with Oakes Park, can you see it?"

Dahl drew a line with his finger across from Oakes Park to River Road. "Got it. We're ten minutes out."

"Good. Because we're putting this baby down right in the middle of the highway."

Drake glanced around the interior. "Why would they lead us right to their lair?"

Trent frowned. "Could be a dozen reasons. Megalomaniac disorder mostly. Their leader believes he can't be caught. That fits our profile, considering how open and willing to take responsibility these Pythians have been so far. They've practically invited us to take part."

"Some say this is only their opening salvo," Mai said.

"Judging by their behavior so far," Trent said, "I guarantee you their leader wants to meet at least one of us. My guess is *that* is what this is all about."

Drake narrowed his eyes, finding the whole scenario hard to believe. Yes they had come up against some evil, crazy masterminds in the past, but someone like this?

"It's their escape plan I'm worried about," Trent said.

Alicia cocked her weapon. "They're not going to get the chance."

Trent looked unconvinced.

At that moment a red Lexus and a light-green Alfa Romeo sped alongside the Hummer. Trent leaned forward to check out the occupants of the Lexus. "Everything okay?"

Collins replied immediately. "Nothing broken."

"Looks like you got hit by a Gatling gun."

"They showed us theirs, we showed them ours. Ours was bigger and harder."

"Y'see," Alicia nudged Drake, "size does matter."

"Oh, balls. Is this another Beauregard thing?"

At that moment a blue and white chopper bounced down lightly in the road before them. All three cars came to a sudden halt. Military helicopters were visible on the horizon, approaching the scene, and more Humvees and other vehicles raced up behind. Drake climbed out and stretched, taking stock of their surroundings. The teams came together again, congratulating each other on still being alive. A tall, broad, haphazard array of green trees and hedges stood all around the eastern side of River Road; dwellings could barely be seen through the dense foliage; the Niagara River flowed to the west. They were stood staring at a corner plot.

Crouch tapped at a tablet as he came toward them. Caitlyn took it off him so he could prepare weapons. "Okay," she said. "The helicopter came down there." She pointed toward the plot. "Twenty eight thousand square feet of real estate, last valued at eight million dollars. Currently owned by Imogen Enterprises, whoever they are. Not enough time to dig, I'm afraid. A one-of-a-kind waterfront estate mansion. There's lake access, three pools, a basement, a dock on the Niagara, a theater, wine cellar, grotto, a goddamn ranch. Everything your well-prepared self-important dictator needs to make good his escape. Even access to a golf course beyond the ranch. It lists farmland separately too. Jesus."

"What's that?" Drake pointed at a tall, brick-built structure. Its walls appeared to have been painted as much to camouflage its presence as anything.

"Some kind of viewing tower?" Dahl commented.

Hayden looked back. "Maybe it offers a view of the falls?"

Alicia cleared her throat. "Are we waiting for something? 'Cause Santa's already been."

Drake fell in beside her. "Do you even remember

Christmas? In Hawaii? With Mano?"

"Yeah. And you pining after the Little Sprite. How's that working out for ya?"

Drake threw a glimpse toward the Japanese woman. "Today? Not so bad. Tomorrow? Who the hell knows?"

"What's her problem? Her *latest* problem?"

"A long story. We don't have time."

Alicia paused as the entire company came up alongside her, readying for one last tremendous assault against the Pythians.

She looked along the line, both ways. "I have time for you, Drake, as much as I have time for everyone who now stands alongside me. If you're interested."

Crouch and Hayden led the way. Drake didn't have time to assess Alicia's underlying meaning—if indeed there was one—before the company came under heavy fire. The mercenaries' last chopper sat beyond the high fence and gates, in the house's grounds, and around it were arrayed a dozen men. Drake ducked behind the wall, watching as Dahl happily relieved a Canadian trooper of his rocket launcher.

"I'll just borrow that for a tick if you don't mind."

The Swede hefted the weapon, grinned toward Drake, and then walked to the lofty wrought iron gate, pointing the barrel between the uprights. If the chopper hadn't been there or the mercs had chosen a different place to stand he wouldn't have had a shot. As it was, the perfect target presented itself.

Dahl fired. The grenade blazed a trail through the air, impacting against the side of the still-ticking, bullet-riddled chopper and bursting into flame. Dahl stepped back and allowed Trent and Radford to deal with the gate. Moments passed and then the wrought iron latticework was falling inwards, bouncing off the concrete. As one the company raced into the grounds, followed by Canadian troops. Bodies lay sprawled around the chopper, most unmoving. Drake headed straight for the picture window, higher and wider than any set of French doors he'd ever seen, and shot over two hundred small panes out, creating a gap wide enough for them to enter. Inside, the house was vast, high-ceilinged with wooden timbers and archways.

He picked his way through the debris, Dahl and Alicia at his side with Mai trailing them, and crossed a polished wooden floor. Through the door lay the entry hallway, as wide as any sitting room Drake had ever seen, and poised above it a railed balcony that led to the second floor. Jam-packed with men.

"Back!"

He ducked back into the room just as a grenade bounced down from above, detonating almost instantly. Shrapnel stabbed the walls. Dahl was already up and inspecting the partition near the door frame.

"Aim there," the Swede told the accomplished soldier with the rocket launcher, pointing just below the vee of the horizontal and vertical wall above the door. "It's plasterboard. Drywall. Gypsum, you know?"

"I'm Canadian," the soldier said. "Not French."

"Sorry," Drake told the soldier. "We're trying to trade him for a girl."

"Sounds like a good deal."

Dahl coughed. Collins leaned over. "I hear on the grapevine that that girl was me?"

Drake blinked. "Um, really? Who told you that?"

"Whatever you say," Collins told him. "I will find out. I know everything."

The soldier fired, sending his rocket blindly through the wall in the direction of the upper balcony. A hole blasted in its wake, giving the accumulated company a view of the mercenaries hit and killed by the blast. Part of the balcony disintegrated but the staircase remained intact. Drake was up and running instantly, heading toward the second floor, confident that Hayden would organize a search of the ground and the basement. Two bursts from his rifle and the coast was clear.

Dahl pounded at his heels, holding the rocket launcher.

"You took that from that poor soldier?"

"Last rocket." The Swede patted the pear-shaped grenade. "Thought I'd make it count."

Alicia was close by. "I hope you guys aren't thinking of replacing *me* with that Agent Collins. Chick's a big-time ballbuster if ever I've seen one!"

Mai snorted with laughter, drawing a grin from Drake. All three of them stared at Alicia and shook their heads as they ran.

"*What?*"

Drake took stock before storming the second floor. Corridors stretched both ways, dissected by still more. In addition to the four of them, following fast, were Trent, Collins, Crouch, Caitlyn and Smyth. Hayden must have literally put a hand out like a nightclub bouncer to chop the team in half.

Drake moved on.

Trent hissed, "Wait!"

Drake froze. The ex-CIA agent was pointing to a shimmering red laser stretched across the corridor. Drake had been about to break it. "Good call. Move back," he said. "We'll have to test it with something. Grab one of their jackets."

Instead, Dahl picked up a dead merc and flung him down the corridor.

Alarms wailed, nothing more sinister. The team headed out, checking every room. Mercs came at them from all angles, so fast and dangerous that they were forced to regularly change their point men to stay fresh and alert. A grenade tore away two structural walls, another blew out part of the side of the house. Timbers groaned. Smyth and Alicia fought hard to pull information from wounded men but all they got was that the Pythians were here, somewhere.

And their boss, it was readily revealed, was here too. He was waiting for them.

Drake shook his head. *Crazy bastard. What on earth could he gain from such provocation?* Notoriety? A boost to his ego? Narcissistic glee?

Probably all three, and more.

They proceeded, listening all the while to Hayden's commentary on events transpiring below. It was only when they reached the far end of the house opposite the high tower that a figure presented itself in a dark, arched doorway.

"Greetings," it said. "I am Tyler Webb. Leader of the Pythians. And . . ." he chuckled "Soon—the world."

Hayden pushed her team hard through the first-floor rooms. This was no time for hangers-on and fortunately she didn't

319

appear to have any. The mercenary attacks were sporadic and hard to gauge. Some of them were die hard fanatics, sacrificing themselves in a hail of bullets, others gave up and laid down their weapons with comparative ease.

Didn't sign on for this shit, and *anything you need to know* were phrases uttered regularly by those they captured. When Hayden quizzed three of them separately about which man led the mercenary arm of the Pythians the harmonious answer was *Callan Dudley,* always *Dudley.*

Good news, bad news, she thought. To have the leader of the Pythians' war division in custody was a fantastic coup, but it also left the door wide open for reprisals and escape attempts. She knew immediately that looking at the situation in such a way was beyond cynical but had felt the consequences too many times before.

Komodo, Russo and Healey took point, engaging the enemy and working as a team. Silk and Radford covered the rear. By the time they reached the narrow basement entrance they were on top of their game, attentive, determined and expecting to win. Russo pursued a final mercenary, kicking the man firmly into the door itself, cracking the timbers.

It was then that they heard a weak voice. "Stop them! Stop them I tell you!"

And Hayden realized they were right on the tail of a fleeing Pythian. Planned or not, fortune or otherwise, they had caught the last man in a rush down to the cellars. It was time to teach these animals a real lesson.

"Take 'em out," she hissed through the comms.

Russo lobbed a grenade down the cellar steps, listening to it bounce twice before the explosion sent his large hands up to cover his ears and stony face. Instantly Komodo and Healey took his place, checking out the top of the steps. Shots were fired from below. Komodo swept his weapon from side to side, unleashing a deadly salvo. Hayden moved to his side.

"There!"

Healey's shout was brimming with enthusiasm. The youngest member of the company leaped down the steps, careful to step across any that were damaged. Hayden caught a glimpse of a tall, thin man with gray hair disappearing into a dark space below. *Damn, do they have tunnels too?*

They clattered down the steps, Healey firing as he went. Another merc collapsed. And then came a weak cry and the resultant grumble of a seasoned, paid mercenary.

"Oh, my ankle. I think I broke it. Help me!"

"If you can't run, asshole, I ain't carrying you. Here."

Hayden leaped off the edge of the staircase and rolled, coming up on her feet and jumping ahead of Healey. The young man's thwarted shout made her smile. At ground level she spied a ragged archway, stone walls beyond. And a man lying on the ground. A man wearing a suit and tie, with gray hair and a pistol waving unsteadily in one hand.

"Put it down!" she cried. "Down, or I will shoot you."

"I can't," the man moaned. "I just can't. After what I've done they'll string me out to dry."

"Who the hell are you?" Kinimaka blurted.

"Robert Norris. I don't suppose you could let me crawl out of here? I have about 10K in my pocket."

"How money solves all problems," Yorgi commented, peering around everyone else. "How it makes world such better place."

Robert Norris? Hayden was thinking. *The* Robert Norris? If this was the same man that sat on the board at SolDyn then that company, one of the richest and most influential in the world, was heading for serious trouble.

"Now wait . . ." she began.

But the shot rang out. Norris, being a certain kind of man, didn't immediately take his own life but tried to take another. His shot flew wide. Both Russo and Healey fired back at the same time.

Beyond the slumped form of the SolDyn man there came a rumble and then the collapse of the tunnel. Hayden knew that whoever had escaped that way was more than likely going to get away.

"Back upstairs," she said. "Let's see if there's any more mischief we can get ourselves into. And bring him."

Drake evaluated the self-proclaimed ruler of the world. Tyler Webb was broad-shouldered and well-muscled. He leaned against the wall with smug confidence. Drake had seen the same kind of confidence exuded by short wiry men when faced with big brawlers they knew they could take down without breaking sweat. This man's confidence though, he imagined, was more likely due to a god complex and a carefully laid plan.

What that might be . . .

"Don't come any closer, Matt. Or you, Mai. And Alicia . . . have you put on weight? Oh, Torsten, why so glum?"

The only reaction came from Alicia, who retorted enough for them all, uttering a string of curses and threats that would make anyone blanch. Not so Tyler Webb. He just grinned even wider.

"The game is certainly on now, huh? Are you ready for what's next?"

"This is you done, Webb," Collins barked. "Get down on your goddamn knees."

"Ah, and you would like that wouldn't you, Claire Collins of the Fucked-up Bureau of Ingrates? *No pleasure without pain,* eh Claire?"

Collins stopped as though she'd hit a brick wall. Drake didn't know her past but saw that Webb had purposely dredged up some tragic memory. It then occurred to him that the leader of the Pythians had collected dirt on each and every one of them. But no matter . . . it wouldn't save him.

"Michael Crouch," Webb went on. "Failed leader. Aaron Trent. How's the wife? You and your so-called Razor's Edge took out my second greatest asset—the Moose. How could you be so cruel?"

Drake glanced sideways at Alicia. *Second greatest?*

"And next, Caitlyn Nash—oh, did your father love your mother, Caitlyn? Did he? And finally—Smyth. Do you even have a first name?"

"C'mere, Tyler. Let me whisper it in your ear."

"We have two of your so-called world leaders already," Caitlyn said, voice trembling with emotion. "Le Brun and Norris are *dead!*"

"Oh dear. Oh no. Well it's a good thing I have a waiting list then." Webb laughed. "So here we are. Let me ask you again—are you ready for the next level? Tesla of Niagara Falls? I mean, why the hell do you think we're even here? Or the apocalypse of Saint Germain?"

"Look." Alicia stepped forward, seeing no reason why this asshole should be allowed to ever talk again. "I think we've given you all the—"

"I have endless resources." Webb held up a hand. "I have a video of you." He nodded at Drake. "And her." He nodded at Mai. "Which you had no idea was taken. I sent men to visit each of your homes and hotel rooms—nothing nasty—just to move things about. Why? So that the next time it happens you'll think of me. Freaky, eh? And so when you *just don't know* if you left that deodorant out on the dresser or if that toothbrush just fell on the floor by itself—you'll think of me. I'll be with you. Always. The stalker of your dreams. The vision in your nightmares. I have text on all of you. Volumes of information. Everything from Internet favorites to Facebook pictures to career evaluations. Did you know a clever man can piece together the entire layout of your house, garden, doors, windows and furniture from putting together the pictures you post on social media? Think about that the next time you upload a selfie. Habits. Routines. I know you. I know all of you."

"Forgive me." Mai's voice was a susurration. "Are you a stalker or a tyrant bent on ruling the world? I forget amid your endless prattle."

Webb blinked, shocked for a second, then caught himself. "Oh, very good. All right then. It's been a blast. Until next time—" He made to move away and then stopped. "Oh, and pictures too," he added. "I have *thousands. Of every last one of the dead bastards that thwarted my very first endeavor!*"

With this final, raging outburst, Webb ducked away into the hole in the wall at his back. Before Drake could move a metal door slammed down in his wake, clicking and whirring as it engaged dozens of locks.

"What's that?" Trent wondered. "A panic room?"

Collins ran to the nearest window. "No. It's the door to a sky-walk that leads directly into that tower. In truth it looks like the *only* way in."

"Hayden remarked on the comms that there's some kind of tunnel network," Crouch stated.

Drake joined her, then looked back at Dahl. "You know what I'm thinking, mate?"

The Swede had carried the rocket launcher without complaint and now grinned widely. "I knew this bloody thing would come in handy."

Drake backed away. Dahl positioned himself at the window, spread his feet apart and hefted the launcher over a brawny shoulder.

"Looks like your reign is already over, Tyler."

The blackest of shadows fell among them. It plunged from where it had been clinging to the high roof, its limbs chopping and whirling and smashing. Dahl was hit first, two feet lancing into his shoulder. The Swede went down with a crash, winded and bruised, and the grenade launcher tumbled away. Drake was next, still trying to comprehend what had happened, struck in the kneecap and throat and left in agony. Mai reacted quicker than the rest, but still she wasn't fast enough, midriff bruised with a flying kick and legs swept mercilessly out from under her. Still the black shadow spun among them. Trent, Crouch and Caitlyn were standing very close, and suddenly found themselves smashing into each other; heads colliding, legs tangling, all ending up in a writhing heap.

Only Smyth and Alicia remained.

Seconds had passed. Smyth loosened his gun, discharged it, only to find his target as elusive as smoke. The black-clad figure was there and then not there and then suddenly right up in Smyth's face.

"What *are* you—" A fist smashed him in the mouth, silencing his sputter. A foot hooked his ankle, sending him to the floor. The same foot stomped on his chest, making him wheeze.

Beauregard turned to Alicia. "I could have used killing blows. I didn't."

Alicia crouched in readiness. "Only for the sake of speed."

"Not true."

"You're not *that* good, Beau. Just tricky. And decent at hide and seek."

The Frenchman appeared to pull a face under his mask. "I am on your side. You will see."

Drake was back on his knees by now. "Let's see how you fight without the shock and awe tactics shall we?"

He stood up, discarding his weapon, fists clenched. Beauregard gave him one stare and then turned back to Alicia.

"I will not go far from you."

"You're working for the goddamn *Pythians!*" she cried into the black, faceless mask.

"Am I?"

The tight-suited figure ran straight at the nearest wall, used its surface to rebound off and leap even higher, grabbed a timber spar and hauled himself up. He disappeared through an open skylight.

Moments later, Drake saw him sprinting across the rounded top of the sky-bridge, jumping through an open window into the tower.

"I don't know what the hell to make of that guy."

"He has helped us before," Alicia said dubiously. "Shit."

Mai took Drake's proffered hand. "I didn't see you all that eager to stop him, Myles."

"Oh, right. And where were the legendary Ninja skills when we needed them? Out worrying about something they can't change?"

Trent helped Collins to her feet. "Who *was* that guy?"

"Beauregard Alain," Drake said. "Kind of a new nemesis of ours. Truth be told," he grinned at Dahl, "I don't believe any of us have landed a real blow on him yet."

The mad Swede gave him a big goofy grin. "Time for that, matey. Oh there's plenty of time for that."

"We're done in here," Hayden said over the comms. "We have men trying to figure out the tunnels and a way into that tower. You might as well head out."

Drake felt as though they'd lost. "Did we just fail?"

"Don't be daft!" Dahl pounded him on the back. "We destroyed their hideout. Their Pandora's Box plan. We killed or jailed three of their members. We even know two of the ones that escaped—Webb and Bell. And most importantly—the plague has been neutralized."

"The world is safer," Hayden said.

Drake took a long look around. "Only until we find out what's next."

327

CHAPTER FORTY FOUR

Drake walked out of the house, rubbing his aching muscles and kneading the knots out of his back. Tiredness threatened to envelop him like a voluminous shroud. But all around strode his friends, old and new, and their heroism and willingness to lay it all on the line for the people they protected gave him a fresh surge of adrenalin and pride.

Outside, the cold fresh air cooled his flesh and, for now, eased his worries.

Aaron Trent held out a hand. "Good to work with you, Drake. I look forward to the next time."

"Any time," Drake said. "And do let me know if you're ever in the market for a Torsten Dahl."

"Ah. We have a code we try to follow in the Razor's Edge, epitomized by a single word. It's called *finesse*."

"Hmm. Never mind then."

Drake shook hands with Silk and Radford and gave Collins a hug. As he stood there a light rain began to fall and his eyes fell upon Mai Kitano.

Staring up at the clouds, up at the rain, the Japanese woman had more water on her face than the light drizzle suggested.

Drake saw the look in her eyes. "It's over isn't it?"

"It has to be. At least for now."

"For *now?* There'll be no more chances, Mai. I couldn't bloody take all this again."

"Until I can come to terms with what I did," Mai said.

"There is nothing else for me. I hope you understand. I don't expect you to. But I do hope. There is something I must do."

"What?"

"I do not know. And I don't know how long it will take. That is why . . . I have to let you go."

Drake felt something break loose inside as tears welled in Mai's eyes. "I don't understand any of this."

"And neither do I. The world shapes us and rewards us and recognizes us. It makes us believe that it knows our name. Only then, when we have accepted our place and our importance, does it destroy us. That is life."

"I can't believe in such hopelessness."

"I hope that you never have to."

Mai turned away from him, her black hair glistening with raindrops, her slim shoulders trembling with what looked like grief. He knew she would make her own way now.

Lost, alone, his first thought was of his friends. Where the hell was Alicia?

Alicia waited amid the rubble, a solitary figure covered in dust and fragments of debris. Her hands were bloody, her face bruised, the side of her mouth bleeding. Her long blond hair was scraped back, tied and hidden away beneath a chunky bullet-proof jacket. A half-empty, battered H&K dangled from her right arm.

Her bright blue eyes watched with extreme vigilance. Every tell-tale sound was analyzed and taken into account. Sounds drifting through the many smashed windows attested to quite a gathering on the lawn below; Drake's voice and Mai's, Crouch's and Russo's and that of Claire

Collins—none of them individually discernible.

And still he surprised her.

"Alicia?"

She turned, half expecting he would sneak up. "That's the last time you take me from behind, Beauregard. Be normal from now on."

The mask was gone so she could see the smile. "The last time? I was hoping it might be the first."

Alicia raised both eyebrows. "You sure got a nerve. Come here."

Beauregard stepped up close so that only inches separated them. Alicia quickly took out her knife and held the tip at his throat.

"I want to know the name of your boss."

"Is that really what you came here for?"

"What the hell else would I come here for? I read your message loud and clear—*I will not go far from you*—I understand you want to get something off your chest. For helping us out, I'll give you the chance. But only one."

"Ah, well then." The French accent grew stronger, distracting her senses. "I work for King Pythian, as you know. Tyler Webb himself. The pay—it is very good."

"I don't believe you."

"Then, *mon amie,* we are at an impasse."

"Not exactly." Alicia brought the knife down, its sharp edge cutting through the top of Beauregard's tight black suit.

"What are you doing?"

"What most girls like me do. I'm taking a look."

The knife travelled further down Beauregard's chest and toward his stomach, parting the thin material as it went.

"This is all I have, if you cut it off me what shall I wear?"

"I don't see where that's my problem." She paused with the knife hovering over Beauregard's navel. "And if this thing turns out to be rolled up socks your leotard's not the only thing that's gonna get spliced. Ya hear me?"

"It's not a leo— *ah!*"

Alicia finished her work and stood back. "Oh, my. You're happier than you sound then, eh?"

Beauregard grabbed her shoulder and drew her close, his mouth mashing down on hers. Alicia allowed herself to be entangled, opening her mouth and using her tongue. Her hands crept around Beau's back, grabbed his behind and forced him toward her.

"That's better."

Alicia's jacket hit the floor. Then her boots flew off. More clothes. Lastly, her rifle. Naked, she finally pulled away from the Frenchman. "Not here," she said. "It's not right. Good men died here today."

Beauregard nodded and led her, carefully, through a concealed entrance into a hidden room. "Webb built several of these. It has many TV screens, feeds from all over. He can interface—"

Alicia pushed him down onto his back and straddled his top half. "Yeah?" she interrupted. "Interface with this."

Beauregard's reply was unintelligible.

A while later Alicia moved her ass to the south. "Don't move a muscle, Beauregard. *Any* muscle."

Much later, after the majority of the authorities were tucked up in bed, the man called Beauregard Alain left the now defunct Pythian HQ. His body ached, and barely any of that came from fighting. Alicia Myles was as demanding a woman as he'd ever imagined. He'd been disappointed to see her go. But it wasn't a goodbye . . .

Farewell.

Until next time.

Even now, the memory sent thrilling shivers down his spine. *Damn, this is the life!* Then that thought sobered him more than a little. Speaking of *his* life, he must move along. One of the surviving Pythians, General Stone, sat in a high security prison cell somewhere in Washington DC.

Beauregard had been told to neutralize him. Not by his true boss but by Tyler Webb. It would be hard to refuse the request but his true boss had excellent connections and might be able to fabricate something. A disappearance could be organized.

And then there was the major discussion they should have—the topic being Tyler Webb, the Pythians and what Beauregard had so far found out.

He opened his cellphone and dialed a number. The call was answered immediately.

"Line's secure. What do you know?"

"Sit down, Michael. This may take a while."

CHAPTER FORTY FIVE

It felt good to be sat inside the spacious, bright bar in the heart of DC. Drake sat back and surveyed the scene, finally relaxing now he knew the whole company was safe. Alicia had returned sometime during the afternoon, fresh, clean and smiling. Drake concealed his relief and affection for her and gave her the dead eye.

"Why the hell are you walking like a cowboy?"

"Piss off, Drake." But she smiled and he grinned back.

Now, the teams were letting their hair down, partying together inside the warm bar as the darkness of night pressed against the lighted windows. Rum and tequila flowed and Collins was up on the dance floor, grabbing every man and woman she could and drawing them into a euphoric, music-filled expression of her love for life. For being happy, because life and happiness can be short-lived.

Drake sat opposite Dahl, a pint in his hand.

"To saving the world," Drake said. "Again."

Dahl clinked glasses. Drake took a deep swig of the heavy nectar. Beyond the rim of the glass he watched Mai, sitting at a separate table with Grace. The young girl's eyes darted eagerly, as if she wanted to jump up and join in the party, but Mai held her back, trying to get some point across.

Drake had been surprised to see Mai tonight. The Japanese woman had explained that she felt honored to be a part of the great team and would respect their celebration;

after all this could be the only time in their lives that these people came together. A sobering thought if ever there was one.

Drake watched as Collins dragged Hayden and Kinimaka onto the dance floor, joining those already there.

"So we have to face the fact that somebody gave away our hotel's location in Niagara Falls," Drake said. "A mole?"

"It was a big team," Dahl said. "With support personnel too. The nurses and doctor. Parts of the FBI and Canadian police. We're unlikely ever to find out. And Webb—like it or not, the man has power. And deep pockets."

"Do you believe the Pythians have suffered a setback?"

"No. Not at all. I believe they have a number of plans on-running and will end when they choose to. If ever."

Hayden came over to them then, a phone pressed to her ear. "Just got word," she said. "General Stone hung himself. Tonight. In his cell. Bastard won't ever stand trial for what he did."

Alicia sat forward. "And Dudley? He worried me the most."

"Still alive. Still in custody. They're moving him to a black site in the next few days."

Drake frowned, wondering if SPEAR should take charge of that operation, and then waved away the work talk. Instead he stared at Dahl. "So? Dropped out of private school, eh? Why did you never mention that?"

"None of your bloody business. I mean, me? Part of the rich crowd? Belonging to the set who already had a job for me in mind when I was eight? Already feathering my bed and shaping my future? Told what to do and when to speak since I could form words? I don't think so. That's *chains,* man, believe it or not. Besides, would it make you treat me any different?"

"Don't be daft."

"Thought so."

"You're a good man, Dahl." Later, Drake would put it down to the beer talking.

"I know."

The music swelled and the drinks flowed. Collins came over and danced by their table, taking them all into a bear hug. The guys from the Razor's Edge were left grinning in her wake.

Drake lifted his glass. "To you."

Trent nodded. "If you're ever in LA . . ."

Silk and Radford dropped down on nearby chairs. "Take the bus!"

Laughter rang out, and the world was happier, safer and full of camaraderie.

For a while.

CHAPTER FORTY SIX

Mai Kitano woke in the dead of night, instantly aware, senses seeking outward for what might have disturbed her. Three seconds later her cellphone rang.

Ah, that was it.

Dai Hibiki, her old friend from the Tokyo police, spoke quickly, his voice full of weariness and strain.

"The days treating you well, Mai? The nights? We've had major problems with the Yakuza since you humiliated them this latest time."

"The last time," Mai said, sitting up. It took only a moment to remember she no longer slept beside Drake, and that this was a new hotel room. She wore a black tank top and white Lycra shorts in bed and now padded over to the window. With one hand she twitched open a curtain, staring over the benighted city below.

"Are you alone?"

"Yes. I needed space to get whatever I did to that family straight in my head. And now, there is also Grace to consider. Life has changed."

"Well, your parents are fine. Chika is fine too. We are . . . happy. I'm guessing that Grace will ultimately go her own way."

"Good. So what do you want, Dai?"

Her friend hesitated. Mai instantly knew the next sentence would be very hard for him.

"This may only make things worse, but the girl that

survived? Emiko? She has been asking about the woman that killed her father. Even in protective custody she is reaching out. I'm scared it will bring her to the attention of the Yakuza. I'm worried she will develop a debilitating hatred."

"Do you want me to come over there?"

"No, no. You shouldn't be here. I only wanted to make you aware of that and one more thing. You remember Hikaru? The Yakuza boss you kind of humiliated in the men's room?"

Mai watched the city breathe below. "I remember him."

"He's a bigger boss now."

"Don't worry. We came to an understanding."

"I only wanted to keep you informed."

"Thank you, my friend."

Mai ended the call and placed her cell carefully on the narrow window sill. Outside, the city lights twinkled, trees swayed to a stiff breeze, and horns honked. The window itself reflected three extra images—the figures of men.

She turned slowly. So this was the noise that had awakened her—not three but six men spread out, all Japanese, who had broken into her hotel room in the dead of night. So ironic that Dai had called her at that moment. So stupid of her to accept that his call, three seconds later, had been the cause of her waking.

Hikaru walked one step forward. "Do not struggle. We know you. We have come for you."

"Did we not have a deal?"

"The Yakuza do not make *deals*," he spat. "We do not forgive humiliation. And you are *twice* guilty. Mai Kitano—come with us now. Do not make this any harder."

Five men spread out to his sides. All of them carried

silenced handguns. Mai wondered then about the trials she had faced in her life, about the girl that sought her, about that girl's father whom she had killed for the Tsugarai clan.

"Have you come to murder me?"

"That sounds like you want us to."

Mai shrugged. "I'm not happy with what I have done."

"Oh, I know that. We took care of the man's family for you. Only the girl escaped. But let us not digress. We're here for you. Do you want to die now for your sins against the Yakuza? If so, you know what to do."

Mai stared down the barrels of all five guns. Would it be simpler to just let go? She had been fighting ever since she'd been dragged screaming from the loving hands of her parents. So long. So . . . damn . . . long.

She looked around. "Only six of you?"

"It will be enough."

Time to decide.

But Hikaru was faster. "Just shoot her where she stands."

Mai moved fast. The first bullet nicked her arm. In a blur of motion, she angled toward her enemies.

The second bullet took her in the stomach and when the pain hit it was like a lightning bolt going off inside. She fell instantly, bleeding out on the hotel room floor. Gasping, gritting her teeth against the terrible pain she nevertheless hunched her body so that she could use her own rapidly draining blood to draw three distinct letters on the worn wooden floor.

Hikaru stood over her, his own gun now raised. "This is what we do to the people that have wronged us."

Smiling, he squeezed the trigger again.

THE END

Please read on for some exciting information on the future of the Matt Drake world.

So the 'crossover' novel comes to an end, about a year in the planning and the biggest adventure to date; it opens up this endlessly evolving romp for even bigger things. I sincerely hope you enjoyed reading it as much as I enjoyed writing it!

Next up, and to be released very soon, will be Matt Drake 10, The Lost Kingdom. I realize cliff-hangers like the one above are not everyone's favorite way to end a book so I made sure you will only have to wait until May 18th to enjoy Drake's next adventure. After that it will be Alicia 2.

As always, e-mails are welcomed and replied to within a few days. If you have any questions or comments just drop me a line.

Please check my website for all the latest news and updates—www.davidleadbeater.com

Word of mouth is essential for any author to succeed. If you enjoyed the book, please consider leaving a review at Amazon, even if it's only a line or two; it makes all the difference and would be hugely appreciated!